"... a tender, thoughtful story of a couple whose once happy marriage dissolves amidst the stress of infertility and infidelity—and unmet expectations. ... quietly compelling. It is by no means a heart-pounding page-turner, but it is a page-turner nonetheless, a subtle story that gnaws and needles long after the cover is closed."—*Chicago Book Review*

"... an annunciation, a miracle, ... this novel of generation, of stasis, and of transformation."— *Newcity*

"... a unique novel that challenges readers to think more broadly about what a family is and what it means to love."
—Windy City Reviews

"... a hauntingly beautiful tale. . ."
Booksie's Blog

"Sloan's evocative pictures of them and their lives, offer a new way or seeing ordinary people. Select this for your book club and enjoy discussing the unexpected twists and turns that lead to the evolving image of an unconventional family."
Hungry for Good Books?

"... a unique novel that challenges readers to think more broadly about what a family is and what it means to love."
Windy City Reviews

"... fascinating and gripping."
Centered on Books

"...appealing to all of us negotiating the often-intricate road of long-term living with another through thick and thin where change seems the only perpetual constant."
Literary Fiction Book Review

"...this is a book which reeled me in slowly.... Any writer who can keep me thinking of their characters even after I have finished reading their story, is an author I can highly recommend. If you love literary fiction, do yourself a favor and pick up a copy of Principles of Navigation – I promise you won't be disappointed."
Caribou's Mom

"Lynn Sloan's novel is nothing short of brilliant and she has accomplished much within the quiet confines of a domestic world."
—*Necessary Fiction*

"...I wanted to turn the page—no, I needed to turn the page. The payoff at the end made me glad that I did."
—*The Collagist*

Principles of Navigation

ISBN-13: 978-1-937677-93-0
Library of Congress Control Number: 2014955920

Fomite
58 Peru Street
Burlington, VT 05401
www.fomitepress.com

Cover Photo - "Untitled" from the series *Beneath the Surface* by Sarah Faust
Cover Design - Sarah Faust Design

Principles of Navigation

Lynn Sloan

for Nancy

with all good wishes.

Lynn Sloan

Fomite

Burlington, VT

For Jeff

1

"We are perfect here, aren't we?" That's what Rolly had said not so long ago.

In the picture, they're standing close, she and Rolly, facing the photographer, grinning at each other, giddy with happiness. She has her arm around his waist, and he towers over her, with his hand draped over her shoulder. Sun slices through the glass wall behind them, lighting the top of her silly curls and glowing in the space between their tilted faces. The inclination of his head says he can't imagine loving anyone else, and she shines back. Yes.

They're in the Chicago art gallery that represented Rolly's work back then, standing in front of an expanse of windows that open onto a garden dotted with bronzes. Both of them wear ivory linen, her dress modern, and his suit vaguely nineteenth century. She barely comes up to his shoulder. Beneath his dark hair, his face is pale and smooth-shaven — his beard came after they moved to Haslett and he decided he needed to look older if he was going to teach college students only a few years younger than he — and she, according to Rolly, looks almost Slavic, with her wide cheeks and jaw, her blue eyes, and her wild, blond hair that has darkened since then. This is their wedding picture, and they appear to be alone, except for a huge powder-blue hip of a woman caught at the right edge. Neither she nor Rolly could place her.

"I don't know anyone who wears a girdle. Must be one of your Detroit cousins," she had said.

"Can't be. Might be your old Sunday school teacher."

"Or one of Patricia's friends. Let's just trim her out."

"No. That upholstered haunch knocks the composition off kilter. We have to keep her."

We're not perfect now. Eight years later, we're so much less than perfect, we're not even normal.

She put the picture back on the mantelpiece.

In the kitchen, she unlatched the back door and stood on the porch taking in the smell of summer morning, all fresh and clean. In a year and a half the new millennium would begin, but even now, change seemed imminent. She could feel it. The wheel of history was about to turn into an unmarked era when the past would slough away, and all would be made new. She didn't believe that, and she didn't believe the dire predictions of the alarmists. But she did believe that good things were possible. New beginnings; a new dawn; a new day, all clichés. Avoid clichés, Journalism 101. But sayings were repeated because they were true. Then they became clichés.

She stepped onto the lawn. In this, the second summer of a record-breaking drought, the dew on the ankle-high grass suggested that it might be easing. Things could turn around for her too. Today was the beginning of her fertile stretch. She wiggled her toes into the wet grass and surveyed the still-shadowed yard that reached to Rolly's studio, on the alley. Overnight, spiders had spun webs on the tips of the arborvitae. When she and Rolly moved in, she'd planned to dig out that spindly shrub. If she hadn't loved its name, arborvitae, tree of life, she would have, but years of coffee grounds and good compost had paid off. Now it had filled out and grown a couple of inches. All around, her garden quivered with energy. She inhaled deeply, imagining her body taking in the generative energy she felt pulsing around her. After three years of trying, she would do anything.

Dr. Petrillo had urged tests. There were some simple procedures, he said, but Rolly was opposed.

"God, Alice, do you want the most private part of our lives dissected by doctors?"

"If this is the way, why not?"

"Just because all this medical technology exists, doesn't mean it's right to try to outwit biology. Let's stick with natural. If it happens, it happens."

How could she argue against natural? But she kept a calendar and thermometer they didn't talk about in the back of a drawer in the bathroom.

She walked to the dilapidated picnic table they never used where a soccer ball had lodged against its broken leg. One of the Faracci kids next door must have kicked it there. With her foot she rolled it forward and saw a flat, heart-shaped stone with a damp patch, shaped like a star, left from the soccer ball's seams. She picked up the stone that fit perfectly in the hollow of her hand. Heart and star, another cliché, but it could be good sign. She tucked it into the brown needles beneath the arborvitae and made a wish.

A finch crossed overhead. She watched it disappear in the treetops.

She'd seen a bird's-eye view of this house and garden in the aerial photograph in the county assessor's office. She and Rolly had just moved to Haslett — he'd finished his MFA and landed his tenure-track job at Wesley College, and she'd gotten a job at the *Haslett Herald* — and that day she was checking the tax records on this house, which they hoped to buy. The clerk had smiled at her enthusiasm when she located this property, a patch of green with a medium-sized house tethered to the street by a straight sidewalk, like most of the others, but that day, it had seemed like the key piece in a jigsaw puzzle. With this piece, everything came together: her and Rolly's first real home and the beginning of their adult lives together. Still one piece remained missing.

The Faraccis' back door slid open. Alice ducked into the lilacs, not wanting to be seen and wishing they could put up a fence, but fences were regarded as un-neighborly in Haslett. When she found this out, she'd composed a mock news item in her head.

RESIDENTIAL FENCES BANNED
After a hot debate at the town meeting, the proposal to lift the ban on residential fences was referred back to committee. Spokesperson for Keep Haslett Open and Friendly Ima Buttinski accused Good Fences Make Good Neighbors of being outsiders "from New England or thereabouts." GFMGN denied these charges and vowed to press on.

"How're they doing?" Bettina Faracci peered through the leaves, her crow-black hair glistening.

"They're late. Probably the drought," Alice whispered, nudging aside the baby eggplants and glancing up at her bedroom window, hoping Bettina hadn't wakened Rolly. Alice wanted to catch him in that lovely drowsy, not-quite-awake state.

"...so I said to Paul, why bother? You can get them at the farmer's market at the same time and you—"

"I can't talk, Bettina. I left the kettle on," Alice lied, hurrying to her back stairs and into the house.

She paused outside their bedroom to brush eggplant powder from her fingers and look at the ribbons of sunlight spilling over Rolly's body. The sight of the dark hair swirling over his pale legs made her feel loose and soft. He turned over. Sweaty tendrils of brown hair stuck to his forehead. He looked like a teenager, not a man of thirty-four. She was as drawn to him as she had been the first time she saw him.

She couldn't tell if he was asleep or playing possum.

"Come here," she said, pulling off her long T-shirt. She lowered herself to the bed and pushed her leg between his. From his taut stillness, she knew he was awake. She trailed her fingertips over his chest until his breath caught.

"Hmm, you're cool." He curled toward her, nuzzling his face into the curve of her neck.

"And you're warm."

"And you're delicious."

He strung a line of kisses along her jaw, and she giggled, then quieted as he drew her close. His breath vibrated in her collarbone. She stroked the smooth reaches of his back and the faint bulge of his waist. Warmth blossomed in her palms and the memory of his hip bones when they first made love, she twenty-two and he twenty-five, and longing spread through her. He rolled on top of her and she laughed, surprised and breathless, as he grinned and moved his hips. She arched into him and wrapped one leg over him.

"Today's the day," she murmured.

His movements caught and slowed and his face turned away.

"Oh no, Rolly, please." She kissed his chest. "Don't do this, Rolly. You're my mate." She pressed her forehead to his, willing him to understand. "I want you *and* I want our baby."

A muscle clenched along his jaw.

"Please, Rolly."

He lifted his head, his eyes avoiding hers, as he traced her cheekbone with his finger. "Oh, Alice, what can I do?"

5

"Just be; just be with me."

She drew his head down to hers, and kissed his mouth, sensing his resistance soften. Matching her breath to his, she lowered her arms to circle his torso, and his chest shuddered. Then he shifted his weight, his hands on her waist, and they made love, each movement marked with a reserve, as if, she thought, they were asking each other for forgiveness.

She did want his forgiveness. Her pretend spontaneity was taking its toll on them both. She wanted this phase to be over. She didn't know how much longer she could keep this up. Others got by without kids. The thought made her feel like she might blow away.

She awoke to the sound of the shower and the sea smell of the sheets. For a moment she thought about joining Rolly under the spray, but closed her eyes.

A fire truck, two, screamed by. She'd fallen asleep. She rolled over and saw Rolly towel off in the doorway, one foot propped on the other knee as he bent to dry his calf.

"I've got the whole day. What do you want to do?" she asked, watching him pull on jeans.

"I'm going out to the studio." He slipped on his sandals.

"It's my first Saturday off in a month."

"I've got a lot to do."

She turned away. When the back door slammed, she dressed quickly, furious, blaming herself, blaming his stubbornness. She shouldn't have hinted about the timing, but at least they'd had sex.

In the kitchen, as she waited for the kettle to boil, wishing she'd kept her mouth shut, she stared at his studio, his private citadel. Through the studio's sliding doors she couldn't see him, only the piece that currently absorbed him: a canoe, eighteen feet long, at least. From where she stood it looked like a gash in the white floor.

His friends, mostly members of the art department, raved about his canoes, but to her they looked like exaggerated copies, not useful like real boats, and not abstract enough to be called sculpture. She didn't say anything, not wanting Rolly to think she didn't get it.

Behind her the kettle hissed. She jerked out of her reverie and poured hot water into the paper cone, debating whether to take him some coffee, and saw herself sliding open the door of the studio, mug in hand, and Rolly looking up, angry. She didn't take down a second mug.

He'd started working on his canoes last spring after their hike along the Indiana River. She'd searched for edible mushrooms and he'd gathered branches. At home she threw away the mushrooms — she didn't know enough about them and they looked evil — and he'd retreated to his studio where he split the branches into flexible lengths and lashed them into shapes that looked like snowshoes, later small boats, and finally into canoes.

"Relics of a lost culture," he'd called them a few weeks ago.

It was almost midnight and she'd spent another evening alone while he worked in his studio.

"Isn't that a little grandiose?" she had responded, sipping the remains of the wine from her dinner.

"Grandiose? Probably." He scrounged in the refrigerator for leftovers.

"'Lost culture'? Not even your culture."

"Words to keep me aimed in the right direction," he said into the refrigerator.

"It's just that I would have liked some company tonight."

He closed the refrigerator, a carton of eggs in his hand. "Right now things are opening up. I've got to keep going. You know how it is."

"Does it have to be this way?"

He cracked the eggs and whipped them into froth. "I'm sorry you had a bad evening."

That was two weeks ago, and his words still stung.

She turned away from the back door, and carried her mug to the kitchen table. Breathe deeply, the infertility books said, to lower stress. She sat down and picked up the latest postcard from her mother. This one featured the Virgin of Guadalupe — Patricia was vacationing in Mexico with her forty-plus singles' group, all of whom were fifty-plus, some sixty-plus — and her taste in postcards veered to tacky. Earlier, she had sent one with burros braying at some joke in Spanish, and one with cockroaches in bikinis lounging around a hotel swimming pool.

But Alice liked this one. The shy Virgin floated on a light blue cloud streaked pink by a postal meter, and she looked startled by the plump red heart she held in her hands. In the postcard factory — Alice imagined dark-skinned women in an adobe cottage — she'd been given a wonderful face, eyebrows rising gaily to her hairline and a cupid's mouth, slightly off-center, which expressed approval of just about anything that might come before her. Alice touched the Virgin's face. "Just a wee baby for Rolly and me," she whispered, then stiffened, but Rolly wasn't there.

Behind her the phone rang.

"Alice, it's me. Did I wake you?" Barry, her boss, sounded rushed.

"No. It's OK. I've been up for a while." She looked over her shoulder, toward Rolly's studio.

"Good. I need you."

"Now?"

"There's been a bombing."

"At the paper?" she asked.

"In Rockton, at JoJo's. But come to the office first before you head out."

"Anyone hurt?" she asked, guessing it was drugs. Meth labs had been found on a couple of abandoned farms.

"No one. The cops think it was a bomb, but they're not saying much else."

"Barry, I haven't had a Saturday off in over a month," she protested, but thought, why not? She wouldn't have to spend the rest of the day rehashing what had gone wrong with Rolly and, with a little luck, by the time she returned, the bad feelings would be buried in the silt of the day. "OK. I'll be there soon."

"Bring your camera."

"Right, chief." She mock-saluted since he couldn't see her. Barry acted like the *Herald* was a serious news organ, a mini version of *The Indianapolis Star*. Setting her mug in the sink, she winked at Patricia's postcard. The Virgin seemed to wink back.

Dressed for work, camera stowed in her bag, she crossed the yard to tell Rolly that she was leaving. She didn't want her departure to underscore or magnify their discord, but she wouldn't mind if her work caused him a little of the irritation his work caused her.

A voice from the bushes said, "Where're you going?"

She jumped. It was Rolly. "Hey, you scared me. What're you doing out here?"

"I thought I'd see if the raspberries are ripe."

He wasn't interested in the raspberries. "Are they?" Had he been coming in to see her?

"Not yet. Another week or so." He noticed her slacks and ironed blouse. "Where're you going?"

"Work. The office, then Rockton, and I'm already late." She tamped down her smile. She'd didn't want him to think she was eager to get away. Or maybe she did. "A fire in a fast-food restaurant in Rockton. Maybe *foul play*." She wiggled her eyebrows. "Barry called his intrepid reporter to sniff out the news."

"Star reporter," he corrected, half smiling.

"I'm not sure when I'll be home."

He shoved his hands in his pockets. "I couldn't get going in the studio, so I thought I'd take a break."

They walked toward the gravel parking spot beside the studio where her car was baking in the sun.

She touched his arm. "About this morning…. I'm sorry if it wasn't quite what you wanted. I'm sorry it's become work."

"I know you want a baby. I want you to be happy. But somewhere in all of this, *I* seem to have been overlooked."

"That's not true."

"It's all about efficiency with you."

"I *have* to be efficient. Three years of haphazardly trying didn't work. Dr. Petrillo said we could find out if there's something wrong, but—"

"Don't start that again."

"I agree with you. Just bad luck. But I want to do everything I can."

He wasn't listening. He was looking toward the Faraccis' yard. One of the girls was on the deck, banging some toy. He kept his eyes fixed in that direction and said, "Something is wrong if all you want from me is sex according to your personal calendar." He blew out a long breath, still not looking at her. "What I'm trying to say is that I'd like sex not to be exclusively about reproduction. I mean, my God, it's become goddamn tiresome."

"You don't mean that." She wrapped her arms around his waist. "It's just hard to do two things at once."

"Let's simplify to *one* thing, making love."

"You know I want you." She skimmed her fingertips across his shirt. He remained stiff. "Come on, Rolly, let's make things right tonight. When I come home."

He said nothing.

She dropped her arms, "I've got to go now." She started toward the car. "I love you, Rolly."

"I know." He squatted, picked up a chunk of gravel, and tossed it in the air a couple of times, testing its weight.

"See you, then." She opened the car door, waiting for him to say something that would turn this around.

He stood facing away from her, toward the garden. He flexed his knees, turned sideways, took a pitcher's stance, gripping the stone with three fingers, drawing it into his chest, then threw it hard. A tiny explosion of wood popped from the corner of the studio.

She slipped into the driver's seat. Two stones in one morning, but hers was about hope and his was about anger. As quietly as she could, she closed the door and fought the key into the ignition. He was acting like a selfish child: stupid, impossible.

2

Rolly stared at the tools above his workbench. At least Alice was gone. He'd been on his way to the house to suggest they restart the day, but her reporter's self-importance had knocked him back. And then her infuriating "I'm sorry if it wasn't quite what you wanted." At least now there'd be no hovering, no, "I made you coffee" or "Can you take a break?" or "When're you going to quit?" or her best, her tautological "It's Saturday," the "Saturday" stretched out with her personal substrata of blame and complaint.

He turned to face his canoe. What he should do was mix stain for the hull's exterior. Instead he lifted from the pegboard his coarse rasp that was clotted with sawdust and palmed its smooth oak handle, its heft a real satisfaction. He liked old hand tools, nothing fancy, garage sales finds, and those he'd inherited from his grandfather. When he held an old, worn tool, he felt a current flow into his hand from all the men who'd wielded it before him. It was the tools, especially the hand tools, that drew him away from metal to wood. He liked wood. Wood was alive. He slid his thumb along the file's clogged grooves. Pain snapped to his first knuckle. A splinter half-inch long. With his teeth, he yanked it out and, feeling absurdly triumphant, spat it into the sink, then wrapped his thumb in a clean rag, one of Alice's old T-shirts.

At the beginning they'd both wanted a child, before her first breezy hope intensified into a gale. He raised his throbbing hand high and squeezed his bundled thumb. If he didn't pay attention to what he was doing, he'd ruin the possibility of making something out of this day.

With his good hand, he lifted down his planes and arranged them in a row on his workbench, largest to smallest. He picked up his favorite — eight inches long, made of maple, with a narrow blade — and rolled his palm over its silky knob, picturing the small bone that protruded like a pebble on Alice's shoulder.

He couldn't make her understand that he wasn't sure about a baby. If she bulldozed him now, how would she act if they had a child? Would everything have to revolve around the kid? There was his work. He couldn't be an occasional artist. Art was an all or nothing calling. You had to be free to take risks. You had to prowl; you had to be quick and responsive. How could you do that *and* be a father? Fathers had to put their child first, always, every time. What fatherhood meant was giving your child whatever was required and shepherding your child toward an independent life. You would want for your child the very thing you had given up for him. Something was wrong with this equation.

But it had been almost three years of trying, so maybe she wouldn't get pregnant. Thinking about what might never happen was pointless.

He pulled out his rag bin, tore a fresh bandage for his thumb, and dug out his whetstones. Cleaning tools was all he was good for today.

When he finished with the planes, he glanced at the canoe awaiting stain — he still wasn't up to it — and dug in a drawer and found an awl with some sticky residue on its shaft. As he wiped the awl's shaft with a rouge cloth, he remembered Meg Saffold's bare arm gliding into the red satin lining of her sleeve when he'd helped her into her coat at last year's Christmas party, her arms milk white, sleek as eels, dimpled at wrist and elbow, like a woman in a fifteenth-century Italian painting.

The phone rang. Glad for the interruption, he cradled the phone between ear and shoulder and walked away from the noisy air conditioner. It was Wolf Lemmen, his office mate, whose heavy German accent was worse on the phone. Something about a hunting trip.

"What are you talking about?"

Wolf, a visiting artist and painter from Bremen, had been given a desk in Rolly's office, and they'd become friends after Wolf, at his first faculty meeting, had argued with the old-fart modernists.

"A barrr…beee…cue."

"Oh, shit. When?" Herman Laasche's annual party. Herman was their department head.

"You want to know when, I want to know why. Exactly. The Old Boar is holding a bar-be-cue next week."

"I'll tell you why, exactly," Rolly said, heavy on "exactly," Wolf's favorite word. "This gives Herman the chance to act like a generous host on the college's dime, booze flowing, grilled mastodon, and when we're softened up, he'll pull each of us aside and assign us some shit job. Revise the student handbook, set up a workshop in toxic hazards in the arts, even—god, please not this—solve the department's Y2K problem." He wondered if Meg Saffold with the lovely arms and an associate in the academic dean's office would be there.

"I will not go," Wolf said, his mouth too close to his phone.

"And miss the chance to lust publicly after the beautiful Irenia?" Wolf was infatuated with Herman's wife, a tall, somnambulant beauty. In their shared office, with the door closed, Wolf would launch into tales of freeing Irenia, the damsel, from the grasp of the Old Boar. Most were set in the Black Forest. He had to be homesick.

"Even for her I will not go," Wolf said. "No. But to pursue my study of American culture, I might change my mind." He hung up without saying goodbye, as usual.

Rolly smiled, returning the polished awl to the drawer. Wolf loved American pop culture: homecoming queens, plastic owls, gilt-framed Renoirs for sale in the hardware store; but nothing of this came out in his paintings, which were abstract geometric objects, rendered in subtle brushstrokes of gray. "Where white meets black in equipoise," as he'd say to anyone who asked. Oddly, Wolf liked Rolly's work, even though his sculpture was rooted in realism.

It was Wolf who'd given Rolly the book on Viking ships that started him thinking about boats. Rolly pushed aside his cleaning rags and searched under the sink for the ingredients to stain the canoe's hull. Now he was ready to get to work.

∗ ∗ ∗

When Alice came home, he was glad to see her. Work had lifted her mood too. She was flushed and excited about what was probably arson. The cops guessed either a disgruntled cook who'd recently been laid off or insurance fraud by the owner, but the fire chief wasn't talking.

Alice asked about his day and cooed over his bandaged thumb. Neither of them mentioned their quarrel. Alice was pleased about Herman's party. Later, in bed, he waited for her to make love to him.

∗ ∗ ∗

Next Saturday they drove to Herman's house in Riverdale Heights, named for the sluggish Wabansee River that skirted the western edge of town before turning eastward to join the Ohio. The neighborhood of large brick houses and gloomy shrubs reminded Rolly of his grandparents' street in Detroit where he'd spent weekends when he needed to get away from school.

"Look, Rolly." Alice pointed to a patch of haze hovering over a low driveway. "A sign the drought may be lifting?"

"Doubt it." She seemed to think the drought was connected to her not conceiving. He touched her shoulder to mask his uneasiness. Things between them had gotten better once he'd decided not to initiate sex. She hadn't said anything. She might not have even noticed.

"I just want a real downpour," she said.

He stroked her neck and her streaky, blond curls. The bright red of the dress her mother had sent from Mexico reflected on her skin, making her look flushed and very pretty. "You look great."

At the stop sign, he glanced in the rearview mirror at his own reflection. His slicked-back hair still bore the marks of his comb. "What do you think, Alice, do I look bad enough?"

"Almost dangerous."

He grinned. He'd spent more time than usual deciding what to wear, finally choosing a yellow T-shirt, black slacks, and a '50s silver sharkskin jacket.

"But maybe too extreme for Haslett."

He reached for the radio to hide his irritation. "Here's some country to get us in the mood for the annual Laasche Pig and Faculty Roast."

A nasal twang keened from the speakers.

"You know I hate country." She pulled away from him and turned it off, and they rode in silence until they reached Herman's cul-de-sac crowded with cars, most of which he recognized.

"Half the college must be here," he said.

Wolf rounded the house's corner. He was carrying a large basket, and his narrow face lit up when he saw them. He, too, was dressed for an art opening: dark gray shirt, high-buttoned, with long sleeves. Too hot for July. Rolly hurried to open Alice's door.

16

"What's this?" He nodded at Wolf's basket of peaches cushioned with ferns, as artfully arranged as a still life.

Before Wolf could say anything, Alice said, "You came. I'm surprised. Rolly said you'd refused."

"I couldn't stay away. I yearn to walk on the same grass as the beautiful Irenia."

"Wolf, quit with that face." Alice stood on tiptoes to kiss his cheek. "You don't look infatuated; you look lobotomized."

"What is lobotomized?"

Rolly grabbed Wolf and pretended to scoop out the front of his brain as Alice ignored them, walking toward the path that led to the back.

At least forty people had congregated in the Laasches' yard, the crowd self-divided into clusters by discipline: the painters, the graphic artists, the facilities staff. Rolly was the lone sculptor in the department. The bursar's office, student relations, and some other administration staff had come too.

Herman hurried toward them from the far side of the patio. Since his hip operation, he'd lost a lot of weight, and the jeans he wore once a year at this party, to prove he was a regular guy, sagged from his waist.

"Good to see you. Great color," he said, touching the sleeve of Alice's Mexican dress. "Matisse-like," then turned to Wolf and his basket of peaches. "Are these for me?"

"No. They are for your beautiful wife."

Herman's mouth tightened. Wolf's rudeness annoyed him. "She's around here somewhere," Herman said, turning to some newcomers.

"You're lucky you still have a job," Alice whispered to Wolf. He grinned, saying he was going to find Irenia and sauntered off.

Rolly turned toward Alice. "A drink?"

Before she could answer, the rosy-cheeked wife of the art department's facilities manager — Rolly had forgotten her name — tapped Alice's shoulder. "You're just the person..." and asked about a commission meeting last Wednesday.

This was why Alice loved parties. Everyone wanted to hear the latest news. Rolly headed toward the drinks cart and Alice called after him that she wanted a soda.

Two teaching assistants served drinks. The one with the shaved head was mixing a drink for a silver-haired woman Rolly didn't know, the boy's contempt for the woman, the party, alcohol in general evident in the way he speared the lime wedge and dropped it into the glass. Smug little shit.

"Two martinis," Rolly said, hoping the kid would disapprove. "Weren't you in my class..."

"Spring a year ago." The boy held the gin bottle at arm's length as if it were toxic.

"With ice," Rolly said, remembering the boy's inept final project, a paper mache male nude. At the edge of Rolly's vision, a red glow advanced.
— Alice in her Matisse red dress. Matisse. Herman, what an ass.

"I said 'soda.'" Alice glared at Rolly, then asked the kid for a ginger ale.

The kid approved. Before Rolly could think of something sarcastic to say, Irenia swooped in, inclined her cheek for Rolly to kiss, and asked Alice about the bomb.

"A bomb?" someone behind Irenia asked, which was an invitation for Alice to launch into her monologue about the various theories.

She should have gone into the theater, Rolly thought, as others drifted over.

"Maybe a bomb, or maybe dynamite shoved into the exhaust fan from the parking lot." She paused to give the newcomers a chance to draw close.

Rolly walked through clusters of people from the administration toward a tree beyond the patio, where Wolf joined him and asked if he'd seen Irenia.

"She disappeared. She saw you coming."

"She is coy, my beloved." Wolf shifted his basket of peaches, then nodded at the crowd around Alice. "What's that?"

"The six o'clock news. Alice is holding forth on JoJo's arson."

"Everyone loves a disaster."

"Alice loves being an expert."

"And you do not love being the expert?"

Rolly gave him the finger.

Wolf repositioned a peach in the basket. "Artists shouldn't marry."

Rolly wrinkled his nose and sniffed. "Is that odor I smell German dogmatism?"

"But this is true. Marriage, it is fine, as long as you marry a woman content to be moon to your sun."

"Did you read that on the bathroom wall at school?"

"What I read was 'Professor Becotte is hot hot hot,' written in your handwriting."

Rolly upended his empty glass. "I need another drink." He didn't move, neither did Wolf.

The garden had filled with people. The late-afternoon light canted through the trees that edged the lawn. After a while, the group around Alice dispersed and she came over, her step springy.

"You're having a swell time, aren't you?" Rolly said.

"And you two look like you're at a funeral. I'll see if Herman or Irenia needs my help."

She walked away, and Rolly watched her enter a band of sunlight, her red dress glowing transparent, and within, her legs scissoring open and shut. A fist tightened in his gut.

Wolf said, "I have no fine woman of my own, so I must seek the divine Irenia, knowing that I will be rebuffed. Where is she?"

Rolly followed Wolf's line of sight to the patio where Irenia was setting out a tray.

Wolf loped toward the terrace, stumbled, caught himself, and made a show of his effort to save the peaches, while Irenia watched, her expression frozen. Wolf tucked in his shirt, selected a peach, and handed it to her, bowing his head in mock humility. Irenia accepted the peach. Those nearby applauded and Wolf bowed.

Wolf was a jerk. Rolly walked to the bar. The kid with the shaved head was gone. Armed with a fresh martini, Rolly strolled through the crowd, wishing he were somewhere else, anywhere else, Chicago, better, New York. At a spot near the pines, he paused and took a long sip of the icy drink, welcoming its sting. Holding the glass in front of his eye, he looked at his colleagues, distorted by the glass. Tadpoles in clothes. This was not where he'd hoped to be when he'd set out, not stuck with the dull and second rate at a backwater, liberal arts college in Indiana. When he'd gotten this job, he'd been considered lucky, the only one in his MFA group to get a tenure-track position, a secure, well-paid day job with plenty of time for his own work. But that's not how it worked.

He watched Evan Maron, the printmaker of the department, carry folding chairs from the terrace to the lawn. Evan was Exhibit A for "stalled career." When the poor schlub arrived at Wesley two years after Rolly, he had a New York gallery, a couple of NEA fellowships. Then his wife had a baby. Two kids now, and Evan made excuses. If Alice should get pregnant, Rolly would not become like Evan.

Draining his glass he saw Alice on the terrace talking to the registrar, and, twenty feet to her left, by the side of the house, Meg Saffold, her wild, coppery hair lit by the lamp above. She'd come. He started to

20

walk in her direction, then her husband, Kenneth, appeared beside her, his white ecclesiastical collar aglow in the dusk.

"When do you think the Old Boar will begin the preparation of the food?"

Rolly jumped. Wolf.

"Why don't you go ask him?" Had Wolf seen him stare at Meg?

Wolf began to natter about some problem with the library as Herman appeared in the distance carrying a platter of raw meat. Rolly scanned the crowd, wondering where Meg was, and spotted her distributing tiki torches.

"Let's move," he said to Wolf, and maneuvered around four women from Student Aid to angle into Meg's path.

She smiled at them. "Defense against mosquitos. Which one of you wants the last one?"

Wolf reached into his pockets. "I have matches."

"Let me." Rolly set down his empty martini glass and took the matches. Wolf glanced at him. Embarrassed, not meeting Wolf's gaze, Rolly took the torch from Meg and drove its stake into the turf, then flipped open the matchbook and handed it to Meg. Wolf said he wanted a drink and disappeared.

Meg held up her hand. "You light it."

Rolly touched a lit match to the wick, and they both stepped back as smoke billowed around them. Waving the smoke away from her face, she smiled at him.

"You're beautiful," he said, surprised he'd said what he was thinking.

"You're not supposed to talk that way to me."

"What way?"

"The flirting way."

"I teach in the art department. Talking about beauty is my business."

"I'm a minister's wife." She cocked her head, mocking or flirting, he couldn't tell.

Behind her, people were drifting toward the barbecue. No one was close.

He said, "You are quite noticeably beautiful."

She looked down, holding her hand above the torch's flame. "Do you think this keeps mosquitoes away?"

He waved away a curl of smoke. "Is it hard being a minister's wife? People expect you to be…"

"Good? Sure. But at least no one expects me to play the organ or organize the rummage sale — I have a job, as you know — but I'm never allowed to miss church."

In spite of the citronella fumes he caught a pear-like scent he imagined was hers.

"Would you like a drink?" He picked up his empty martini glass. He'd forgotten how flirting felt: risky and exhilarating.

"I'd like to eat."

Darkness had fallen while they were talking. Now each table shone with candlelight and was ringed by rosy faces. Near the patio Alice sat at a table with Wolf, her back toward Rolly. Careful not to walk too close to Meg, Rolly led the way to the buffet. Plates filled, he pointed to a couple of unoccupied chairs where the registrar and the art historians, Shep Holloway and Curtis Bey, sat.

Meg looked around. "Where's Ken? Oh, he's surrounded. OK, over there is fine."

As soon as they sat down, Curtis asked Rolly about the Rockefeller fellowships. Rolly explained what he knew, wanting to cut this short, his awareness focused on Meg beside him, who chatted with Beverly Heersma. When Meg bent to retrieve her napkin, her hair brushed

Rolly's arm. His chest folded in on itself.

Another bottle of wine was emptied. Nearby tables began to clear, and Meg said she should find Ken. Saturdays had to be early nights for ministers. Rolly hoped his disappointment didn't show as he helped with her chair.

After she left, Shep took her seat and waved over Wolf. While they talked about teaching, Rolly thought about Meg, and whether her holding his gaze meant what he hoped it meant, or whether her see-ya-around farewell was what she really meant — until Alice found him.

In the car she said, "I saw you deep in conversation with Meg Saffold."

Rolly adjusted the side mirror. "We talked about the incoming crop of freshmen. Their SAT scores are a notch lower than last year's, but that's not important with art students."

"You looked very interested," she stretched out the word. "I didn't know you had much interest in freshman students."

"What's that supposed to mean, that I have an excessive interest in upper-level students?" This was the wrong distraction. Rumors circulated around him and Wolf being chick magnets, though he'd never done anything. He reached over and ruffled her hair. "Sorry I'm so irritable. I wanted out of there hours ago."

"It's your department; they're your friends. Can't you make an effort to put yourself out, just a little?"

"Oh, please, Alice. Herman's party isn't about having a good time."

"No, I mean it. This is just like you."

"Being bored at a faculty party?"

"An unwillingness to extend yourself, even a little, for anyone else."

He said nothing.

"Did Herman buttonhole you for any special assignments?"

She was seeking neutral ground. He was grateful. "No, but he probably figures since my sabbatical is awaiting approval, he can get me to do anything. And he's right."

"It's hard to think that your time off is about to end."

"Summers aren't *off*. I work like crazy in the summers, and I'm supposed to for every reason, including my job depending on me having an active exhibition record."

"I meant that you'll be working more regular hours again, like a regular husband."

"Is that what you want? Me to be like Paul Faracci? Can't wait to come home at the end of every day because that's all he's got. Come on. Are you really sorry that I love my work?"

Her jaw was clenched. She wasn't going to answer.

"You knew who you married, Alice. I haven't changed."

"That's the problem."

He refused to respond. In front of their house, he turned off the ignition. Through the car's windows, the roar of the crickets sounded accusatory.

Alice turned to him. "I'm sorry I said that. I didn't mean it."

He knew he was supposed to say he was sorry too. When he didn't, she opened her car door. "Well, I had fun at the party, even if you didn't."

He followed her up the walk, but paused at the bottom of the steps, envisioning their front hall, the mail stacked in the basket on the table. He imagined the floor creaking as she rounded the landing and saw their bed leap into view when she flicked on the lamp. He couldn't imagine taking off his clothes and lying down next to her. He said, "I'm going out to the studio for a while."

She glanced over her shoulder. He knew she wouldn't bother to coax him in; she was no longer in her fertile period.

"Night, then," she said and closed the door.

3

The end of August was as hot as mid-July, but for Alice, the slow days at the paper ended. The beginning of the school year required interviews with the new teachers, stories on new educational initiatives, and dozens of short pieces on the various clubs' proposed activities. Church and civic groups, coming out of their summer doldrums, wanted their fall activities covered, and the continuing drought demanded a couple of inches in every edition. The cops arrested a disgruntled former cook for the fire at JoJo's. The days got shorter and colder and Alice covered the crop and livestock sales. Halloween, Thanksgiving, Christmas. Rolly joked she could just delete last year's date and plug in 1998, but she insisted that she loved finding new angles, and she did. Most nights they made dinner together and talked about their days. She didn't mention where she was in her cycle, or her sadness each time her period began.

But in January, when she was two weeks late, she told Rolly that she was going to sleep in. After he left for the college, she hurried to the bathroom. Behind the stacks of toilet paper, she found the pregnancy kit she'd hidden last year. The first few times she'd been late, Rolly had stood by her, but now she didn't want him involved, not until she knew for sure. She read the instructional leaflet. "Test results may be unreliable if used after the expiration date." She picked up the box. 11/98. Two months out-of-date. She should have checked last night. Sickened, she reread the instructions. She might as well go ahead, as practice.

Afterwards she took a shower, and emerging from the steam, she glanced at the pee stick she'd left on the sink. The lines seemed to match up, but the mist was thick and her eyes wet. Not believing it could be true, afraid, she wiped her face and reached for the wand. The lines were thick and straight. She *was* pregnant. Elation shot through her, then vanished. Pregnant, if not a false positive. Pregnant, if the out-of-date pee stick could be trusted.

She needed to see Dr. Petrillo, today. She grabbed a towel and dashed to the bedroom and the phone. The doctor could squeeze her in at noon.

＊＊＊

In an hour she would know. Breathless, shaky, wishing she could stop time so the possibility that she was pregnant wouldn't be snatched away, she paused half a block from the office of the *Haslett Herald Weekly* and tried to locate the faint clicking deep inside her, more felt than heard. The sound of her body changing? She strained to listen, but all she was certain of was the wind in the awnings. Across the street, in the town square, workers dismantled the nativity, and on the lamppost in the front of the *Herald*'s office, a man stood at the top of a ladder, taking down ancient tinsel garlands. From her purse she pulled Patricia's postcard with the Virgin of Guadalupe. Looking at the Virgin's merry face always calmed her. She kissed the card and tucked it back in her purse, then wrestled open the door to the *Herald*.

"Bitter out there," she said to Fritzie Janke, who sat at her desk behind the counter that divided the reception area from the working space. Alice blinked in the glare of the new fluorescent lights that Barry had installed in response to Fritzie's complaints. Barry did pretty much

26

as Fritzie asked. Fritzie had worked for the *Herald* since Barry's father had been the editor, and she knew where every file, every photo, every scrap of paper could be found.

Alice swung up the panel in the reception counter to enter the workspace. Behind Fritzie's desk were two long worktables and rows of file cabinets topped with Little League and bowling trophies from teams the *Herald* had sponsored over the years. The back three doors guarded a drafty bathroom, the furnace room, and the stairs to the second floor where Alice's cubicle sat outside Barry's office. In its heyday when it was the only newspaper in this part of the state, the *Herald* employed three reporters.

Fritzie poured Alice a cup of coffee, without bothering to ask. Behind her pink-tinted lenses, she looked weary, and her pre-Christmas perm had lost its snap. "Try this. It's the good coffee. Weren't you going to the county board meeting?"

"No coffee for me." Not if she were pregnant. "And unbelievable, the meeting started on time, and ended early. I thought I'd stop in before heading out again." Dr. Petrillo's. Fighting a spasm of nerves, she stared at a new snapshot of a little kid in a snowsuit taped to Fritzie's desk lamp. Fritzie treated the office like her living room.

"Cute kid," Alice said.

"Donnie's Emma."

Wondering if Donnie was Fritzie's nephew or her great-nephew, Alice glanced at the messages Fritzie handed her. "What's this? 'Interview visionary. God'. "

Fritzie tapped a cigarette from her pack. "Barry got a call from some farmer. Seems there's a girl who claims to have seen the Virgin Mary, out west of here." She patted the papers on top of her desk. "Here's the name, address, phone. Girl's a senior in the high school. Go see if it's a hoax."

"Either that or weed behind the barn."

Fritzie snorted, and Alice crossed her arms and intoned, "A high school senior on her family's farm in the county reports seeing the Virgin, eight months before the arrival of the millennium. Could this be millennial madness or…a bible-thumping nut? A Nostradamus believer? A hallucinating junkie? A fifteen-minutes-of-fame seeker?"

Fritzie laughed and offered Alice a donut, which she declined.

The second floor had been remodeled long ago into one open space, with four cubicles and one real office, Barry's, in the front, overlooking the town square. It had no privacy, just glass walls that set if off from the rest of the floor. Barry would sit in his father's green chair, at his father's massive desk through which he'd drilled holes for computer cables, and worry about declining subscriptions and revenue. This week he was in Indianapolis at a workshop on how to deal with the Y2K problem.

The staff had shrunk to Alice and two part-timers, Harry Mack, a coach at the high school, who wrote sports, and Lorett Clifford, who wrote obits. And there was Tracey, a high school student intern, who came in once a week after school.

Alice's cubicle sat next to Barry's glass wall. It held two wide desks that met at right angles with just enough room to move her chair in and out. In college she'd assumed she'd work for a big news outlet, but it turned out that she loved the easy pace of this small paper. Since 1921 the *Haslett Herald Weekly,* previously the *Haslett Herald Daily* and before that the *Haslett Daily Siftings and Herald,* had dispensed local news: weddings, auctions, crop, feed and stock prices, real estate closings, church functions, and, most important to its subscribers, school athletics. Barry might include an abbreviated national story, if there was a local slant, like legislative farm bills or wheat prices in

Ukraine, but he favored oddball stories for the front page, like the car running on root beer or the Salt Lake City boy who could type sixty words per minute with his toes. Last week it was nighttime curling on Lake Superior. Nothing big ever happened in Haslett or the county, which was a point in favor of this Virgin sighting. Alice might work in the millennial angle.

She hung her coat on the hook and reached for the phone.

A woman's voice said hello over a roar, probably a dishwasher.

Alice introduced herself, said she was with the *Herald*, and would like to speak to, she straightened the note, "Heidi Fender." Fender. English? German?

The woman hollered "Heidi." Alice listened to the dishwasher.

"Yes?" A girl's voice, thin and hesitant.

Alice introduced herself again, saying that she'd received a message that Heidi had seen a vision. The girl said nothing. Alice went on. "This seems like important news. I'd like to talk with you about this. Would that be all right?"

"OK."

"May I come out, say, this afternoon?" Barry would want pictures.

"I got to check with my mother."

Alice waited with the phone wedged under her jaw, stuffed her notes from the morning's meeting into a folder, and cleared her desk. Except for the dishwasher, there was no sound on the other end of the line. Was the girl coming back? Had she left? Alice said, "Do you think the Virgin might want you to tell others?"

"I dunno."

"Maybe what she wants is for you to tell others. If it's a miracle. Why don't I come out and we can talk?"

In the background, the dishwasher shifted into another cycle.

"OK."

Alice glanced at the clock. In half an hour she would be at the doctor's, then lunch with Patricia. "How about two this afternoon? Hey, why aren't you in school now?"

"I didn't feel like going."

She might be a dropout. This was going to be a waste of time.

* * *

"Mrs. Becotte, I've got good news. You're going to have a baby."

After a blood test, urine sample, and quick exam, she was sitting in Dr. Petrillo's office, facing him across his wide desk with a forest of family photos. He asked again for the date of her last period. What else had he said that she'd missed? Her brain wasn't working. "You're five weeks pregnant. So, adding fourteen days, because this is your first, August thirteenth, that's your due date."

"Please not the thirteenth." She knew she sounded foolish, superstitious.

He gave her a look, but said, "We'll make it the twelfth then. We'll know better in a month or so. I'd like to see you regularly, once a month, and you can go about as you usually do." He gave her a prescription for vitamins and a handful of pamphlets and told her to eat normally, a sensible diet, expect a moderate weight gain, nothing big, and avoid alcohol.

"I feel silly. I'm so happy," she bumbled. Her mouth hurt from smiling.

"Relax and enjoy this."

Her purse clattered to the floor when she leaned across the desk to kiss him.

"Thank you, Doctor. Thank you."

He laughed. "Nothing to thank me for. Thank your husband."

* * *

At the pay phone in the lobby, she picked up the receiver to call Rolly, then put it back. Not over the phone. This had to be in person.

She phoned Patricia and cancelled their lunch, saying an interview had been moved forward.

Not quite believing the good news, she ate a slow lunch in the medical center's coffee shop and read the pamphlets Dr. Petrillo had given her, remembering nothing. She imagined a baby growing inside her. Images flowed into one another — of white blankets enfolding, wisps of hair dark, like Rolly's, or curls, like hers, and flower bud fingers.

✳✳✳

In less time than she'd expected, she reached the address Fritzie had given her. The *Herald*'s yellow plastic cylinder was attached to the mailbox at the end of a long, potholed driveway. She parked next to a sawed-off tree stump that probably held a planter in the summer, and looked at the dingy house hunkered beside a line of spruces planted too close, maybe forty years ago. No bathtub Madonnas, no concrete saints, no hand-lettered "repent" signs.

A middle-aged woman with fallen cheeks and a tight ponytail stared at her through the storm door.

"Hello. I'm Alice Becotte, from the paper."

The woman didn't move. Alice showed her press ID and the woman waved her into a cold living room where an ugly, stiff brown couch faced two matching armchairs. "That reporter's here," she shouted, then left Alice alone.

Above an old TV hung an oily crucifix with palm fronds from last Palm Sunday, almost a year ago. Overhead a board squeaked. Alice waited, her eyes on the stairs beyond the archway. Black cowboy boots appeared, then a long expanse of bare legs under a tight black miniskirt. Lots of silver jewelry, bleached, spiky hair, and heavy eye makeup.

"Heidi?" Alice said. The girl had to be a drama queen. "I'm Alice Becotte."

"I've seen your name in the paper." The girl raised her hand to her mouth and bit the skin around a black-painted nail. "That series on foster kids who get screwed up. That article on drownings in the old quarry." Her washed-out blue eyes finally met Alice's.

Alice said, "I'd like to learn about what you've been through. Can you tell me about it?"

"I guess so." Her eyes flicked toward the back of the house where the woman, the mother, must have gone.

Alice reached for her notebook and began to sit down.

The girl said, "I'll get my jacket."

Outside, wind tunneled up Alice's sleeves, and the zippers on the girl's too-big black leather jacket clattered like wind chimes. They started off across the frozen field, the girl leading but saying nothing.

Alice was eager to get this interview moving and done with. She wanted to be alone in her own home. She wanted to concentrate on being pregnant.

"If you didn't feel well enough to go to school, should you be out here?"

The girl stopped. They were in the middle of a frozen field with corn stubble rising from the ridges.

"I don't feel sick now." She kicked a stone. The soles of her black cowboy boots were clotted with mud. "I didn't want to talk in the house. Mom listens to everything. She can't decide."

"Can't decide?"

"Whether it's real."

"Natural to doubt, don't you think?"

From under mascara-laden eyelashes, the girl stared at her, flat-eyed. "I don't lie."

32

This girl looked made for lying. "But she thinks you…might?" Alice said.

"That's her problem."

Birds broke from some bushes along the field's edge.

Alice thought about the crucifix and the withered palm fronds. "You're Catholic?"

"Sort of. I mean, *they* are, my parents. I'm not sure. Wasn't sure."

"And now?"

"Do you believe in miracles?" the girl asked.

Alice thought of her postcard Virgin. "I might."

The girl pointed and they walked toward a clump of trees. "That's where she comes."

Alice took out her notebook. "When did you first see her?"

"October twelfth, I remember. Dad hadn't harvested these fields yet. Before the corn is cut, no one can see you if you sit down here."

Standing within the stand of scrubby trees, Alice scanned the flat horizon broken only by the Fenders' house and their unpainted barn. Would this soul-crushing place induce visions? Or was the girl making this up? Or smoking pot? Probably not meth. No twitchiness or the red eyes.

"What were you doing, when you first…?"

"Sitting here on this rock." Next to the flat rock, twisted pop cans protruded from a leftover crust of snow.

"Tell me what you saw."

"The first time I was just hanging out, and I sensed someone close. I was alone. Everybody had gone to town. I hadn't heard anyone come up, you know, through the corn. And I would have. I looked around and saw her out of the corner of my eye. But when I tried to look right at her, she kept moving, always off to the side. I knew right away who she was though. She was so beautiful and so…I guess, peaceful."

The girl was telling the truth or what she believed was the truth. Alice felt like an intruder.

The girl went on, the wind snatching away some of her words. "…wears…a blue…you know, like in…pictures." Alice strained to hear. "Her face, I knew it was her, but her face was so faint…I couldn't see…just the glow."

From the corner of her eye, Alice saw the girl's lips draw together, as if she was working something out, then she turned to Alice. "You're going to have a baby."

Softness spread through Alice. "How do you know?"

The girl didn't respond. She gazed up, her eyes reflecting the churning sky.

"How do you know?"

Turbulence filled the space between them. Alice felt as if she were pinned between the barren sky above and the scoured, frozen ground, and her flesh had become porous, the thinnest of filters for the wind to stream through. All that anchored her was an impossibly small weight, the baby.

"Did she tell you?" she whispered.

"I just knew."

Afraid to press, Alice bent to snap off some dried weeds, waiting for more, wanting more.

Near her shoulder, the girl's boot dislodged a stone. "She never says anything, so far, anyway. She's not here now, or you would have seen her."

Alice looked at the Fenders' house. A wisp of smoke rose from the chimney.

"I've seen her now four times," the girl said. "After that first time, I saw her a week later, here again. Then it was December second, I saw her down by the creek." Alice followed her gaze to a curving line, maybe a quarter mile away. "Then on December twentieth, I saw her near the barn." She turned to face Alice. Her eyebrows were pinched. "I try to hold on to her, but I can't. Do you understand?"

Alice did, although she couldn't have said exactly what it was that she understood.

"Once I felt her touch on my hand. It was tingly-like, and it spread through me and it made me feel... I can't describe it."

"Do you have any idea why she's come to you?"

The girl's eyes looked bright, as if she might cry. "No. Not yet, no. But I think...she'll show me." She lifted her face to the sky, her mascaraed eyelashes trembling. "Let's go back."

At the house, a curtain moved. Alice thought about the girl going into that grim house. They began to walk.

"If there's anything I can do," Alice said, not knowing what she meant. "Or if there's anything else you remember." She handed the girl her card.

The girl tucked it in a pocket, then reached for Alice's right hand. With her index finger, capped by a black-painted nail, she drew a circle on Alice's palm. "Baby," she said, cupping Alice's fingers within her own.

Alice felt softness encircle her, like a warm bath, rising from her feet to her head. She felt steady and safe. She'd been blessed. She wanted to sing.

"Bye," the girl said.

Alice remembered she should get a photograph of the girl—Heidi, she must think of her as Heidi—and called to her as she reached the front steps. Alice framed her looking away, cropping out anything that might give away the location. She wanted to protect this girl, Heidi, from becoming a spectacle. She would keep the story short and simple. "High school girl," no details, not even that she was a senior.

As she drove away, she kept Heidi in sight in the rearview mirror until she disappeared into the house.

✳✳✳

Abuzz, Alice drove to the mall, filled her vitamin prescription and bought an expensive bottle of wine for dinner, for Rolly. She was exploding with energy. The baby's room, she could start planning. In the paint store, she was overwhelmed by the choices. She grabbed a bunch of pastels.

In the room that she and Rolly used for guests and storage but that she'd always seen as a nursery, she taped the swatches to the wall. The greens reminded her of school, the yellows looked yucky, and the blues were nothing like the blue on the postcard that she hadn't wanted to pull out in the store. The postcard had become sacred. She retrieved it and saw that the Virgin's robe was much lighter. She did not have Rolly's visual sense.

"14 Abril…Mex…" The rest of the postmark was smudged.

Her mother had written, "Dears, What a city. Modern and decrepit. In the museum an ancient, pre-Columbian doll whose face, not body, looked just like you, Alice. A fertility doll. An omen??? Love, P."

Thank you, Mom. Alice turned the card back over. Had Heidi Fender's Virgin looked like this? Probably not the colorful garb and the multicolored halo, but maybe the same sweet smile. She put the bent card in her bedside drawer, for safekeeping.

In the kitchen she flicked on the lights. Outside the five o'clock sky was as dark as iron. Watching a headlight from the alley climb the side of Rolly's studio, she wished he were home. His ambivalence about having a baby had sprung from all the disappointments, month after month for more than three years, she knew that. Uncertainty was corrosive.

When he got home, she rushed to meet him, wrapping her arms in around his thick parka. He pulled away and began talking about his classes. She plucked sawdust from his beard. She would tell him when his mind wasn't halfway somewhere else.

"And then Herman stopped by and asked for every damn detail connected to my sabbatical."

Norway. She'd forgotten.

As he talked about what Herman had said and how he'd responded, they walked to the kitchen. She handed him a glass of the fancy wine she'd bought.

"Aren't you having any?" he asked, drawing her close.

She murmured no, liking how the curve of her belly fit perfectly into the depression of his pelvis, their baby held secure between them.

"Nice wine. So what about you? How was your day?" He rearranged his arms to reach for his wine glass.

She held her breath, to make sure she had his full attention. "We. Are. Going. To. Have. A. Baby."

He stared at her, two pink spots on his sharp cheekbones, above his beard. He didn't move.

She opened her eyes wide, waiting for him to take in the news, then spun away like a top, three, four turns from refrigerator to table and back, before twirling back to him. Dizzy, she grinned at his puzzled expression. "Ta-da. We're going to have a baby."

"Oh, my god." His face flattened, then lit up. He fumbled his wine glass onto the counter and wrapped her in his arms.

She sagged against him, his heart's double pulse against her cheek, and they swayed. She lifted her feet, one then the other, on his shoes, and he began to walk, widening his steps into a waltz.

"I love you so much, Alice."

His steps carried them to a chair, and he sat, holding her close. Silence settled around them as if the whole world beyond this room had vanished. Absolute quiet. Not even their breath. Suddenly, like a geyser, she exploded. "Isn't it wonderful? Rolly. A baby growing in here." She lifted his hand to her belly.

"I can *feel* the heat," he said, blowing on his fingertips. "God, is it true? A baby. I'm going to be a father. Me?" He mimed terror, eyes popping. "It's not possible." He laughed. "I guess it is, right?"

She nodded and he bent down to kiss the base of her belly. Her heart lurched. She touched the sliver of skin above the neck of his shirt.

"I'm going to be a father? God. Like my dad, his father, his, all of them stacked up behind me. I can't believe this."

"Well, believe it," she commanded and they both laughed.

"I'll drink to that." He kissed her nose and reached for his glass. "Can I pour you some?"

She shook her head. "No. I'm going to be perfect. No wine, no caffeine, no junk food, no additives, no chemicals of any kind." She remembered the paint swatches upstairs. "You'll have to do the painting. No fumes for me, but I got samples." He looked confused. "The nursery. You know, we'll fix up the guest room."

"We don't have to start tonight, do we?"

Alice hugged him. "And I better not go into your studio if you're using any resins or adhesives or anything."

"Oh. Of course. Are you supposed to do anything special? Take vitamins? Avoid anything besides the obvious?"

"The doctor said pregnancy wasn't a disease. Prenatal vitamins, yes, but I'm supposed to go on as usual. And I'll get bigger and bigger." She stretched out her arms.

"I'll pretend not to notice. No, that's not right. You'll be beautiful and I'll sculpt you," he thought, "out of roses. I'll sculpt you out of roses."

She nestled into his chest, hearing him ask when the baby was due.

"August, the twelfth." Not the thirteenth.

"August?" He lifted his hand from her belly and pulled back. "What about my sabbatical?"

"You'll do your work. You won't be teaching, but you'll be around a lot for the first year."

"I'll be around a lot? What about Norway?"

"Babies are portable. You'll sculpt or do whatever, and I'll be a hausfrau. Think about those immaculate Swedish root vegetables and fish and clean frosty air. What could be better with a baby?"

She watched him calculate. The plan had been for them to go after the school year ended, in June. She said, "We'll leave a few months later. That's all. But you'll still be free of the college come summer. You can get started on your projects here." Why did she have to explain this? She watched his mind race. "Rolly, please, this will work out. You don't, we don't, have to figure out all the details tonight, just like we don't have to paint the baby's room tonight." Not even a smile from him. "People do this all the time, rearrange things for a baby. It's called *life*."

His gaze remained fixed on some point beyond her. Fighting to suppress her dismay, she put her arms around his neck and rocked her hips on his lap. "Come on. Can't we just be happy and enjoy this tonight?"

She tried to look into his eyes, but the part of him that was connected to her had gone underground. She wanted to cry. "If you want to go to Norway earlier, you can, in June, if you want, and come back in August." She hated this idea.

4

Rolly stood at the icy window of his third-floor studio in the art building, wishing he could remember who said that an artist was someone who could hold two opposing ideas and still function. Kant? Hemingway? Buddha? By this standard, Rolly was no artist. He was stuck. He couldn't function. He was elated about the baby, a new human being originating from some of his tossed-off cells. Never would anything else he might create equal this. He'd had his worries before, but in the last couple of weeks, he'd come to see how things he hadn't thought about would change. Like his and Alice's connection. They wouldn't be a couple anymore; they would be part of a triangle. Two against one, or two close and one left out, and he knew who'd be left out. When he first realized this, he'd thought this would work to his advantage—even now, he wanted more time for his work—but he didn't want to be reduced to running support services for Alice and the baby. Yet, he was excited about becoming a father. He felt larger, more expansive, like he'd have a bigger footprint in the world. But right now he felt stalled.

His classes were fine—students always brought him out of himself—but when he was alone, he couldn't concentrate. He cleared a spot on the frosted window. Across the snowy plaza, a couple of students emerged from the social science building, turned, and walked backward into the fierce wind. That's what he wanted, to be pummeled by the elements. A walk, that's what he needed, and maybe he'd try to catch Wolf for lunch. He might tell Wolf about the baby, even though he and Alice had discussed waiting another month, until the end of her first trimester, before they let the news out.

Outside, the wind bit through his jacket. He gave up the idea of a walk and headed straight for the student union. Heat hit him as soon as he entered the glass building, and plinking sounds wafted from the game room. A few scattered people sat at small tables in the dining court, no one paying any attention to the overhead TVs. On the far side, floor-to-ceiling windows overlooked the snow-covered soccer field. In spite of the wide-open expanse of glass, this place reminded him of an underground bunker. Wolf wasn't here; his 2-D design class must be running late. Rolly sat at a table by the windows, blinking into the glare.

Last night at dinner, Alice had talked about getting a new car. "Ours feels like I'm driving a Band-Aid box. I want more protection for the baby."

When he'd protested—they'd be leaving for Norway when the baby was six weeks old, and their cars would remain here in a garage—she'd come up with the idea that they could buy a car over there and, after the year was over, bring it back. Up to now, they hadn't talked about a car for Norway; he'd assumed they'd buy a junker.

"And we'd save on storage," she'd added. "Our cars wouldn't sit idle for a year."

"Good idea," he'd said, feeling boxed in. Why did everything have to change?

She'd spread out brochures for baby paraphernalia: car seats, bassinets, changing tables.

"Do we really need all this shit before we leave?"

"Some we'll take."

"How much?"

She smiled her big-hearted, infuriating smile. "Don't worry. We'll get the minimum. I just wanted your opinion."

His opinion? So he now was a baby products consultant? "It's all fine with me."

He stared at the white soccer field, still annoyed, scraped back his chair, and headed for the cafeteria line. These days he and Alice were on a balancing scale: What lifted her up brought him down.

Returning with a loaded tray, he saw Wolf wend his way through the tables.

"Good class?" Rolly asked, recognizing the excitement of teaching well and feeling envious.

"A very good class." Wolf pulled off the gray sweater he used for a winter coat. "Some of them are getting it, the idea of movement edge to edge. I'm hungry. That looks good." He eyed Rolly's sandwich. "And you?"

"Nothing's going right."

Wolf shrugged, then mimed that some force was tugging him toward the cafeteria. "I'll be back."

His Terminator routine was growing old, Rolly thought as he picked up Wolf's sweater from the floor to spread it on the heat vent under the window and noticed a skinny, balding guy with a baby in a back carrier stop at a nearby table. The guy wrestled out of the unwieldy contraption holding the baby. The kid, who had to be at least a year old, giggled as the guy plucked off the kid's hat and mittens, unzipped the jacket, and pulled out one arm, the other, then tried to strap the squirming kid into a highchair. The baby put up a good fight. Once in the highchair, he began to bang his fists. Patient Dad cooed something

42

while he took off his own steamy glasses and wiped them on the front of his jacket. It was tropically hot and the guy hadn't even had a chance to unzip.

Wolf slid his tray onto the table. "Chimichangas and Chinese fried rice, side by side in the cafeteria. This is America's great contribution to civilization: voluptuous variety. This and your beautiful on- and off-ramps."

"Ramps?" Rolly turned from the kid now squawking over a juice box Patient Dad had produced from somewhere.

Wolf, who'd noticed the kid and Patient Dad, turned his back to them. "For your highways. Ramps."

"Don't overlook our indestructible plastic lawn furniture."

"Indestructible and so ugly. No prize there." Wolf took a bite of fried rice. "Tell me what has been going on with that girl Alice interviewed, the one with the visions?"

"Your interest in American culture is limitless." Rolly watched Patient Dad arrange Cheerios in front of the kid. "That was a month ago. There's been a stampede out to the farm. The father is charging admission. Alice feels guilty, as if she's been a shill."

"She portrayed the girl sympathetically, I thought. I haven't been following this. My neighbor now takes his newspaper in as soon as it arrives. I have no opportunity to keep up."

"Alice's sorry she gave her the exposure. You know Alice, journalism: the fourth estate, serving the community, etc., etc."

Rolly watched as the father unpeeled a banana.

Wolf nodded toward a copy of the *Herald* someone had left on a nearby chair. "Cows and ritual slaughter, satanic marking found in — what was it? a public pavilion? — by the river."

"I don't follow this stuff. Ask Alice."

The baby threw the banana on the floor.

Wolf shifted to see what Rolly was staring at, then shot Rolly a look that said the man had no business bringing a kid into the Union. Rolly agreed. Today he wasn't going to mention Alice's pregnancy. To divert Wolf from baby and dad, he said he'd gotten a travel grant of five thousand dollars.

"Still the Vikings?"

"Their shipbuilding, in particular."

"The Bayeux tapestries, that is what I know of their boats." Wolf stared with suspicion at his untouched chimichanga.

"Great designers, spare use of materials, the simplest means. And their wayfaring interests me too."

"Ah, your canoes."

"In a way, right, that's where it started. But you know how it is, I began with the materials and a curiosity about native people here, America, and that leads to other preindustrial, precolonial, pre the discovery of America, pre—"

"Didn't the Vikings discover—"

"I want to learn how their goals affected their boat design. See, sometimes travel is about exile, and sometimes it's about discovery. And there's journeying itself that I want to learn about, if I can. What's necessary? What's essential? What's at the heart?"

"And you will find this out by traveling yourself?"

"Right. I hope." It was a relief to talk to Wolf, who understood. "I'll, we'll, need a home base too. Herman has a friend who might allow me to hook up with a university in Bergen, a fair-sized town, according to Herman, along the western coast."

The baby behind Wolf wailed.

"Bergen, that is a beautiful town." Wolf threw aside his balled-up

44

napkin. "When I was a teenager, my family camped there. It has an ancient, restored center and harbor. The mountains come right to the edge of town. Grieg's house…"

A loud crash. Beneath the kid's highchair, an overturned tray wobbled in a puddle of coffee. Patient Dad noticed Rolly and Wolf staring and said, "I guess I better confine this fellow to home for a while," as he dabbed at the coffee with a handful of napkins. A kitchen worker rushed forward with towels.

Wolf shook his head. "I do not understand why having children is such a common practice. Children are like puppies, briefly cute when they are young, but forever afterward a nuisance."

"Let's get out of here." How was he ever going to tell Wolf about the baby? "Come to my studio. I want to hear what you think about what I've been working on."

"I thought you were stuck."

"I started something new as a break from my canoes. I was starting to run dry." This wasn't true. With the baby being the nonstop focus at home, he'd decided to work at the college and begun fiddling with some tree branches he'd collected awhile ago and had not bothered to take to his home studio. "I want to see if you think there are any possibilities. Maybe I'm overlooking something."

Opening his studio door rattled the big windows opposite. His studio was like a large shoebox, thirty by twelve, with high ceilings, a white linoleum floor, and a bank of east-facing windows that leaked wind and rain. But here, unlike at home, he felt unwatched. On one long wall he'd positioned bookshelves, a desk, a cluster of photographer's lights on stands, and a beat-up couch covered with a Navajo blanket. Heaped near the windows were the casts he'd made from branches that suggested human gestures.

From each limb, he stripped the branchlets and most of the bark, then wrapped what remained with gauze, strips of handmade paper, a thin mix of plaster and polymer, creating white, deeply textured casts. These he slit open to discard the original wood and left the hollow, hinged cast open along one side. Their watery shadows flickered on the white wall from the draft.

"It's freezing in here," he said. "Maintenance must have turned off the heat." He hooked his parka on the coat tree he'd made out of showerheads, wishing he hadn't invited Wolf.

The casts looked puerile and stupid. He'd been fooling himself to think he might be onto something.

Wolf looped his sweater near Rolly's parka and strolled toward the cluster of casts. He picked up one that looked like an anorexic's arm, balanced it in his hand, tipped it this way and that, then snorted and replaced it among the others.

Rolly cringed.

Wolf said, "You, I see, have been reading the French. Everything must be recast — is that it? — in this age when we have all been so divorced from reality that we are only stirred by copies. Authenticity is no longer possible, yes?"

Rolly turned away, to his desk, picked up a squash ball, and hurled it against the far wall, not aiming at Wolf or the casts, but coming satisfyingly close. "The problem with intellectuals is they're full of shit."

Wolf shrugged. "You are right, of course. Give me a few moments, will you?"

Hiding his embarrassment, Rolly sauntered to where the squash ball had come to rest. "Look all you want."

He couldn't think of a way to ask Wolf to leave without making a big deal, so he juggled the squash ball and stared out the window.

Outside, a misty snow was falling, leaching the scene of substance. It looked like a Whistler watercolor. To the south, past the plaza, was the administration building, a featureless gray box. Meg Saffold's office was on the second floor rear, not visible from where he stood. Sometimes he thought of her sitting at her desk in the outer office of the dean, her red hair afire. He hadn't spoken to her since Herman's party.

Wolf stirred. Rolly turned.

"Rolly, I must tell you: This work has no soul. Not like your canoes—that's good work, I told you, but this — Rolly, you must avoid this — the only word is 'pretty.' An interior decorator would put these in the lobby of a corporate headquarters. Or spray them silver and hang them in a shopping mall."

"Don't be shy, Wolf; speak your mind."

"You asked for my views. Now you don't want them? But you know I tell you the truth. I am your friend. Would you rather I flatter you?"

Yes, he would rather be flattered. "You're right. You're saying what I know. I guess that's why I asked you. I just don't like having it confirmed." Rolly walked up to Wolf and squeezed his shoulder. "You're a good friend, but you don't have to be such a good friend."

Wolf grinned.

Rolly nudged one of the casts. "Wolf, this shit embarrasses me."

"The canoes were good. What happened to you?"

He couldn't tell Wolf about the pressure from Alice, about the baby, about not being able to work on anything that meant anything real. He picked up a prism. The room, the windows, Wolf, everything was upside down.

"I got sidetracked."

"Lost your nerve?"

"I don't think that's it." What if this was just the beginning?

Wolf peered at him, waiting for more. After the silence expanded, he said, "You must move on or back. The boats, that has promise."

Outside, the sky had darkened. When Rolly turned to face Wolf, the studio seemed too bright. "That's what the sabbatical is about."

Wolf said nothing but Rolly knew he was thinking that the answer wasn't to be found in traveling to someplace new. Wolf walked toward the coatrack and reached for his sweater. "You can't wait for some intervention. Right now, you must hold tight or you lose. Like fishing, you must not slacken when the fish fights. You play it wherever it goes. Even when it plunges deep, you must not weaken. If you don't do this, you become," he paused to pull his sweater over this head, "like all the others around this school: safe and dead."

Rolly waited for the door to close. When he no longer heard Wolf's footsteps, he flipped on the spotlights and aimed them at the cluster of casts. He was humiliated to have made this shit, furious that he'd tried to delude himself that it wasn't total shit, and upset that he'd wasted so much time. He picked up a cast that had reminded him of a woman extending her toe into cold water and tore it in half, then grabbed another one, much shorter, shredded it, and in a fury, ripped and tore every one, paper and flecks of plaster flying, until nothing whole remained. Out of breath, he gathered what was left and stuffed it in the trash. Garbage: that's all he'd produced since the summer.

Panting, he stared at the overflowing bin. Next to the black plastic, a scrap of white paper had lodged next to damp coffee grounds, causing a brown stain to seep into the paper fibers. A jagged coastline appeared. He retrieved the soggy triangle, pinned it on the wall next to some drawings, and stood back. Maybe what he'd been trying to do wasn't entirely worthless. Maybe he'd let the baby business undermine him. With sufficient concentration, he could figure out how to salvage something worthwhile. Wolf was right. He'd lost his way. But there had been some good impulse at the beginning. He'd collected branches that had reminded him of gestures. What he should have been looking for was branches that suggested wounds. Not the pretty but the painful.

He pulled from his cupboard scraps of leather, coils of copper wire, and metal fastenings. He would start again, make new casts, then pierce, cut, and tear them; then he would repair them with sutures, splints, bandages. He would make casts for his casts. He laughed, thinking of it. He would undo the natural prettiness of the branches he'd selected and make pieces that ached. As they should.

✳ ✳ ✳

He worked intensely and the days sped by. He found new materials, mulberry tissue, unbleached linen, handmade papers, and experimented with different threads for stitching. With each material, he tested how it performed, wet and dry, and how it took dyes. When he was convinced he had what he could work with, he made thin plaster casts from a couple of tulip tree branches that had barely any bend. When the casts were dry, he ripped them from the branches and stitched them back together, misaligned, so that they looked mysterious and otherworldly, yet obviously of the natural order. These satisfied him. He cast more branches and realized that it wasn't the baby that had been the problem; it was that his work had just foundered, which was a normal part of the process that could happen anytime. He just had to stick with it. The usual solution.

He felt guilty about how he'd been with Alice: difficult, irritable, not interested in all the baby stuff she was researching. Sitting on his studio couch, studying the ripples in cheesecloth he'd dipped in gesso and hung to dry, he got an idea for how he could make it right with Alice. He would show her that he was ready to be fully part of this baby business. He would design and build her a crib.

"Alice."

No answer. He dropped his jacket on the newel post, excited to show her the cribs he'd sketched, and walked into the kitchen. The three o'clock light blazed across the floor and up the stove. He'd left campus early to catch her before she left for some teachers' meeting at the high school.

From the basement, she called, "That you?" and appeared, half-dressed in bra and slacks—her belly only slightly curved, two months pregnant—and carrying a couple of ironed blouses. "I've been attacking the pile. I didn't have anything to wear."

She reached up for a kiss, and he drew her close, careful to put his cold hands on her slacks, not on her bare skin.

"Rolly, you're freezing. Please."

"Sorry. I've got some sketches I want you to look at."

"Don't ask me to talk about your work, not now. I'm in a hurry. Besides, I never know what to say." She started for the front hall.

"They're of cribs."

"Really?" She stopped and hooked the blouses on a cabinet knob. "Let's see."

He spread his drawings on the kitchen table. "I want to make something special for the baby."

A lighthouse smile lit her face. "Oh, Rolly, thank you." She shivered and hugged herself.

"Aren't you cold? Do you want me to get you—?"

"I'm fine."

She sat and pulled the top drawing toward her. As her eyes followed the lines he'd drawn, a buttery warmth spread through his chest.

"I like this one, Rolly. I like it a lot. It reminds me of Carl Larsson."

She'd given him a book of Larsson's watercolors last Christmas. Larsson was a favorite of hers, too saccharine for him, but he wanted her to see that he recognized her inclination. He kissed the top of her head. "I thought you'd like it, but keep going, there's others you'll like too."

"This one's wonderful. We could paint the room a soft yellow…"

"Yes, but keep going." He loved her enthusiasm.

As she bent over the next drawing, he watched the sun catch the tiny hairs on her bare shoulders.

"Too early American, don't you think?" she asked, looking up.

He nodded. "You've got a better eye than you know. But I wanted to give you lots to choose from."

She grinned.

The next couple of drawings were very spare, austere really. He knew she wouldn't go for these, but she studied each carefully, without comment. He couldn't remember the last time she'd looked at anything he'd done this intently. He liked the feeling.

"These look Shaker-esque." She kissed his cheek. "Did the Shakers make cribs? They were celibate, weren't they?"

"But they adopted kids. Little bundles left at the gate."

"They must have made cribs." He smiled at her and she smiled back.

She picked up the last drawing, his favorite. It resembled his canoes, but was much smaller and wider and would hang from long wooden ribs from a universal ball joint on the ceiling. She studied the sketch and he explained how it would work.

"Why does it have to be attached to the ceiling?"

"So the baby will feel like he's floating." He fought a flicker of annoyance. "Think of it. He'll be suspended from above. His orientation will be to the sky. I'll paint a sky on the ceiling and he won't be tied to the ground. In a regular crib or bassinet, if someone knocks it, the baby is jarred, but if someone bumps this crib, the baby will glide. He'll have the sensation of free motion. Wouldn't that be perfect? Wouldn't you want that for yourself?"

"Can't it have a base?"

"A base would make it too rooted."

"Why would legs and wheels, which would allow you to actually roll the crib from place to place, make it too *rooted*? You aren't thinking practically." She tucked her chin in.

"Alice, this is supposed to be fun." He put his arm around her waist. "Come here. I'm sorry. I don't mean to be stubborn. The point is for our baby to have a wonderful crib. You want the Larsson one, I'll make it. You like that?"

Her chin quivered. He drew her into his lap and stroked her cheek, relieved as the tension ebbed from her body, but wishing that his compromise didn't feel like defeat.

"After I finish that work for the exhibition in L.A., I'll start on the one you like, OK?"

Alice looked up at him, her eyes shiny with tears held back. "Thank you."

✳✳✳

He bought the boards for the crib, set them aside, and returned to his casts, working long hours at his college studio. He needed twenty pieces for the L.A. show.

He'd just arrived at his studio after his special projects class, when someone knocked on his door. A student with a question, he guessed; but when he opened the door, there stood Meg Saffold. Startled, he stepped backward. In the dim and chilly hall, she stood with her coat unbuttoned. He'd forgotten how the air surrounding her seemed to pulse. She reached into her bag and pulled out a small, white envelope.

"I was downstairs in the office, putting these in a few of the boxes. Jocelyn mentioned that you were upstairs, working. I hope you don't mind being interrupted."

"No, come on in, I was…" Her freckles were astonishingly vivid.

"I thought I'd come up and deliver this in person." She walked past him into the studio.

He took what looked like an invitation to some college function. "Would you like something to drink?"

She spotted his hot plate. "Tea?" and unwound her scarf. "Can I?" She nodded toward the showerhead coat hooks.

"Let me help you." His arms prickled with pleasure as her coat slipped into his hands, hoping she wouldn't notice his casts at the other end of his studio, near the windows. They weren't finished and he wasn't ready to have them be seen or to explain them. Not yet.

He filled the kettle and settled it on the hot plate. "Earl Gray, regular, lapsang souchong?"

"Lapsang souchong." She faced him. "I've never been here before. I guess I've never been in any of the art studios. This is huge. Hard to heat?" She pulled down the sleeves of her dark green sweater. "It's…I don't know…it's great that you have so much space. If I had this much space all to myself, I'd live here."

"In a way, I do." He thought of Alice. A knot tightened in his stomach.

Meg walked to his bulletin board, skimmed his class lists, paused to examine his array of sugar packets that were printed with drawings of Great American Women, then strolled to his drawing board where she peered at some sketches, touching nothing. The way she regarded what she was looking at reminded him of Farley, his white cat from when he was little. When Farley got out of the house, he'd stop at the edge of the patio and stare at the grass. Slowly, he would extend a paw over the grass, but not touch it, curious but wary. That's how Meg moved. At his woodworking bench, she picked up a rib he'd cut for a canoe last summer and set it carefully in an open space in the middle of the bench, not in the heap where she'd found it, as if she noticed something special about it. Then she moved to his shelves and stared at the odd constructions that were experiments with different adhesives. Her attention made everything spring into high relief.

"Here's your tea." He felt shy and exposed.

She cradled the mug in both hands and held it up to her face. "Hmm. It makes me feel we're meant to live outdoors, under trees, like those," she nodded toward his casts — his stomach clenched — "with smoke from our fires swirling around us, keeping us warm."

He and Meg in a wintry birch grove: He pushed the image aside and put down his mug to reach for the invitation she'd brought. The envelope held a thick white card. An embossed circle surrounded Daisy Duck, who spun coyly on pink high heels while beaming at Donald Duck. Little hearts danced around her head. "Be mine." A valentine? Not an invitation. It was a joke, had to be, just a friendly gesture, but he felt like a cartoon character who'd raced off a cliff and was scrambling in midair. Heart pounding in his ears, he looked from Daisy Duck to Meg, who was resisting a laugh.

"Of course, I'll be your valentine." To cover his confusion, he turned his back to her and walked toward his bulletin board. "I'll pin this here, next to favorite women," his Great American Women sugar packs. "Eleanor Roosevelt, meet Daisy Duck." He was afraid to face Meg.

"How did you make them look like real sugar bags?" she asked, coming up beside him.

"They *are* real. I found them in a restaurant supply house in Mobile, Alabama."

"Daisy is too much of an airhead for Eleanor." She pulled out the pin, lifting the card. "Next to Clara Barton is more fitting."

"Why?"

"She was a cross-dresser during the Civil War."

"I thought she started the Red Cross."

"*And* was a cross-dresser."

"You're not serious."

"Who can say for sure who anyone really is?" She suppressed a smile.

What game was she playing? The radiator hissed. There was no other sound. The campus might have been deserted. Rolly realized how alone they were. He hoped she couldn't see that he was shaking.

"I meant, *why* the valentine?"

"I thought you meant why Clara Barton. I give valentines to my friends."

"I'm your friend?"

"Aren't you?" She gazed at him, her eyes, bright and intense, almost mean.

"Well, I guess I am." His heart clenched.

"I gave one to Shep Holloway and one to Herman. Not your friend Wolf, whom I do not like."

He was pleased and embarrassed to be pleased. "Any friends in your husband's congregation?" He couldn't tell if the twist of her lips expressed mischievousness or disappointment with him, for connecting whatever this game was with anything real.

"No." She pointed toward the tree casts. "Tell me about those… whatever, in the corner."

"They're what I'm working on right now and probably a waste of time," he answered, uncomfortable with his fatuous modesty, but relieved to have the conversation move away from the game. He liked the frisson of flirting, which shook off the pall of same old, same old that characterized this place, and, at the same time, was glad she was a minister's wife, and thus bound by stiff rules. He walked away from her, to the counter where he'd left his tea. The cold, smoky brew puckered his tongue.

She stood by the casts, which towered over her. "These whatever *are* beautiful. Why do you say they're a waste?"

"Please don't say they're 'beautiful.' That's the worst." He thought of Wolf's disdain.

"They *are* beautiful. Why be afraid of beauty?"

"They're not finished yet. I've got to get rid of the beauty. More binding. More discoloration. Tie them up in twine. Like…I don't know, corpses, or at least packages that would never get through the post office." She laughed and touched one. Her laughter bubbled inside him, like soda pop bubbles, painful and delicious. He said, "I might tie them up, dust them with powder. Give them a mummified aura. I'm not sure yet. I want something tougher than beauty, *punctum*, that which pierces. What most people mean by beauty is what they expect to see, only better. Beauty confirms. Hell, beauty sedates."

She watched him, weight on one hip.

Why was he saying all this? If she didn't understand, he didn't care. He inhaled and walked away from her to look out at the snow-covered plaza below. Within an hour the solid gray cloud cover would darken and, without a sunset, night would fall.

He said, "I want these things to break your heart."

Behind him he heard nothing, not even her breath, and wondered if she'd heard him or if he'd spoken. It didn't matter. He was a husk, a dead thing. If he cracked open, a handful of silt would spill out on the floor. He turned to her.

She wasn't facing him. She was running her finger along the cut edge of one of the casts. On the wall above her head, its pale shadow wavered among the others, a movement like water.

"They're so light. I thought they were clay." She picked up one of the short branches and balanced it on her open palm, as Wolf had done, but her eyes shone with delight.

"They're just molded paper," he said. "Let me." He took the cast and settled it among the others and reached for another, a longer one. This he pried open and snapped over her arm. The top of it arched backward, about two feet higher than her head.

"Is that OK?" he asked.

She nodded and raised her arm slightly, making the branch dip behind her. "Will it break?" She lowered her arm to her side.

"It doesn't matter." He selected another cast, about the length of the other. "OK?" he asked, touching her other arm, thrilled by the strangeness and familiarity of her warmth within her sleeve and snapped this cast on her other arm.

With her eyes fixed on some point behind him, she held herself rigid, with the two papery limbs rooted at her hands and towering over her head. In her black leggings and green sweater, she had the presence of a dancer waiting for her cue, the personification of contained power. And beautiful. That word again. She was beautiful. He stared at her. A wire coil had slipped over him and was being drawn tight, pressing on his flesh, cutting into his skin. He was trapped.

He swallowed. "You redeem these casts. What do you think, you willing to wear these in my next show?"

Meg started to raise her arms, but stopped when the branches wobbled precariously overhead. "Sure. Maybe the next faculty show at the gallery in the Union."

"Never." He slipped the casts from her arms and placed them with the other casts, the back of his neck tingling.

"I could."

"Not in this town you couldn't."

"I could," she whispered.

Something inside him took a dive. He looked around the studio, at the shabby surroundings, at his tools and armatures, scraps of wood, the casts, at his incomplete and unrealized efforts as his hand moved up her back to lift the hair from her neck and letting it fall. She smelled of oranges and wool and something like crushed cypress.

"My god, not this," he whispered, bending to kiss her.

"No, not this." She offered her face to him and his heart jerked.

5

Alice reread her headline, "Doggie Bones Exhumed," then hit the delete button. A fur-matted, gruesome lump, no resemblance to a dog, but "doggie" made it a joke. A joke? What was wrong with her today? She was eleven weeks pregnant, had no sign of morning sickness; she should be floating on air, but she was in a sour mood, vexed by everything, and, for no good reason, wanting to stick it to Mrs. Leonard Gruenke, what a name, who'd demanded that Alice put this damn pooch story on the front page. Alice straightened, planted her feet on the floor, and breathed deeply.

> On Friday, February 15, Mrs. Leonard Gruenke of 1021 Maple called police to her home to investigate the disappearance of her Pomeranian Daisy. Daisy was not just any dog, she was special.

Special? Alice hit the delete button again. Without Barry on the other side of the glass wall, she was regressing to high school. No, middle school. "Like my own flesh and blood," the woman had said. Maybe it was this that repelled Alice. Loving a dog that way, the way that Alice loved her thumb-size baby. She touched her belly and started again.

On Friday, February 15, police, responding to a call from Mrs. Leonard Gruenke of 1021 Maple, discovered the body of her five-year-old Pomeranian, Daisy, buried behind her garage.

Mrs. Gruenke had recently returned from a two-week vacation in Florida and found Daisy missing. During her absence, Mrs. Gruenke had hired a neighbor's seventeen-year-old son to housesit and care for Daisy. The boy told her that a car had hit Daisy, and he had buried the dog behind the garage. Mrs. Gruenke became suspicious and asked the police to investigate.

Alice had used the woman's name too often. She would change this. She wasn't going to write that this woman had insisted the cops take the dog's remains to her vet. And why hadn't Jet Bower, who was usually so sensible, talked the woman off the wall once she started ragging on the boy? A member of a cult that planned to take over in the new millennium? The supermarket tabloids fed this stupidity. The *Herald* carried a lot of nonsense too — "That's what people want to read," as Barry said — but even he refused to give space to the crazy stories that came in now, with the year 2000 only nine months away.

The phone rang. Fritzie, from downstairs: "Do me a favor? Pick up the publicity information on the Methodists' Spring Renewal conference? I told Ken Saffold, you know him, the minister. I said I'd stop by the parsonage, but the garage just called. My car won't be ready today."

"Sure, after I finish this damn dog story and inflate the crop forecasts to six graphs." Alice hung up, then called Fritzie back to apologize.

"You're allowed to be moody when you're in your condition, but will you see to the Methodists?"

Alice assured her it would be no trouble, feeling especially guilty because Fritzie had promised to crochet a baby blanket. How could Alice say she didn't like marching ducks? She hadn't meant to tell anyone about the baby, except Patricia, for two more weeks. The ugly blanket coming her way was her just reward.

She fixed her gaze on her monitor. She was having a hard time taking anything seriously except the baby. She played at being a reporter, made the calls, covered meetings, wrote swiftly — not this morning — and kept the banter going with Barry and Fritzie and the others when they came in. With all her friends, even Bettina, she played at being interested in whatever it was she was supposed to be interested in. With Patricia, she played at being the good daughter, phone calls, lunches, questions about what she was up to. With Rolly, she played her regular role: girlfriend-wife. She tried to look pretty, makeup first thing in the morning, no sweats, even after work when she was tired, and she didn't complain when he came home late. After those weeks when he'd acted so distant, like he wasn't sure, he'd come around, but she could tell that what he felt more than excitement was pressure. What she wanted was for him to join her in "expecting." Expecting, a perfect word. Expecting a new, beautiful, soft baby who would nestle close, like her own beating heart. Expecting each day to be arranged around a purpose greater than herself. Expecting to love without limits. Expecting them to be a real family. But Rolly had taken on too much work. The show in L.A., a new one next fall in Seattle. Even the crib had added to his list.

Wanting to think about something else, she turned from her blinking monitor and phoned her mother.

"What's up, dear?"

"I'm going crazy. Barry's gone. I can hear mice in the walls. The big window overlooking the square is frosted over. I can't even see out. I'm trapped. Help!"

"Well, I've got to drop off Dr. Mueller's books this morning." Patricia worked as a bookkeeper for several dentists. "Lunch after that?"

Swiveling to see the wall clock, Alice said, "It's not even eleven yet, and I'm starving. How fast can you get here?"

"I don't believe you! When I was pregnant with you, I practically didn't eat for the first five months. My doctor put me on an all-ice cream diet. I've been fighting those five ice cream pounds ever since."

Patricia had never forgiven Alice for those imaginary five pounds. "I'm different from you. I'm ravenous all the time. Can you make it by a quarter to twelve?"

Alice finished the dog piece, a story about the county commission meeting, and the crop forecasts, after she reached a professor from the ag extension who gave her a couple of good quotes about the continuing drought and an estimate of how much crop yields would be down. Slipping her coat from the hanger, she touched her belly. The same slight bulge, not bigger yet, but softer.

Downstairs Patricia stood next to Fritzie's desk, admiring something in one of Fritzie's magazines. The two women were the same height and about the same age, but they couldn't be more different. Patricia, with her smooth blond hair, pert face, and aerobicized body, evident even under her stylish slim coat, looked like a TV anchorwoman, while Fritzie's roots showed in her mud-dull perm, her freckled skin sagged — no fancy facials for Fritzie — and she was shaped like a barrel. Fritzie, who'd never married, was the one who looked like Alice's idea of a grandmother. Patricia looked too self-involved. It had surprised Alice, and Rolly too, when she moved to Haslett a year after they did. She could be a bookkeeper anywhere, she said. She wanted to live near her daughter. That was a surprise too.

"How about Chan's?" Patricia waved good-bye to Fritzie and kissed Alice.

A year ago, Alice had written a story about Irene Chan and her restaurant. Irene's family had come over as boat people, like lots of Chinese-Vietnamese.

"How about the drugstore?" Alice countered, recalling Chan's fried garlic stench. "I'm kind of in the mood for a tuna fish sandwich."

"But Chan's sizzling rice soup would be just the thing on such a cold day." Patricia hugged herself. "This wind is whistling up my sleeves."

"OK," Alice agreed, not wanting to make a fuss. "Soup sounds good."

Chan's was on the far side of the square. Sickening food smells rushed at Alice when she pushed open the door. Tea might settle her stomach. As usual at lunchtime, nearly every table was taken. Patricia chatted with Irene at the cash register as Alice nodded to Josie Ott, the town manager, holding court in the front booth. At a table near the fake bamboo planter sat Steve Grimp and Jet Bower, her two favorite cops, whom she'd last seen yesterday in Mrs. Gruenke's backyard. Both men were wearing their winter hats with the furry earflaps down.

Mei, Irene's insolent cousin with waist-length black hair, led Patricia and Alice to the one empty booth and threw a couple of menus on the table. If Rolly were here, he'd goad Mei into a smile. He regarded making Mei smile a personal challenge.

"I'm glad we came," Alice said, calling after Mei to bring some tea. She'd thought she wanted to talk to her mother about Rolly, but now she wasn't sure.

Patricia said, "What I hate about winter is what it does to my hair."

"You look perfect as always." She waited for Patricia to struggle out of the tight sleeves of her coat. When Patricia folded it beside her purse, Alice said, "You haven't seen Rolly in…how long? Come over for dinner on Sunday. I'll get a ham."

From her purse Patricia pulled out a green flyer. "Here's something I picked up for you at the gym. They've added a new low-impact aerobics class, which would be ideal for you."

Alice set it aside. Keeping her figure wasn't high on her list of concerns. "If not Sunday, what about Saturday night?" Afterward, Alice could ask if she thought anything was going on with Rolly.

Patricia glanced up from the menu. "Taking a few measures now will make getting your figure back after the baby that much easier. Has the doctor said it's risky for you?"

"He said take the vitamins, avoid the usual, and live normally."

"Well, if you think that's enough…" Her tone said it wasn't. "About this weekend, I can't. I'm going to Las Vegas."

"Las Vegas? You don't even gamble."

"Don't scowl, Alice, you'll look old before your time." She patted Alice's hand. "I've met a new man. Warren Jenks." She glanced at the nearby tables, as if someone might be eavesdropping, as if anyone might be interested. "He lives in Indianapolis and he sells irrigation equipment all over the Midwest. I met him at Betty and Fred's about a month ago. We've gone out twice."

"You haven't mentioned him to me, and now you're going to Las Vegas with him?" Alice pictured Patricia in a sparkly, low-cut dress, too much makeup, on the arm of some bald guy with a fake tan.

"I don't think you have a right to mind." Patricia unfolded her napkin and smoothed it carefully across her lap as Mei set a pot of tea and two cups on the table.

When she was gone, Alice said, "Don't have a right to worry about you becoming pathetic? You just met the guy. Do you even know if he has a wife in wherever you said he came from?"

"Alice, you're being silly. Are you feeling OK?"

"I'm fine." Alice knew she was being petulant. Peering into her little cup, she poured tea that hadn't steeped enough.

Patricia reached across the table to squeeze her hand. "But how about dinner Tuesday or Wednesday, a week from now?"

"I'll have to check with Rolly. I hardly see him during the week."

"Is that what's bothering you?"

"No," Alice lied.

"Don't worry, honey. He's getting adjusted to the idea of everything being different from now on. For men, it's harder. Their bodies don't lead the way as they do us. My guess is that Rolly is working like a devil now to prove something to himself."

Mei set two bowls in front of them and dumped hot rice into a basin of soup. Heads nearby turned as the dish sizzled.

Patricia continued, "Your dad went through something similar. Worried he wasn't earning enough, not that I cared. He wanted to be a good father. And he was always that, wasn't he, dear?" Alice nodded. He'd died when Alice was eleven. "He worked so hard the six months before you were born that I joked about being a single mother."

That's how Alice felt. She sipped her soup. "I haven't been worried, not really. It's just that he doesn't work at home anymore, only at his studio at the college. Is it because he doesn't want to see more of me than he has to?"

"Don't get clingy, Alice. He'll come around. Make yourself busy too. Take the aerobics class." The restaurant's door jingled. Patricia glanced toward the sound. "I'm hoping to introduce you to Warren. He was supposed to be here with some customers from the co-op. But maybe…"

So that was why she'd insisted on Chan's. Annoyed, Alice said, "I'd hoped you'd go with me to Weiland's to look at maternity clothes." She hadn't thought of this until this moment.

"All they have is tents, and you're not even three months pregnant. I'll take you shopping in a month. We'll go to Indianapolis."

Alice pretended she wasn't hurt while Patricia talked about her neighbor's new car, what she should pack for Las Vegas, and whether she should get a fresh haircut, all the time keeping her eye on the door. No Warren. Not exactly Mr. Reliability, Alice thought, with satisfaction. She said she had to get back to the paper. Mei brought their check.

On their way out, Alice paused at the cops' table. "Anything new with the Gruenke dog?"

Jet shook his head. "That woman's something else, but Doc Bear," everyone made fun of the vet's name, which was really Bernstein, "says the dog was sexually abused."

Alice's stomach lurched. "How's that possible?"

Jet shrugged. "Doc is turning in a report. Should be available at the station later today."

"What's all this about?" Patricia asked, turning back. Before Jet or Alice could answer, Patricia glanced at the door where a group of men were coming in.

"Warren," she gasped, grabbing Alice's arm and urging her forward.

"Warren, I want you to meet my daughter. Where... Alice, this is Warren Jenks."

Alice produced her professional smile and shook the hand of the nondescript man in the gray parka. "Patricia was just telling me about you."

He didn't look like the smarmy loser she'd pictured. More like the men who hung around the hardware store on Saturday mornings: bald, with a fringe of dun-colored hair, pale eyes behind thick glasses, wide mouth,

66

and saggy jowls that slid downward into a heavily starched, white collar beneath his maroon scarf. Alice had never liked that shade of maroon.

"And your mother's told me so much about you too. She's quite a fine lady, your mother. Here, let me introduce you to…" And he turned to the middle-aged men he'd come in with, one she knew from the bank, the other two, strangers.

When the introductions were over, Warren said, "Won't you ladies join us?"

Before her mother could respond, Alice said, "You stay if you want, Patricia, but I've got to get back to the paper."

Patricia made her good-byes and followed Alice out to the sidewalk.

"He wasn't what I expected," Alice said.

"What do you mean?"

"I expected him to be at least good-looking. Somehow the Las Vegas thing…"

"He's good-looking enough," Patricia interrupted, flexing her fingers in her gloves, then smiled tightly at Alice. "Don't worry about me, honey."

"But I do."

*** *** ***

Fritzie barked, "Don't talk to me," when Alice entered, "one eighty-four, eighty-six, eighty-eight. There." She looked up from her knitting. "Come take a look at this crib blanket I've started for my niece in Merrillville. Here." She held up a magazine folded to a picture of a vile, color-splashed afghan.

"Psychedelic?" Alice asked, her stomach turning over.

"Something different. It's what she wants. How'd you like me to make one just like it for you?" She peered at Alice over the edges of her glasses. "Oh, you should see your expression. Don't worry, I'm joking."

"I like one with the ducks," Alice lied, her chin wobbling, the precursor of tears. Fritzie was making her a baby blanket — yes, it would be ugly, but it was an expression of her affection — while Alice's own mother offered her a lousy aerobics flyer. And she was running off with a new boyfriend to Las Vegas, of all miserable places.

"Then ducks it will be."

"I'll love it," Alice blubbered, hugging Fritzie, then grabbing a tissue from Fritzie's box. "That dog story has gotten to me."

"You're allowed." Fritzie flicked her eyes at the ceiling. "Barry's here."

"Good."

"Don't forget the Methodists."

"I won't." Alice unbuttoned her coat and touched her belly, cursing Chan's fried garlic.

Behind the glass wall Barry was hunched at his desk, his white shirt and thick shoulders a reassuring sight. He glanced up and nodded.

Alice waved, hung up her coat, walked into his office, and leaned against his desk. She felt queasy.

He clicked "save" and swiveled to face her. "Front page is done. I've tightened your county development story."

Barry was only twelve years older than she, but with his gray hair, paunch, and confident air, he seemed much older. "I spent the morning at the bank, talking to their board about this development deal. I'm glad to be out of there. How're you doing? You look pale."

"Not great." She told him about what Jet had said about the dog, adding that she'd stop by the police station to get a look at the report.

Barry shook his head. "You go on home. *I'll* update your story. You don't look so good."

"Thanks, I will." She pressed her fingers against her belly and tried to smile. "After I run over to the Methodist church to pick up their copy on their Spring Revival Conference."

"Call and tell them if they want the notice to appear, they have to bring it in. I'm not having you run around in this weather." He rifled through a pile of papers. "But take care of this before you go." He handed her a slip of paper.

Roger Fender. After her story on Heidi ran, he'd put up a five-foot-sign: "Visit the Holy Site where the Blessed Virgin Appeared." Alice had written her piece to minimize sensationalism for the girl's sake, but her father wanted maximum sensation. Alice had heard he charged admission.

"I'll take care of Fender," she said, her stomach churning. At her desk she popped a mint in her mouth, hoping that would help.

After the interview ran, she'd called Heidi to see how she was doing, but the girl had been cool. She didn't want to talk. Alice had been disappointed and confused. They'd shared a connection, she thought. The next two times she'd called, the mother answered. She said Heidi wasn't home. Probably lying.

Roger Fender answered. Alice introduced herself.

"I want to speak to the boss," he said.

"Mr. Holtzer asked me to call you. Can I help you?"

He breathed noisily. "We got big news out here, and I want to know why you ain't writing about it."

"Has something else happened? How's Heidi?"

"Has something else happened?" he shouted.

On the other side of the glass wall, Barry grinned. Better Alice than he.

"What are you asking for: a fresh miracle every day? You *know* what happened. Who'm I talking to, anyway? You say you're a reporter. Why don't you report on the biggest thing that ever did happen in Langford County or anywhere else in the state of Indiana? A new age is dawning and right here is the evidence and you..."

"*We* covered the story. Front page, center. I take it Heidi hasn't seen anything new. Is that right?"

Barry walked past her desk, bugging out his eyes, and pointing north, in the direction of the police station. She made a face.

Fender whined, "This is something that people need to know about. Who knows what might come next?"

The jerk just wanted to keep the crowds coming. She pictured Heidi trapped in that dreary living room with the grim palm fronds. "Mr. Fender, I'm afraid the paper can't run another story. But if something new comes up, let me know."

"You better believe I'll let ya know." He muttered something she couldn't catch.

"Can I speak to Heidi?"

"She ain't here."

He was lying. "Then if you'd give her the message—"

"After your kind have enticed her away from the Christian values?"

"Mr. Fender—"

"She's took off. Emptied my wallet, stole my brother's CD player. Ten days ago. We haven't heard from her since."

Alice sat up, caught between hoping Heidi had escaped that miserable household and alarm. "Have you informed the police?"

"That bunch of lame-asses? No. But if you was to run another story about what happened here with her and the Virgin, I know she'd see it and feel the call to come home."

He was playing her, but she was worried. "I'll be out to see you tomorrow, and we can talk about this. How's four o'clock?" If Heidi hadn't gone missing, she'd be home from school by then.

"Four's fine."

Alice hated the triumph in his voice. She called the police station to find out if there was a Missing Person out on the girl. There wasn't. Alice felt queasy. The mint hadn't helped. Silently thanking Barry for telling her to go home, she hunted for her shoes under her desk, then remembered the Methodists. After a couple of deep breaths and a sip of water, she dialed the number. A woman answered. Alice asked to speak to Ken Saffold.

"This is Meg Saffold. Ken's not here right now. He's been called to the hospital."

Red hair, tall, connected in some way to the college. Alice was sure they'd met. "Hello, Meg. Alice Becotte here, from the *Haslett Herald*. I'm calling about the publicity packet for the Spring Conference."

A beat of silence, then, "Ken told me a Fritzie Janke would be picking it up."

"Unfortunately, Fritzie Janke can't make it. Will someone from the church be able to drop the packet off here before three-thirty? That's the latest, if we are going to run something in next week's paper."

"Are you asking *me* to bring the information to your office?"

Or you could stuff it. "We're shorthanded at the moment."

Silence. Finally, the woman said, "I'll see if anyone is available."

What a bitch. Alice hung up without saying good-bye. Not an ideal minister's wife.

The sky hung heavy and gray when Alice stepped outside. Snow was on its way. She swung out of her parking spot and turned south at the corner, galled by the minister's wife's unhelpfulness, and aggravated by Patricia's la-di-da attitude, Warren Frog-face Jenks, Fender's games, and the ugly blanket with ducks that Fritzie would spend so much love and labor on. Why couldn't Fritzie make something pretty?

At home she filled the kettle and headed upstairs to change. In the bathroom she sat on the toilet, sleepy. When she opened her eyes, she saw a dark spot on the white saddle of her panties. Her period? She touched it. Dry. Some mark from the laundry? But she hadn't noticed it before. It looked like blood. There shouldn't be blood.

She slid from the toilet to the floor, with her back pressed against the side of the tub. Nearby, the towels hung crooked from the hooks. Above them, the fish poster was dimpled from moisture. The shower curtain was bunched at the end of the tub. Everything was as it should be. Nothing had changed. She put a finger into her vagina. There was blood. A little, not much. Very little really, just a few black-red streaks.

She heard a distant yowl. The kettle.

She worked her way up from the floor, pulled up her pants, and walked carefully downstairs, hand on the walls, afraid to jostle herself. Turning into the kitchen, she gripped the doorframe and held on. Steam billowed from the screaming kettle. Not hurrying, she moved toward the stove, picking up the pregnancy book she'd left on her desk as she passed. She turned off the stove, dialed Dr. Petrillo's office, left a message, and stared out the kitchen window, seeing nothing, waiting for his return call.

***

"Could you describe the blood for me?"

She did.

"And would you say that it's flowing?"

"No."

"Like a light period?"

"Not even that much. Just a little."

"Well, Alice, I don't think this is anything to worry about at this point. Breakthrough bleeding is not uncommon in the first trimester, and, let's see you're in your—"

"Eleventh week."

"I want you to relax. I can hear how worried you are. Take it easy. Rest, go to bed, not that you need to, no, but I think it's best for you not to exert yourself. Have that husband of yours fix dinner tonight. And call me tomorrow. Of course, if there's any change, if the flow increases, if there is any cramping, call me immediately — you have my emergency number, right? — but I don't expect that. Call me tomorrow, just to check in."

Terrified, half believing him, half not, she dialed Rolly's office number, but couldn't think of what she would say. Crying, she hung up.

Afraid to turn around, sensing that panic was crouched behind her waiting to lunge, she searched for the postcard of the Virgin of Guadalupe and found it under the phone book. Cradling the card next to her chest, she carried it upstairs. In the bathroom, she checked to see if there was more blood. There was: thin, bright red, but not a lot. She wished she had asked Dr. Petrillo how long this bleeding could last and still be called normal.

The bedside clock said 4:05. It was impossible to believe that less than an hour ago everything had seemed fine. She propped the picture of the Virgin against the bedside lamp, got undressed, and climbed into bed. Tilting the card so that she could see it, she called on the Virgin to come to her aid, seeing Heidi's face overlap with the sweet Virgin's. Heidi's heavy mascara, the Virgin's pink lips, flickered as she prayed.

She phoned the art department. It took a few minutes for Jocelyn to find Rolly in his office.

"What's up?" A scuffling sound came next. "Wolf says hi too."

"Could you come home, Rolly?"

"What's wrong?" His voice had become alert.

"I'm bleeding."

"Are you OK?"

"Just come."

6

Rolly gunned out of his parking space behind the art building, nearly clipping Herman's aged Mercedes, reminding himself that no one was healthier than Alice. He couldn't remember her ever being sick. Not enough to stay in bed. Not with colds. Not the flu. Never. Once she'd sprained her ankle, needed crutches for a week, that was it. He sped through town, wishing he knew more about pregnancy. It wasn't risky the way it used to be, that's what he did know, and Alice didn't even look pregnant yet. Their visit with that ass Petrillo hadn't explained much. Week nine, week ten, week eleven. He talked as if pregnancy was a ski course and these were slalom gates Alice would career through, flags snapping. Alice had beamed, exhilarated by the coming run. No mention of problems.

He rounded the corner of their block and saw that their house was dark except for their bedroom window. The length of the street was lined with grimy embankments of snow, notched for cars. He pulled into the space he had shoveled that first morning when he and Paul Faracci had bet on who would finish first. Snow crunched under the back bumper.

On the phone Alice's voice had been small, not a whisper but tiny, like she was shrinking. "I just want you here with me."

"Alice?" he called, opening the front door. No answer. In the kitchen the drawers of her desk gaped open, and a cup of tea sat forgotten beside the stove. He took the stairs three at a time.

She was in bed, the blanket pulled up to her neck, her eyes closed, giving no sign that she'd heard him. The covers were smooth, as if she'd slid herself between the sheets and not moved. He tossed his jacket on the rocking chair and sat gently on the edge of the bed, not wanting to wake her, but wanting her to tell him she was all right.

After a moment she blinked, her eyes hot and shiny.

From crying or trying not to cry? "Are you OK?"

She struggled to sit up and straightened her spine against the headboard. He wanted to wrap his arms around her, but saw that she was working to hold herself together. He lifted her hand and held it against his cheek. Her fingers were cold.

"This afternoon when I got home from the office," she spoke in a rush, "I thought my period had started, but I'm not supposed to have a period. I called Dr. Petrillo and he said..." She stared at a point above his shoulder. "It's called breakthrough bleeding. I should take it easy."

"And?"

"Rest but not worry."

From the bedside table he picked up *Pregnancy: A Guide to Bringing Well Babies into the World*.

"It says if the bleeding goes beyond spotting, if real bleeding starts, there's a chance...it says a chance...of a miscarriage."

He put down the book and gathered her close, her torso rigid, but she didn't pull away. After a moment she patted his back as if he, not she, needed comfort.

"But that also means that most of the time it *doesn't* happen, right?" he said. "Everything will be OK."

She nodded, her curls scratching his neck.

"Is there anything we're supposed to do?" he asked.

"The doctor said wait. That's all. If there's a change, call him."

"That's it?" He reached for the phone, but she held him back. From under the sheets, she withdrew an old postcard he recognized as Mexican.

"What's that?"

"I've been praying. Remember Heidi Fender? She *knew* I was pregnant. I didn't tell you — you would have made fun — but it had to be her recognition, had to be her blessing from the Virgin Mary. I know it was."

Rolly felt an inward folding. "That's just great, but I'm calling the doctor."

"No, Rolly, don't. Please. He said there's nothing to do now. Go get us some dinner. Don't call."

"Calling the doctor won't make matters worse." He watched her eyes widened with dismay. "You want me to wait until the morning?"

She nodded.

"OK, then I'll wait."

He drove to the mall half a mile away and chose a couple of old sci fi movies at the video store before entering the pizza parlor where the steamy air was thick with shouted orders and teenagers clowning near the counter. He wanted to call Meg, wanted to hear that little catching sound she made at the end of some of her words, and hated himself. Yesterday, after they'd made love and wrapped themselves up in his Navajo blanket from the cold of his studio, he'd begged her to say words that end in 'g,' just so that he could hear that delicious snag in her voice. "Shoppin-ga," "washin-ga," "holdin-ga," she had offered, and he had prompted, "How about, dancin-ga, kissin-ga, love makin-ga?" Standing in front of the pay phone, he thought about her picking up and saying "hello." He wouldn't have to say anything. He could just listen to her breathe. He latched the receiver back in its cradle.

76

On the way home, it began to snow.

In the kitchen, still in his parka, with the pizza box stacked with videos, he stared at his hulking reflection in the window, reluctant to go upstairs. He didn't want Alice to see him scared. Snowflakes big as cotton balls stuck to the screen he had left up last fall, blocking the view of the backyard, cutting off what was inside this house from everything out there. He took off his jacket, made a salad, and carried their dinner up on trays. They ate in bed, watching one of the dumb movies. Alice ate very little.

"I'm OK, really, just not hungry."

He cleared up. When he returned to the bedroom, carrying a brandy for him and cocoa for her, she'd closed her eyes. He couldn't tell if she was sleeping. On the TV, guys in black commando suits were thundering along the corridors of a space ship. He set her cocoa next to the alarm clock and lowered the volume so the explosions were no louder than a cap gun's. As he settled against the pillows, she nestled close. On the TV, silent explosions rocked the space ship. He listened to Alice breathe, while he watched a near miss on the end of the world.

When she'd told him about the baby, he'd pictured outsized baby gear à la Claes Oldenburg, strollers with bulldozer wheels, gigantic rubber nipples, glow-in-the-dark pacifiers expanding, and his own life contract. How was he going to hang on? Somehow, Meg shored up his balance. Instead of feeling overwhelmed, he was energized by all that he was keeping afloat. What he had with Meg was the glue that held his spinning-out-of-control life together. His drive, which had deserted him when Alice began blocking all the exits, had returned. Meg loosened the cords that Alice wound around him, and, oddly, she didn't diminish his love for Alice, she made it easier.

He'd always believed that men who claimed to love two women at the same time were self-serving, self-deluding, and cruel to both women because they withheld something essential from one or the other, more likely both. But now that it had happened to him, Rolly could see that what was withheld was something that rightly belonged to only him, something so personal he would have been embarrassed to give it a name. What Meg had done was restore this essential thing to him. Or he'd misplaced it and she helped him find it. Having rediscovered himself — that's how it felt — his bond to everything he loved, especially and unexpectedly to his wife, had grown deeper.

He flicked off the VCR. In the dark the window opposite the bed, a perfect rectangle of white, advanced toward him, a curtain of snow lighted by streetlamp. Fear crept over him. Inside Alice, something life-changing was going on, and he was a powerless bystander. The future was already set in motion. He couldn't change it or affect it.

Meg was the only one he'd told about the baby. She had held his head tight to her chest and whispered, "It's OK, Rolly," and he had believed her.

When he woke, it was still dark outside and Alice was missing. He listened. No sound. Outside the window the snow had stopped falling. He swung his feet to the floor, glanced toward the hall, and after a moment could see that the bathroom door was closed.

"Alice." He pressed his face to the doorjamb. He heard a low sound. "Are you OK?" She didn't answer. "Can I come in?"

"No." She hissed. "I feel terrible. I threw up."

"I shouldn't have gotten that damn pizza."

"It's not the pizza."

He opened the door. Alice was on the toilet, bent over, her head down, arms around her knees. In the faint light from the frosted window, her back glowed with the sickly iridescence of a fish curling on ice. He knelt beside her and brushed the sweaty curls from her neck.

He found a washcloth, soaked it in water, and Alice pressed it to her face, but she remained hunched over. Through the unshuttered top of the bathroom window, the snow clouds had broken apart and raced across the black sky.

"I'll call the doctor."

"No." Her pale face floated near his hand. "I better go to the hospital."

In a blur he yanked on clothes, ran outside, started the car, and left it running while he grabbed her coat, boots, and upstairs again, got her robe, before returning to the bathroom. She was in the same position, curled on the toilet; on the tiled floor were pink smears where she'd tried to clean up blood. Fighting nausea and trying to look calm, he draped her robe over her shoulders. The toilet water was scarlet.

He held her upright and threw her coat over her robe. As she slipped on her boots, he saw that her legs were streaked with blood. He had a vision of her withering as blood drained out of her, pooling on the white tiled floor. Panic pulsed through him and he clutched her.

"I've got to get towels," she said, "for the car." Her teeth were chattering. He seized a stack from the cabinet and led her downstairs.

He sped through empty streets and into the country, afraid to take his eyes off of her, but trying to stay focused on the road.

The hospital door sprang open at his touch. The wash of greenish light blinded him for a moment, and Alice flinched, tucking into his side. A sea of shining linoleum welled up in front of him. Far away, behind a glass panel, he saw movement, a nurse. Alice moaned and started to keel over, but he held her tight, shepherding her slowly across the slick floor. Off to the side, stretched out on the connected orange plastic chairs, a heavy man in a down vest slept. Behind the glass window the nurse's hat turned. Alice slid her feet as if she were walking on ice. Hard as he tried to guide her forward, they didn't seem to be moving. The nurse grew no closer. Her cap bobbed cheerily. She was talking on the phone. They inched forward. The nurse stood, eyeglasses flashing aluminum.

"My wife, she's bleeding," he called out, but the nurse turned away. He wanted to scream but was afraid of frightening Alice. When they reached the window, she put her hand on the glass to steady herself, her fingers fitting into the circle of a NO SMOKING sign.

The nurse's glasses turned in their direction. "If you'll fill out these…" She slipped some papers through the opening, then stopped, squinting to look past them. Rolly turned and saw animal tracks, blood smeared by Alice's boots.

"My wife needs help now."

The nurse sprinted around the partition, and men in blue scrubs appeared as Alice buckled forward. They took her arms and guided her toward swinging metal doors.

"Where are you going?" his voice echoed.

"If you'll just take a seat, sir."

"It's OK, Rolly. I'm OK," Alice said, her eyes wide with fright.

"I'm coming too."

"You'll be able to join your wife in a moment, but first—"

"No. Wait," he said, but a couple of orderlies he hadn't noticed stepped close.

"Hey, man, be cool. They're just taking her in. They got a job to do, see. You don't want to be getting in their way now." They backed him through the swinging doors and toward the orange chairs where the guy was sleeping.

"Take your hands off me!" Rolly yelled, ready to strike.

"We're not touching you, man. Now come on, take it easy," the other one said.

Rolly stood against the wall, refusing their offer of coffee, trying to imagine what was happening to her now, but old images came to him: the triangular scar on her forearm from the iron, her hands folding a napkin, opening letters, peeling fruit; her neck, with the tight short curls that stuck to her skin in the summer; driving, sunlight sliding over her throat and shoulder as she lowered the visor; her wide, Slavic cheekbones; the way her lips tensed when she was in pain.

✳✳✳

He flinched. One of the orderlies had tapped his arm. "The doc says to come in now."

"Mr. Becotte." The emergency room doctor.

"This is not a crisis, but we're going to have to proceed. I've spoken to Dr. Petrillo, and he's on his way. There is some risk to your wife of hemorrhaging, and if we perform a dilation and curettage immediately, we can reduce that risk. We can remove any remaining tissue that could set up infection and future trouble. Further, this procedure will allow us to discover if there is some fetal abnormality that might have caused this."

"Come."

He followed the doctor through the swinging doors and into a curtained area where Alice lay on a gurney behind nurses fiddling with tubes and an IV stand. He tried to touch her, but a nurse stepped between them.

"What're you doing?" he demanded.

The doctor was still talking, "—a spontaneous abortion is a miscarriage."

Abortion? Miscarriage? A small creature was running loose in the hollow of his skull, but his eyes could see nothing except white.

Alice whimpered.

"What the hell are you doing to her?"

Someone caught his arm. "This is for the IV. We have to begin fluids."

If he took his eyes off Alice, something bad would happen. A nurse bent over Alice and raised a vein between the bones on the back of her hand. A clipboard with legal forms appeared. He took a pen. They began to push Alice away.

She gasped, "Stop."

"What are you doing?" he demanded. A nurse was tugging at Alice's wedding band.

"We have to take this off before surgery. It might fall off. Get lost."

Alice started to cry. "It doesn't come off. It never comes off. Please don't take it off. I won't lose it. I promise." She tightened her hand into a fist.

The older nurse bent down. "It's all right, dear. We can tape it on. Everything will be fine." She nodded as she unlocked the gurney's wheels again.

"Rolly?"

"I'm right here." He shoved between the nurses and leaned over to kiss her. Her skin was an unnatural ocher.

"Am I going to die?"

"You are not going to die." The nurses were pressing him. "The doctor said everything will be fine. I love you."

"The baby?"

Tissue, not baby, not fetus. Tissue, that's what the doctor called it.

"Alice," he whispered. "There is no baby anymore."

She stared at him, uncomprehending, as the nurses closed around her, nudging him aside. Words were spoken and the women, all in blue, glided the gurney down the corridor. Double doors swung open, then closed behind them.

✳✳✳

After the surgery, after the nurses had settled Alice in for the night, he sat with her, holding her hand, her wedding ring bundled in tape,

82

neither of them speaking. She looked washed clean of feeling, not yet sad. He felt as if a giant hook had lodged in his chest. She said she had to sleep and he should go home. He was relieved.

The streets were dark. Daybreak was an hour away. When he reached their corner, he saw that their front door gaped open and yellow light spilled down their steps. Burglarized, too, on this night of all nights? But it was fitting, wasn't it, that more destruction should rain down on him. He walked up the stairs on jerky legs. Alice's plaid scarf hung on the coat tree. A matchbook shored up the wobbly leg of the walnut chest. The crooked top on the newel canted to the right, as always. He should have fixed it. Through each room he walked, looking for signs of the break-in. Upstairs, bedclothes were tossed on the floor, drawers open, blood swipes on the bathroom floor, but nothing seemed to be missing. Then he realized that this was how they'd left it. He walked downstairs and closed the front door, disappointed. He wanted evidence of a crime. He wanted to nail an intruder. He wanted to have a reason to beat the shit out of someone. In the linen closet he found some old towels and a bucket. On his hands and knees he washed the floor of Alice's blood until all that he could see on the shining tile was his own shadow.

A few hours later he returned to the hospital, carrying a garish bouquet from the supermarket, the only flowers he could find at 7 a.m. Alice was sitting up, her face wan, her hair brushed flat, her curls gone. Dr. Petrillo stood by her bed. Now that the crisis was over, he'd managed to get here, freshly shaved, dressed for breakfast at some country club. Alice barely glanced at Rolly, her attention locked on Dr. Petrillo, as if she were afraid of missing something.

He greeted Rolly, saying that he had just arrived and was pleased to see Alice doing so well. They wanted to keep an eye on her for a few more hours, but she could probably go home that afternoon. When he began to say what a good a patient Alice was, she interrupted him. "Why did this happen?" A muscle twitched in her cheek. Rolly squeezed her hand.

"Alice, Rolly, I know how hard this is for you, but first trimester miscarriages are quite common, more than you'd guess. They're nature's way of eliminating unsound fetuses." Unsound. The other doctor had used the word tissue. "You couldn't have done anything differently. I know you, Alice. Don't worry that you did something wrong. I can even say this: If I could, I wouldn't interfere in these early miscarriages. These pregnancies would only yield babies with horrible defects. Unsustainable, that's the point."

Alice tightened her grip on his hand, and Rolly's chest ached, grateful, for what he wasn't sure. For her love? For a monster baby that wouldn't be born? For the justice of punishment for him not wanting the baby enough?

"When can we try again?" Alice asked, drawing Rolly's hand toward her heart. Her question sideswiped him. He held tight, sick at the possibility of the nightmare repeating itself.

"Well, anytime really. There shouldn't be any problem, as soon as you feel strong enough. But I'd wait maybe, for six months or so, just to make sure your body's back to normal."

Six months would come in late summer, when they would be in Norway. Everything simple. He could keep his work going, and they'd start a new baby. He envisioned a picnic in a Norwegian meadow, he, Alice, and a baby in a basket. Behind them the sun yellowed the sky above red and purple flowers in a wash of green. He recognized the scene from a children's book and realized how deeply he wanted to give this to Alice. Leaning down, he kissed her forehead, smelling unfamiliar cotton.

Alice stroked his cheek, but spoke to Dr. Petrillo. "Of course, we'll try again."

As Petrillo explained details of Alice's release later that day, Rolly tried to listen, but he felt as if he was gliding away in one of his canoes.

"Sometime after two." Dr. Petrillo waved as he walked from the room.

Rolly returned to the house to get something for Alice to wear home. In her closet he pushed hangers back and forth, searching for the shift she'd asked for, exhaustion making him clumsy. A silky blue dress slid to the floor, one strap looping over his shoe. As he hung the dress back up, he realized he hadn't told anyone what had happened, and now the need to tell someone pressed on him. Alice had called her mother after Dr. Petrillo left and cried, and he'd talked to Patricia too — he couldn't remember what they'd said — but he'd told no one about the pregnancy, not even Wolf, no one except Meg, and he couldn't call her. He looked around the bedroom, half hoping to find someone nearby, and remembered the guy in the emergency room, the one sleeping on the orange chairs, wondering if he was still there. Rolly could go back and shake the guy's shoulder and say, "My wife just had a miscarriage." The guy would blink, push himself up shaking his head, and grasp Rolly's shoulder.

Rolly sat on their bed and stared at the Kathe Kollwitz print above the blanket trunk, noticing for the first time how the fevered black lines describing the mother and child looked like barbed wire. When Alice had hung this print a couple of years ago, he hadn't liked it, but he'd said nothing. Now he hated it. He rose from the bed, lifted the picture from its hook, and carried it down to the basement. He couldn't throw it out, but he shoved it into a gap behind the boiler. Feeling as if he'd accomplished something vital, he returned to the bedroom, folded Alice's clothes into a small bag, then returned to the hospital.

For the next week, he and Alice stayed home together. He told Herman Alice was sick and arranged for an adjunct to cover his classes. Alice didn't notice the missing print — he'd hung a mirror in its place — and she spent most of her time reading in the living room or in bed sleeping. He puttered around, staying close. She said she didn't want to talk about the miscarriage. Often he'd find her staring at nothing. If he asked what she was thinking, she didn't bother to answer. He knew what she was thinking. What else was there? Once she said, "This isn't fair," but that was all. He tried to think of ways to comfort her. Fixed the meals. Read to her from the paper. Bought her a short-sleeved green sweater for spring. He did not spend any time in his studio. He did not call Meg.

Each night in bed, he held Alice and tried to talk about the things they would do in the spring. She pretended to be interested, and this pretense saddened him further. Only when she said that she wanted to try again at the end of the summer, and he agreed, would she relax into his chest and tuck her head into his shoulder as she always had, but her head felt light, as if she were holding herself back in some internal way, even after she fell sleep.

After a week and a half, she went back to the paper, and he resumed his normal workload.

"Maybe at dinner we'll have something new to talk about," she said.

After his morning class, to avoid seeing Wolf or any of the other Monday regulars, he grabbed a sandwich at the Union and took it back to his studio.

The place had become unfamiliar, the air smelling stale, of dust and some lingering scent he was afraid was Meg. The white paper castings standing in bins along the west wall, a month's worth of work, looked like birch trunks that a deranged bone-doctor had practiced on with saws and plaster and splints. Wolf had blasted Rolly's earlier versions as display props. These weren't even that meaningful. Was it a few stolen hours with Meg that had made him stupid? How else to explain this junk? A load of shit, that's what he'd produced.

The next day he borrowed a pickup and brought to campus the four canoes he'd left at home. After struggling with the balky freight elevator, he lined them up in the middle of the floor, buoyed by his sense of purpose and what he could now see as their strong, totemic presence. He sighted down their lines from different angles, surprised by how fine they were. Why had he abandoned them? He picked up the smallest canoe by its center thwart and felt it flex. This one was perfectly carved and aligned. He set it down and brought over the other small canoe, aligning them together. Neither was more than a yard long. The thin light filtering through the ice-frosted windows shone on the copper-glazed bark exterior of the hulls. Squatting, he inspected the interiors, which pulsed with darkness.

When he began with the canoes, he'd planned to make ones that looked like Ojibwa or Algonquin birch bark craft, authentic and water-worthy, but with enough details that were just a little off, just a little unsettling, that would require the viewer take a closer look. This second examination would reveal subtle irregularities that nudged aside ordinary assumptions, and what would emerge, he hoped, would be mythic and powerful: the eternal journey. Man leaving home, hunting, exploring, returning home, only to set out again. Voyaging with no final destination, all passage, the ancient quest revisited and made ironic, and yet not entirely ironic. These two small boats achieved that. He had dismissed them and moved on into a morass. He'd been a fool.

He turned to his two larger canoes. Hoisting the bigger one onto his shoulder, he carried it into the center of the floor and set it carefully beside the small ones, nudging the stempieces into a straight line, then retrieved the last canoe and aligned it with the others. He backed off and sat on the windowsill. Their sleek, deliberate forms, aggressive as weapons, thrilled him. He had never looked at them carefully enough. But they weren't complete. He'd been stymied and lost his way, but he could see that the next step was to make them into funereal vessels. The Celts, the Vikings, and even the Sumerians had funereal rituals connected to rivers.

He saw a river misty in morning light, its gray surface peeling open as a blade-thin boat rose up, and kept rising. Cataracts of white rushing water swirled away from the glistening black hull until all that remained was blackness. Death and the river, River Styx, Dante and Virgil, Osiris on the Nile, beyond the Great Waters, journeying to the edge of the world: this was what he had been looking for. He would build a flotilla of canoes or maybe solitary ones. He might stick to sleek low vessels, but if he decided to work in multiples, he could give them canopied roofs like floating temples.

He opened a drawer, hunting for a notebook, and there was Meg's Daisy Duck valentine. He pulled it out and everything slowed down. Daisy smiled at him, her head haloed by little hearts.

He hadn't allowed himself to think about Meg since the miscarriage. When he did, he felt pulled apart. He was too much of a coward to face her, but he longed to explain what had happened. When he thought about what he would say, anything, everything seemed like a betrayal of Alice. Her loss, her anguish, and his couldn't be summed up in words, and even if he could, he shouldn't, not to the woman he'd made love with while Alice was bleeding.

He put the valentine back in the drawer and pulled out a sketchpad. Focus, that's what he had to do. He had to concentrate on his work.

Near the midterm a few weeks later, he'd finished a new canoe and was cleaning up for the day, when he heard tapping on the door, quick tapping, Meg's knock. She stood in the hall blowing on her fingers, her hair spun loose from the wind, red blotches from the cold flowering on her cheeks. Elation and dread took away his voice. She walked past him into the center of the studio where he'd left a pile of black stones next to his two smallest canoes. Propped against the wall where the cast branches had been stood his four large canoes.

"What happened to those white casts?"

Not trusting his voice, he shrugged and didn't answer.

Giving him a querulous look, she tucked her skirt behind her legs as she knelt next to the smallest canoe that was no longer than a skateboard. He'd coated its exterior with a gray polymer, which make the burrs and ridges gleam like scars, and the interior he'd lined with black-dyed fur that drank the light completely. She lowered her hand into the fur. "You've started something new."

Her words thrummed through him. He leaned against his drawing table to fight the shake in his chest. "Not really. Awhile back I'd begun working on canoes, then quit, didn't know where to go with them. That was before…" Before they had come together. "A couple of weeks ago, some ideas hit me."

"Is that why I haven't heard from you?" She turned to face him.

He looked for signs of accusation, but her candy-blue eyes were clear.

"It's not that. It's…"

"Alice."

"Yes."

"Did you tell her about us?"

He shook his head.

She looked down at the pile of stones near the hem of her skirt. "What are these for?" She nudged one.

"I'm wrapping them."

He walked toward where she knelt, and from under the side where she couldn't see, he lifted a grapefruit-size stone that he'd wrapped in black rice paper and lashed with scarlet twine. He held it out to her, wanting her to understand its weight as an expression of what he couldn't put into words. His distress, his love, his regret.

She took the wrapped stone without looking at him and transferred it from one hand to the other carefully, as if it were breakable, then handed it back to him. "What's it about?"

Angry with himself, and with her, he said, "I call it a 'successful soul.'"

Her face hardened. She stood, wiped her hands on her skirt, and walked to his workbench. "What's that supposed to mean?"

"I've been thinking about what Freud said." He felt like an idiot, but couldn't stop. "We all have two basic urges, one, for generation, that's the libido, and the other, the desire to die, to return to the state of the stone, Thanatos."

"So whose successful dead soul are you holding? Yours? Your desire for Thanatos?"

"I'm talking crap. It's a goddamn rock I'm sticking in this canoe, that's all." He dropped the stone into the canoe, causing it to wobble with the sound of rattling bones.

"Alice had a miscarriage."

The ends of Meg's blazing red curls shook, but she said nothing. Rolly let out a breath and waited, watching her features draw together, her lovely eyebrows pinch into a worried line.

"I'm so sorry, Rolly."

She walked toward him and pressed her face into his chest. An ache welled up in his throat. He blinked back tears. He had forgotten how he felt with her. He breathed in the clean, toasted smell of her hair. How could he have forgotten this? He held her close, wanting not to let go.

She leaned back against his arms and raised her hands to his face. "Rolly, you're a good man. But goodness doesn't require conventionality. There is space in every life for privacy, don't you think? We could keep it simple." The corners of her lips turned down in her tantalizing pout.

"Meg, I can't do this."

The muscles in the small of her back tensed. He cradled her more gently, wanting the love he felt and his anguish to flow through his hands. "I thought I could hold it all together—and God knows, I need you. But in the hospital…it wasn't the baby's dying…I know it was…but…I felt I was tearing out Alice's insides. Because of you and me." Her face hardened, but he went on, needing to persuade her. "I can't do it. She's… I just can't." He dropped his arms. "I don't know what comes next."

Meg backed away. "You don't give me any options here, do you? Do you want me to say," her voice curled, "I understand?"

He reached for her.

"Get away." She held up her hand as if stopping a blow. "Or do I say, I never want to see you again?" The cords of her neck stood out as she swallowed. "The miscarriage, I'm sorry. But it didn't happen because of you or because of you and me. You say you love me…" She spit the words at him. "Go to hell."

She stalked to the door and yanked it open.

He listened to her steps retreat in the hall, listened to the stairwell door open and slam shut. He waited for the next thing to happen. Slowly he surveyed the clutter on the walls, the shelves of junk, his tools, the worktables, sink, desk, the empty bins that had held the tree casts, the canoes, a few maquettes he had made years ago. Revulsion lapped into his chest and rose like floodwater.

He closed the door Meg had left open. Outside in the corridor, students passed.

He picked up a stool and threw it at the nearest canoe, snapping its spine and piercing its skin. He grabbed its stempiece and hurled the canoe across the room. On impact it shattered and fragments of bark and wood flew up and fluttered down. He watched as everything that trembled quieted.

7

Alice stood at her kitchen sink, waiting for Patricia to arrive, listening to Rolly bang around upstairs, and staring through the window at Ariana Faracci's dingy pink wading pool, left out all winter. Last summer, kids were always playing in it, their fun a pleasure to hear. When the days became too cold for water play and it filled with leaves, she'd wondered when they'd take it in. Thanksgiving came and went, and Christmas. Snow fell on New Year's Eve and the pool disappeared. When the snow began to melt after her miscarriage, the reappearance of the grimy saucer with the faded mermaids had seemed like a perfect emblem for the way she felt, but today it infuriated her.

She shouted up to Rolly, "How long are you going to keep this up?"

No answer.

She glared out the window. The Faraccis were good, share-a-cup-of-sugar neighbors, and easygoing, but both Bettina and Paul let things slide, were careless with their kids — more than once Alice had to take the children in when Bettina forgot they were in the yard and locked them out — and they were too damned happy-go-lucky. Nothing ever went wrong for them, while Alice did everything she was supposed to: ate lots of vegetables, seldom drank, never smoked, exercised now and then, and Bettina had just popped out her two, beautiful baby girls, and today the sight of that damn pink wading pool was like a stick in Alice's eye. She dropped the sponge into the sink, stomped to the back door, down the back steps, and charged through the bare lilacs into the Faraccis' yard. Wrestling the dented saucer from the frozen muck, she kicked out a half-moon of ice, dragged it into the alley, and flung it against their garbage cans. The crash of hard plastic on metal startled the mourning doves on the Faraccis' garage roof, and up they rose in a cloud. Alice grinned, pleased to have disturbed the clucking birds, and maybe half the neighborhood, wiped her hands on her skirt, and made her way into her own backyard.

A sudden explosion shattered the Saturday calm in a peaceful alley in Haslett around 11:50 a.m., sending doves reeling. Sources close to the birds say a woman in a brown skirt and beige cardigan was seen fleeing the scene.

"That you, Alice?" Bettina stood on their deck, her arms crossed.

"I'll buy you a new one come summer," Alice yelled, racing up her back steps.

She slammed the door behind her. Overhead, Rolly was still hammering in the bathroom. Could she get no peace? At least lunch with Patricia would get her out of here. She reached for the faucet and got a sputtering gasp. This was just like Rolly, not to mention that he was going to turn off the water. Then she remembered his passing through on his way to the basement and saying he had to cut off the water. Her indignation seeped away, leaving her disappointed. It wasn't right that she was wrong.

How lucky she was, everyone said, to have Rolly fix up the house. First he'd hauled his damn canoes to the college and begun working

94

there again, which was where he should confine his work, but then he quit again, fickle as always, and given his spare time over to the house: cedar cabinets in the basement — as if they needed them — replacement windows in the living and dining rooms, and now redoing the bath.

"Rolly's so handy. I'm envious," Bettina had said. Paul never lifted a clumsy finger. "Of course, he's working out his feelings," she'd added, in case Alice was an idiot.

Sure, he was sad, but from the beginning he hadn't wanted the baby as much as she had, and as far as she was concerned, he could work out his feelings somewhere else instead of colonizing the house. When she'd asked why he had to remodel now, he'd said, "I want everything finished so there'll be no risky fumes or particles or stress when we try again." The logic of this frustrated her.

She looked at the stove clock. Just past noon. Her mother would be here soon. Patricia had called after getting back from her trip to Florida with the wonderful Warren Jenks.

Upstairs, a single loud thump shook the house. She walked into the front hall and stared at the stairs where Rolly's boot prints had lifted the dust to show the true green of the carpet. The place looked like a war zone.

"How much longer do you have to keep this up?" she shouted.

The banging stopped. "Did you say something?" he called from inside the bathroom.

"Patricia'll be here any minute. Can't you stop for now, wait until I've left?"

"What time is it?"

"After twelve. Any minute and I'll be gone."

"Just let me…this last…"

"Sure." She set her hand on the newel post knob, the dome no bigger than a baby's head.

She hated weekends. During the week at work, she was fine talking to people, writing, chasing down facts, having coffee with Fritzie and going back and forth with Barry over headlines and priorities, but at home, she wanted to be left alone.

The doorbell rang and she jumped. Her mother, radiant in a burst of yellow. Alice unlatched the storm door, forcing a smile. "What an amazing suit. You look like a canary. Did you buy it on your vacation?"

Patricia laughed. "Before I left. This is the first chance I've had to wear it here. How are you, dear?"

They hugged. Alice was surprised by the rush of relief that flooded her. Rolly thundered down the stairs.

Patricia drew back but held tight to Alice's hand, reaching for Rolly's too. "You're both so wan."

"Just because you're nicely toasted." Her mother looked dazzlingly chic, and Alice felt even more like a schlub.

Patricia tickled Rolly's dust-filled beard. "What's this? Premature gray?" she laughed and hugged them both again. "What're you working on now?"

Alice answered before he could. "Still the bathroom. Now let's get—"

"Want to come up and see?" Rolly said, wiping his hands on a rag.

"He's nowhere close to finished," Alice said. "Let's go."

Rolly stuffed the rag back in his pocket. "If it hadn't been for the back order on the faucet and the damn toilet cracking, I'd have been done a week ago." He looked over Alice's head. "Maybe I should have called a plumber."

So with Patricia here, he was willing to admit Alice was right.

Patricia squeezed Alice's shoulder. "Oh, you kids, my god, you've done so much. And I'd love to see what you've done, Rolly," she patted his arm, "but we're running a little late. My fault."

Alice hid her annoyance. Since the miscarriage, an alliance had sprung up between Patricia and Rolly, but how could she accuse them of plotting to make her feel better?

Rolly tried to catch her eye. "Are you OK?" he whispered, bending to kiss the top of her head.

"You don't have to hover."

She ignored the glance he and Patricia shared as he opened the storm door for them.

Pausing on their front steps, Alice took a deep breath and lifted her face to the sun, feeling like she'd been sprung from prison.

"Lunch is on me," Patricia said. "And we're both going to have a glass of wine. If wine's OK?"

"Wine's fine. I'm not pregnant."

"Well, that's… In time."

In the car Patricia glanced at Alice to make sure she'd fastened her seat belt as if she were a child, then launched into vacation talk. "Perfect weather…rain forest…lizards." Alice half listened, enjoying the car's cushiony sway, like riding in a hammock.

Once they reached the county road, a brownish haze floated above the fresh-tilled fields. The drought. She'd already written two pieces on the dry spring and another that was an interview with the guy from ag extension. Barry cut the phrase "El Niño." "Use 'cyclical'."

Patricia adjusted the rearview mirror and looked over. "How are you…"

"When are you," Alice interrupted. She hated when Patricia probed. "When are you going to get rid of this gas-guzzler?" It was a ten-year-old Lincoln.

"Warren asks me the same thing. Says I should get a little sports car." She laughed. "Maybe I will."

Patricia in a sports car? Alice disliked Warren Frog-face even more.

She smoothed her skirt. "Would you do something for me? Would you get Rolly to stop on the house? You saw the mess. He won't listen to me."

"Dear, he's almost finished. It's going to be wonderful…"

"I don't care."

"But he can't stop in the middle." Patricia swerved to pass a tractor. "It's too bad he didn't get 'home fever' awhile ago. You won't have long to enjoy it before you go to Norway."

Norway. A couple of days ago a packet had arrived, sent by the agency that was finding them a house in Bergen, the coastal town near the university where Rolly would be a visiting artist.

"But you'll come back to enjoy it, dear." Patricia patted Alice's skirt.

The pictures showed icy blue fjords beneath mountains so jagged, it hurt to look at them. Valleys dotted with cows. Red-cheeked children picked wildflowers. Storybook cottages nestled beneath pines. Alice couldn't imagine herself there. She couldn't imagine herself anywhere.

Patricia turned into the driveway of the Saddle Club Inn. "Look how crowded…" She spotted an opening. "But today I've got Warren's parking karma."

Fierce red geraniums, artificial — it was too early for the real thing — spilled from the planters that lined the sidewalk to the club's portico-ed door. "Hope they haven't given away our table. We're only a little late."

They were seated in a snug room crowded with tables of tastefully dressed women. Patricia fit right in. Alice didn't.

"What's wrong, dear?" Patricia flicked open her napkin.

Against the green silk walls, Patricia in her yellow suit looked like a parrot. "You're so…I guess, bright," Alice said. All the women were dressed in spring colors. Why'd she chosen this baggy brown skirt? And this tatty cardigan?

"That sounds like a reproach, but thank you anyway. I feel bright."

A waitress handed Alice an oversized menu, and Patricia interrupted the waitress's recitation of the daily specials to remind Alice that the chicken salad was excellent. The waitress smiled patiently, and Alice wondered what it would be like to be a waitress, not here, but somewhere far away, a waitress in a diner where the daily special would be meatloaf and mashed with a side of canned green beans. If you were a waitress, you could pick up and go anywhere. There were always jobs for waitresses. She imagined herself swabbing a rag across a luncheonette counter and setting down a thick-lipped mug in front of a UPS deliveryman. Sunlight blasted in the plate glass window behind the guy, and a bell tinkled when someone came in. A desert town as far away from Haslett as you could get, where she would live alone, above the bus depot, where no buses ever came. After her shift she would walk across the dusty town square and mount the white-tiled stairs to her apartment. At her kitchen table she would sit, smoking a cigarette, staring at nothing.

"I think I'll take up smoking," she said.

"Oh, please." Patricia said to the waitress, "Two mesquite grilled chicken salads on," she flipped open her menu to read, "'on a bed of locally grown mâche and fiddlehead ferns.' It sounds like the forest floor. I never heard of mâche, whatever that is, growing around here."

"Locally grown in California, then flown here," Alice said.

Patricia smiled at the waitress, covering for Alice's snarkiness. "And two glasses of California chardonnay."

When the waitress left, Patricia said, "Honey, I'm worried about you. You're so down."

"Only compared to you."

"No, really. I am worried."

"I'm fine."

"You *will* be fine, I know that." She patted Alice's hand. "So tell me what's going on in town? Anything happen while I was away?"

"Well, a couple of drunks broke into Edie's Bar — Edie hadn't been paying his alarm bill — and drank enough to burn off half their brain cells. Gin, vodka, schnapps, crème de cocoa." Wicked delight bubbled in Alice. "You have to give them credit. Most burglars aren't this fastidious, to stick to the clear stuff. Then they decided to make sandwiches from the ham Edie had left in the fridge. They turned on the meat slicer — and this is where they weren't so fastidious…"

"Stop. I don't want to hear it."

"Amputated three fingers."

"That's enough." Patricia lifted her wine glass and held it like a shield.

"OK, not three whole fingers, just the tips. Of course, this ends Frank Critch's potential advancement to safecracker. That's a career that depends on intelligent fingertips. Even stupid fingertips are a basic requirement."

Patricia glared at her. "What the devil is going on with you?"

That's what Barry had said too. "Just joking," Alice responded.

The waitress appeared with their salads. When she was gone, Alice leaned forward, and said, "You want to know what Frank Critch said? 'That it wasn't fair.' I like that, don't you? Fair? He'd broken and entered. I can tell you what's *not* fair."

"Oh, Alice." Patricia reached for Alice's hand.

"Dr. Petrillo couldn't find anything wrong with me. I would have been such a good…"

Patricia uncurled Alice's tight fingers and stroked her palm. "What it takes is one day and then another and then another. In time, you'll feel better. You and Rolly going away, that'll help."

Shut up, Alice thought.

"It won't be long before all this will be behind you, honey."

Shut up, shut up, shut up. Alice withdrew her hand. "Let's see how this forest floor tastes. Now tell me about your trip."

Patricia hesitated, her eyes searching Alice's, before a subtle easing in the lines around her lips signaled that she would back off. It was, after all, her damaged daughter's right to snap and be hostile: That's what her long exhale said. She picked up her fork and, keeping a wary eye on Alice, talked about the huge drinks served at cocktail hour, the little black things that Warren had found between his toes when they returned — some burrowing parasite; he was on antibiotics now — and the amazing sunsets. Oh my god, she'd never seen anything to compare.

As her mother nattered, the straitjacket around Alice softened, and she could swallow the salad without wanting to retch. Patricia's face was animated as she relived her vacation, but Alice could see new lines between her eyebrows. Her mother was getting old. Alice was sorry for causing her mother so much pain.

When they left the restaurant, Patricia asked if they might stop at her alteration woman's house to pick up the dress she was going wear to Warren's brother's thirty-fifth wedding anniversary party.

"That's fine," Alice said. She didn't care one way or the other. She had no desire to go home.

The woman lived deep in the county. The smell of loamy soil flowed through the open windows. At the farmsteads, the cattle with clotted mud halfway up to their knees looked stunned by the intense sunlight. Alice hadn't been out this way since the day she had interviewed Heidi.

Patricia turned at a bullet-pocked mailbox and drove up a potholed driveway to a shabby, low farmhouse. From inside, a dog barked.

"I'll stay out here," Alice said.

The dog stopped when the door opened for Patricia. Alice stared through the dusty windshield at clouds piling up on the horizon. On that bitter cold day in January when she met Heidi — had it been less than three months ago? — the zippers on the girl's jacket had jangled like wind chimes. Alice closed her eyes. That day she'd been filled with hope.

✳ ✳ ✳

"So you got a little nap?"

Alice jerked awake. "How's the dress?"

"Fits like a glove." Patricia hooked the plastic garment bag in the back.

"I dreamt about Heidi Fender. She lives not too far from here."

"Out past Behm's farm stand, right?" Patricia slid into the driver's seat. "I was by that way yesterday. No crowds now. They must have wised up."

"Even I was half persuaded," Alice said. Before her pleas to the Virgin had made no difference.

"That's your superstitious nature. Where you got it, I don't know. Certainly not from me or your father."

She wasn't superstitious. But forces beyond logic seemed possible. Not that any forces had worked for her.

"Would you like to drive by there now? See if there's a crowd."

"You just said there wasn't."

"But I thought you might be curious since you took such an interest."

"Nope. Nothing more on the Fender sideshow, Barry said, unless something new comes up. It hasn't."

Alice had tried not to think about Heidi since the miscarriage. She'd put away the postcard too. But now she wondered if Heidi had run away, even though she was sure Roger Fender's story about his daughter being a crook was bogus. Heidi would have a good reason to escape, with a father like that. She might be out west, living off the land. In the mountains, maybe. Or waitressing.

Patricia took the road that led to town.

"You'll feel better soon, dear," she said, pulling up in front of Alice's house. "Try not to brood."

"I'll do my best."

Inside the house Alice held her breath until she heard Patricia's car turn the corner.

"Rolly?" No answer. She smiled. She was, at last, alone.

***

After the endless weekend, Alice drove out to the Melody Acres Retirement Community to interview the new director. On the way back to the *Herald*, she came to the intersection where the hand-painted sign, "Visit the Holy Site where the Blessed Virgin Appeared," with a series of arrows pointed to the high-walled enclosure Fender had built to cash in on Heidi's visions. No freebies for the curious or the believers, but none had come by in a while, judging by the new grass that had sprung up in the ruts that had led to the enclosure. Alice turned her car in the direction of the Fenders' house. She'd been thinking about this since she'd told her mother she had no interest in coming.

Tulips bloomed at the base of their mailbox, which surprised her. The daffodils in her own garden were spent, but she'd expected this place to remain as it had been the day she'd interviewed Heidi: cold, gray, locked in winter. The trees had leafed out, and the patchy lawn had greened. The house looked the same, the peeling paint maybe a little worse. Beyond the house, the lopsided maple held a tire swing she didn't remember from last time. She parked beside the split rail fence and turned off the ignition.

Mrs. Fender answered the bell quickly — she must have been watching — and said that Heidi was in the barn and Alice should go around back. Alice had assumed Heidi would be home, even though it was a school day, even though she hoped Heidi had gotten away from this miserable place and her rotten father, but she knew that Heidi would be here when Alice came.

The barn doors were open. Inside, the air was cold and smelled of cows and hay.

"Heidi?"

The girl's head appeared in the far shadows, over a wooden stall.

"Remember me, Alice Becotte, from the *Herald*?" She sounded like a fool. Why wouldn't Heidi remember?

But she gave no sign that she did remember as she walked forward with a rake in one hand and a coiled rope in the other. Minus the leather jacket, but wearing jeans, black T-shirt, the same black cowboy boots, she looked much the same, except her hair wasn't white but magenta, like a joke wig. A couple of years ago, Alice had written about a bank heist in Clydesville where the robbers had worn clown makeup and wigs. The disguises worked. They were never found.

Heidi looped the rope over a hook by the open doors. "Sure, I remember."

"I wondered how you are doing. I'm not here for the paper." Heidi said nothing. "Your father said you'd run away." No response. "That you'd stolen money and a VCR from your uncle, and his truck, and taken off."

A smile flashed across Heidi's face. "I went to my uncle's. He lives in Kentucky. School got to be too much. People thought I made it up and didn't like me getting in the papers and all. Why stick around? My uncle said come down there for a while and let things chill. I just got back."

"Why'd your father tell me you'd run away?"

"He doesn't like you."

Where was Fender? Alice looked toward the open doors. In the yard a couple of crows cawed.

"He's in the far back pasture," Heidi said.

The girl could still read Alice's mind. "So how're you doing?"

Heidi shrugged.

"I didn't come to find out if you've had any more sightings of the Virgin."

Heidi hung the rake among others. "She has come but I don't want to talk about it." She dislodged a clump of hay on her boot and leaned against the open door. Past her, sunlight sparked off the winter-scoured yard and the house where the mother now stood on a ladder, washing a window.

"I was pregnant then. You knew it. I hadn't even told my husband." Alice fought tears by keeping her eyes on the mother fifty feet away. Through her wet eyelashes, strands of sunlight connected everything: the window's reflections with the aluminum ladder and the clothesline, the power cables to the house, and the split rail fence with the fields and the distant trees. Everything was connected. Only she was cut off.

"I lost the baby."

No response from Heidi. Alice waited, squeezing her hands into fists, listening to the wind whip through the dry grass in the yard. The girl had to explain what had gone wrong. There had to be a reason. Alice turned away from the yard. The girl's face had closed down, like a sullen teenager's. Humiliation washed through Alice. Heidi was a teenager and Alice had no right to ask anything of her. She was only a kid. And Alice had no right to ask anything of a Virgin she didn't really believe in. Why did she want answers, when answers wouldn't change anything? She straightened, wiped her hands on her slacks, and put on her calm face. "Well, I just stopped."

"I got to get back to work."

In the distance Heidi's mother stepped down from the ladder. Alice walked toward where she'd parked, concentrating on each step. She was pathetic.

Rolly was gone when she got home. She didn't want to see him, and she didn't want him seeing her with red eyes. He'd vacuumed the stairs and dusted. She gazed into the living room: the barrel-shaped chairs, the lamps Patricia had given them, the empty fireplace, their wedding picture gone. After the miscarriage, hating their happier, innocent selves, she'd put it somewhere. She couldn't remember where.

She hooked her jacket on the banister and climbed the stairs. Rolly's cleaning efforts hadn't extended to the upstairs hall. Plaster dust floated in the sunlight streaming from the baby's room. That door was supposed to remain closed. Reaching to pull it shut, she saw a worktable and the floor littered with junk: 2 x 4s, sawdust, boxes of ceramic tile, loops of metal strapping.

Rolly had trashed this room.

Outraged, she tossed his tool box into the hall. Whatever she could seize, she flung out the door: chunks of wood, paper, C-clamps, and, one by one, ceramic tiles, each exploding with a satisfying crack. A loop of metal snapped back and cut her neck. She ignored the pain as she wrestled lengths of board together, knocking over Rolly's coffee cup, which sent coffee flying over the wall. Coffee dripped over the swatches of nursery colors she'd tested — apricot, peach, and yellow, good for either a boy or a girl — slid over the baseboard, to puddle on the floor. Panting, she turned to his worktable and knocked the scarred top off the two sawhorses. The plywood was too heavy to lift, so she dragged it across the floor, delighted by the gouges it cut in the oak.

"What the hell?"

Rolly stood in the doorway.

She shoved past him to twist and kick the plywood against the bathroom door.

"You have no right," she said, over her shoulder, then turned to face him. He didn't get it. His uncomprehending eyes searched hers.

"I've had it," she said, stepping away from him onto something sharp. "You've got your damn studio out back. You've got one at the college. Isn't that enough? How much goddamn space do you need? I can't breathe in my own house, and now this."

She pushed her hands at him, to make sure he didn't come closer. "You spoiled this. This wasn't supposed to be touched. Why did you set your crap up in here? Just get out. Get the hell out." She bent over, gasping. "I want your foulness gone, out of this room. I want everything cleared out. I want the walls washed down. Then, do you hear me, this door will remain closed."

"I didn't know..."

He *knew*. He didn't care. His teary eyes were a pretense of caring. He tried to put his arms around her.

"Don't touch me." She slid down, pressing her back against the wall. "Get away from me."

"I didn't know." He knelt beside her. "I was trying to keep the construction chaos contained. It wasn't a secret." He spoke softly, murmuring that they'd try again, when her body was back to normal, when they were away from all this. "You'll see. In Norway, you'll sleep late, drink lots of milk, and become a hausfrau. We'll make love all the time. You'll get pregnant."

She hated him.

His fingers touched her cheek. She raised her eyes to meet his. "I don't know you anymore."

"Alice, I'm sorry. Come on now, come lie down."

He had never really wanted the baby at all. This fact held her steady as she allowed him to guide her to their bedroom and lift her legs between the sheets and fold the blankets under her chin. Beneath his tenderness, she recognized treachery.

8

The next morning Rolly looked for fallout. Alice had slept heavily and didn't stir when he slipped out of bed. When he returned with coffee, she was sitting up, a long red scratch across her cheek. "Are you OK?" he asked, slopping coffee, but what he'd thought was a scratch was only a pillow mark.

She nodded, eyes averted, and accepted the cup.

"Do you want me to stay?" Where should he sit? Maybe in the chair?

She didn't answer.

"I'll be downstairs."

Half an hour later, she came down, dressed in old jeans and a soft white shirt, looking more like herself. She was pale but the red mark was gone. She smiled without parting her lips, opened the window over the sink, and, after glancing at the toast he'd started, began to squeeze oranges for juice, as she always did on Sunday mornings. He spread out the Sunday *Indianapolis Star*, hoping that her outburst had exhausted the last of her bitterness.

She offered him a glass of juice, and he said, "I was trying to control the disruption. For you."

"I want you to quit." Except for a slight jittering beneath her left eye, her face was expressionless. "You clean up the baby's room and leave the mess in the bathroom. We can bathe in the kitchen sink for all I care. I want this over."

"I'm sorry. I didn't know that room was so important."

She walked to the coffee maker, filled two mugs, and carried them to the table, keeping her eyes on the coffee's swaying surface.

He intercepted one of the mugs before she could put it down. "How could I know that the room had become sacred? We hadn't done anything to it yet. Slapped up some paint samples, that's all."

Still not looking at him, she took a sip. He watched the corners of her mouth tighten. "How could you *not* know?" she said. "We shut the door together."

"But I didn't think *permanently*. It's just an empty room. It's there to be used."

How had she not noticed that he'd been using that room as a shop for almost three weeks? He'd moved his worktable and tools up there while she was at work, so she wouldn't be bothered, but she saw the bathroom demolition, she saw the new construction. They discussed faucets and tiles. Where'd she think he was doing the sawing? Where'd she think he was keeping the stuff?

He said, "When a baby comes, it will be back to normal. I'll refinish the floor." He stood behind her and wrapped his arms over hers. "I'm sorry."

"I want it kept closed," she said, but she didn't stiffen or push him away. "OK."

By dinnertime he'd cleaned the mess upstairs and taken his tools to the basement. On Monday, after Alice left for the paper, he began on the bathroom again, but he only worked when she was out of the house. He brought in his TA, paying her double the rate she got from the college, and finished in a week, all except the painting. Alice said she liked the new shower and the new medicine cabinet.

He waited for her to thaw. April into May, she remained cool, but she no longer looked at him with scorching resentment or walked out of the room when he was talking. They hadn't yet made love since the miscarriage, more than two months, but she settled close to him when she fell asleep. When her breath slipped into an almost inaudible rustle, he sometimes thought of Meg.

Fixing the broken had become his theme, personally and professionally, as he'd told Wolf, letting his friend assume "personal" meant his home remodeling and "professional" meant Rolly was back to creative work. But he wasn't. He brought home the two canoes that he hadn't completely destroyed in his rampage after Meg.

Repairing an old piece instead of making something new was pathetic, a total lack of inspiration, but as he patched and laced and reconsidered what was possible, the distinction between creation and repair began to blur. He told himself that art was always, in some way, a kind of reclaiming of what was essential, that all creation was excavation. Whether this was true or not, he enjoyed what he was doing.

The days lengthened, spring merged into summer.

In mid-May he took Alice to a recital at the college, something she always liked, and they stopped for dessert at the Sugar Bowl. As they eavesdropped on a girl heavily tattooed with vines and roses tell her friend how cruel it was to brand cattle, Alice caught his eye and whispered, "Maybe not if the brands are roses," and smiled at him in their private way.

Slowly, her depression lifted. At the dinner table she told stories from the paper, and she asked about what was going on in his classes.

He brought home a fax confirming their house rental in Bergen, beginning September 1. He set it on the kitchen counter.

"Is that the house with two upstairs bedrooms and the orange rug?"

she asked, slicing a pepper. The evening was warm and she'd rolled up her T-shirt sleeves, showing off her nice arms.

"And surrounded by forest. You said you could live with orange."

She swept the pepper strips to the side of the chopping board. "Hand me an onion, will you?"

Recently, she'd cut her hair so short, it bristled in spikes under the light. He missed her curls.

"If I don't hear from the university about studio space by the end of the week, I'll call them but Herman said that he'd sent in the paperwork. Have you firmed up with Barry when you'll begin your leave?"

She kept chopping. "Not yet."

"Oh, come on. We've got to settle on a date. How much time do we want to tour around? We can leave anytime, say, after July fifteenth. I need to put finishing touches on the canoes before packing them off to Jacqueline in New York. She'll store them until the exhibition next spring. After that, I can figure out what tools I'll take to Norway." He reached for the dishes.

"July fifteenth is too soon."

He hid his annoyance. "So August first. Let's pick a date and you tell Barry, or talk to Barry, and then pick a date. We have to settle this."

With the tip of the knife, she pierced another onion.

"OK?" he asked.

"OK, what?"

"OK, you'll talk to Barry?"

"OK, I'll talk to Barry."

She slid the peppers and onions into the hot pan and stood, one foot propped against the other knee, like a crane, watching the vegetables sizzle. "Once Barry starts thinking about my replacement, he may decide he doesn't need a full-timer. He's used to me, used to paying my salary, but after a year, what'll I come back to?"

"That's a year. Lots can happen." She might get pregnant, he didn't say, since whenever he brought up the topic, she withdrew; but she would get pregnant, even if it took going the fertility-doctor route.

"Open the back door, will you?" she said. "It's too hot."

Outside, the Faracci girls yelped in the sprinkler.

"You'll talk to Barry on Monday, right? I've got to get the tickets."

"I said I would."

***

The final weeks of the term were, as always, a headlong skid toward graduation. Herman made sure Rolly's leave didn't exempt him from last-minute committee meetings and, squeezed between final critiques and portfolios reviews, there were last-minute pleas from students for course extensions or job recommendations. By the final Friday of the academic year, the campus was empty.

Collecting slides he'd left in Studio B where the walls had already been stripped bare of the students' manga-influenced portraits and awkward nudes, he realized it would be more than a year, a year and a summer, before he'd be back. He felt free, free and elated, like when he was ten and the bell had rung on the last day of school and his friends were waiting outside with cans of shaving cream. All that was ahead beckoned.

Wolf had offered him a ride home — Rolly's car was in the shop — but Rolly'd said he wanted to begin his sabbatical by walking the five miles between school and home.

For the first time since he'd broken it off with Meg, he walked past the administration building. The gray-filmed glass of her window gave nothing away. He hadn't seen her, not even at a distance, since he'd broken it off. A few weeks ago in the bookstore, over a shelf, he'd glimpsed frizzled red hair, and without thinking, he hurried down the aisle and around the corner, startling a girl in a Jimi Hendrix shirt. He tried not to think about Meg. Whenever he did, longing overwhelmed him. But he was wedded to Alice. He knew that now. He hadn't understood what that really meant until he'd seen her suffer in the hospital.

Turning south, away from the administration building, he took the curving path that cut through lawns already browning from the drought, followed it under the Wesley College arch, and set off down the strip of fast-food joints that bordered the campus. As he walked, he felt the college receding and taking with it his teacher-self, harried, schedule-keeping, answerable-to-everyone Rolly Becotte.

He walked through quiet streets, past a middle school, and Haslett's Triple A baseball field, enjoying the sun on his head and the weight of his shoulder bag on his hip. When the sidewalk ended and the road divided at unincorporated woods, he took the fork that edged the outskirts of Haslett. Overhead, a small airplane circled low. Putting aside thought of the school year that had ended and the grades he hadn't yet filed, he took in what was around him: the laundry flapping on the line, a rusted Plymouth on cinderblocks, kids trying to master wheelies. When he reached his own neighborhood of straight streets, he stopped to adjust his shoulder bag and noticed his shadow on a well-watered lawn. His torso curved into indentation where a tree had been removed and the soil had collapsed from decaying roots. He stepped sideways, pulling his shadow out of the hollow. He grinned. This was his life. He was free. Joy almost lifted him off his feet.

At the corner of his street, he paused. The lawns blazed white and sun-shot green under cascading sprinklers. All of this, his home, Haslett, the college, was halfway to being a memory.

"Alice," he called, unlocking the front door.

No answer.

On the refrigerator was a Post-it note: "Back around 8:30. Will

114

bring dinner," and her initial, A, that looked like a reaching sailboat. He picked up a pencil and drew a cloud blowing into its curve and waves below, then opened the refrigerator to find a fancy salad with carefully arranged pepper rings and a bottle of red wine chilling in the door. She'd planned a celebration. Happy, he popped open a beer, noting fresh-cut peonies on the table and the candles. He pictured Alice's candlelit face, her pushing aside her plate to reach for his hand. Maybe tonight they would make love.

But she wouldn't be home for hours, so there was time for him to get something done in his studio. He hadn't decided what to take to Norway. All spring, he'd found it hard to work up the enthusiasm against the drag of Alice's indifference. The salad and wine signaled that this phase was over. He headed for his studio, envisioning a future in which Alice would be close, his longing for Meg would no longer ambush him, and his work would flourish. The stillness of his studio welcomed him.

He started putting away the tools he wouldn't need for a year. After that, he selected what to take: a dozen chisels, his grandfather's drawknife, a crooked knife, his favorite rasps, some sketchpads, some art catalogues. While he flipped through his stack of plywood, looking for pieces to make crates, the screen door rattled. It was Wolf, his nose flattened against the mesh.

"Come on in." Rolly glanced at the clock. It was time to quit anyway. "I did tell you I was walking, right?"

Wolf shrugged, surveying the disarray. "Ah, *Herr Meister von Handwerkzeug.*"

"Figuring out what to take. How'd you decide, when you came here?"

"What fit in my suitcase, nothing more." He sauntered toward the shelf where Rolly kept odd things. "Anything new?" Wolf leaned forward to inspect Rolly's beaded African dolls, his right foot coming too close to a small canoe half-hidden in the shadows.

"Careful," Rolly said. It was one of the child-size canoes he'd crushed the afternoon he'd ended it with Meg, the one he'd been able to salvage. He'd cut out the mangled center section, but instead of replacing it with similar materials, he'd accentuated the break by linking together the fore and aft sections with steel rods, thin as needles, which maintained the gap and declared that this canoe would never float. The piece was now about rupture.

Wolf pulled out the canoe.

"What have you been keeping from me?" He spun the canoe until it pointed toward him. "I like the surgical quality of these." He touched the metal rods and the canoe wobbled. "It is like pinning together a broken statue, um? No. It is more. It is fine. Intellectually demanding, um? If you are not careful, you could become too emotional for me, but that said, this is the best work I've seen from you." He stood up, his knee clicking. "Have you others? Over there?"

Wolf flipped back the tarpaulin on the full-size canoe that rested on a cradle — Rolly had to ship it to New York soon — and peered down the length of the dark hull as he ran his hand along the long, curved sheer line. Remembering Wolf's scorn of his cast branches, Rolly hung back, nervous. This was more conventional than the small canoe. The outside of this one was stained a dark red-brown, the inside a black-blue so dark Wolf had to lean in close to examine the interior. The ribs of the interior were black; the center rib, which would normally be covered with planking, was a glistening scarlet, like a fresh incision.

"Is it wet?" Wolf asked, with his finger hovering above the red.

Rolly shook his head.

Wolf touched the rib, then rocked back on his heels. "You have got it, my friend. No doubt. Do not let go, do not stop, until you have taken this...*Macht*...as far as it will take you."

"You approve?"

Wolf spied down the gunwale. "It's not what I do, but yes, I think it is quite good."

Rolly pushed back his hair, more gratified than he wanted Wolf to know, and expelled a deep breath. "Thank god for this sabbatical. I'm ready to get serious now, after this last hellish year." Wolf look puzzled. Rolly hadn't told Wolf about the pregnancy or the miscarriage, and he wasn't going to now. "I'm half worried that when I get to Norway, I'll lose what I've got going here. A different setting, different materials, new things all around. It could be good; it could be bad. In my proposal, I wrote that I'd research Viking ships, visit the sites in Godskap and Bodsköy, breathe the air, walk the land, but now I don't want to get so involved with research that it might pull me away from what I've started."

Wolf shot him a disdainful look. Why was Rolly complaining?

"OK," Rolly laughed. "It'll be great. I just need to get away from here. Want a beer?" A beer and goodbye. It was almost eight and Alice would be home soon.

He rummaged in his under-counter fridge as Wolf talked about misplacing his grade sheets. "They were on the desk. Did you pick them up? I am thinking that when you took yours, mine became mixed in."

"I'll check." Rolly handed him a beer. "My bag is in the house." He twisted off his bottle cap, wishing Wolf wasn't making himself comfortable sitting on the floor. Fifteen minutes and out of here was what Rolly had in mind. He took a long swallow of icy beer.

"In a few minutes I'll close up for the day, and we can go see if your papers are in my bag."

"Good. I was beginning to worry that I had come too early."

"I was ready to quit anyway."

"I meant for dinner."

Rolly started to say not tonight, but Wolf interrupted. "Alice invited me when I ran into her downtown."

Rolly set down his beer. "She invited you?"

"She said it was a celebration for the end of the school."

But not an exclusive celebration for the two of them, not a celebration for the beginning of something new. Rolly walked to the open screen door to hide his dismay. The upstairs windows of the house flashed copper from the sunset, and the white siding glowed like a schlocky home-for-the-holidays commercial.

Alice had sucker-punched him with her cheery note and the goddamn salad, but he wasn't going to let Wolf see this. Rolly hoisted his beer bottle. "To the end of school. And to work, which is the only thing we can be sure of, isn't it?"

"Even that..."

"Yeah, even that. But at least we own it."

Furious and ashamed, Rolly listened to Wolf rise.

"When will Alice be home?" Wolf asked.

"I want you to go."

"Go? But..."

"Just go. I want you to leave. I planned something else for tonight. Alice doesn't know." He kept his back to Wolf.

"I am sorry," Wolf said behind him. "I guess she didn't..."

Rolly didn't move as Wolf pushed past him to slide open the screen door. "Tomorrow I will call you about my grade lists."

The shadows climbed the back of their house. When the last of the red had retreated to a small triangle at the peak under the roofline, he heard Alice's car on the gravel beside his studio. He stepped into the yard when she opened the gate.

"Here's dinner," she said, handing him a bag from the butcher's.

He took it. "I sent Wolf away."

"What?"

"I told him I wanted to celebrate alone, just the two of us."

She stared at him. "But that's… "

"He's a friend. He didn't mind."

"A good friend doesn't mind being *uninvited*? A good friend doesn't have feelings?" She glared at him, her jaw heavy with disdain. "I thought you'd like this. It's the end of the term for him too. He's alone. He doesn't have anyone here. A nice dinner for both of you. Fun, for your benefit, not mine, that's what I'd planned."

She stalked toward the house. At the bottom of the porch steps, she paused. "When'd he leave?"

"Twenty minutes ago or so."

"OK." She pulled herself taller. "We'll have him over next week."

Rolly preceded her up the stairs, and when she didn't follow him inside, he set the butcher's sack on the counter and returned to the back door. She was standing in the center of the dark yard, looking at the sky. He descended the stairs and walked to her side. "I wanted the evening for the two of us."

"So you said."

"Can we get on a better footing?" he asked.

"It's very hard."

"Come inside. Let's make dinner."

"I thought I saw a nighthawk."

"What does a nighthawk look like?"

"I don't know, swift. Could have been any bird."

He couldn't see anything against the dark sky. "Are you still mad at me?"

"I don't know. Let's go in."

She went upstairs to change, and he uncorked the wine. He shouldn't have sent Wolf away. Disappointment was no excuse. He'd seen little of Alice's edginess lately, and he'd made the mistake of thinking it was gone. He would apologize. When she came down, dressed in shorts and her favorite T-shirt that featured a cartoon dog reading a newspaper, she looked as if she, too, had resolved to make something good of the evening.

He handed her a glass of wine. "I'm sorry. I shouldn't have sent Wolf away. You invited him. You were being kind to our friend. And I was selfish wanting you to myself."

She clinked his glass. "OK."

OK? She was going to make him grovel. If that's what it took, he would. He watched her sip wine, a ruby reflection dancing across her cheek. "You're beautiful."

"You always say that."

"You are, but if you don't want me to…"

She put down her glass, opened the refrigerator, and asked him to set the table.

If he showed her that he had nothing against Wolf, that might help. "A couple of days ago, Wolf suggested you and I meet him in London at Christmas. He's returning to Germany after the fall term here. What do you think: Christmas in London?"

Alice stood, one bare foot resting on the other, heating oil in one pan for the chops and stirring risotto in another. Had she heard him?

"What do you think, midnight service in a Christopher Wren church, figgy pudding, whatever that is, a little Good King Wenceslas?"

"Here, you keep stirring." She handed him the risotto spoon. "I need to get a platter."

She was pulling her passive-aggressive shit. He could ignore it.

After she found a platter, she joined him at the stove. He stirred the risotto; she tended the chops, the fragrance of the rice and thyme-scented lamb underscoring how unlikely was the kind of evening he'd hoped for. Instead, a delicious dinner eaten without warmth, a ruinous end to a day that had started so well. To break the silence that was becoming awkward, he asked about her day. She talked about the software guy coming to test the *Herald*'s Y2K patches. And Harry Mack, the paper's sports guy, wanted to write a column on fishing, but Barry wasn't convinced.

"So what did Barry say about your leave? July or August?"

She lifted the chops to the platter. "Can we talk about this after we sit down? Bring over the salad, will you?" She flicked off the light above the stove.

She was determined to make him pay for fouling up her plans.

She was already seated with her hands knotted in her lap when he brought the salad to the table. She hadn't bothered to light the candles but left on the glaring pendant lamp.

He sat opposite. "Say what you want to say."

"I'm not going."

"What do you mean?"

"I'm not going to Norway." Her face was hard as ivory.

"What're you saying?"

"What I just said."

"You've got to come." He reached for her wrist and she tugged free.

"I don't want to go anywhere. I want to live my own life. I want to fall asleep in a chair and not have anyone tell me to come to bed. I don't want to be watched all the time. I want to be myself…by myself."

"What the hell are you talking about?"

She refused to look at him.

"Please, Alice. What are you saying? I love you."

"I don't care if you love me. I don't care if I love you. That's not enough."

"Not enough? How can that be 'not enough'?"

She shoved aside her dinner plate and placed her fists on the table. "I'm not ready. I don't know what enough is, what it would be, but I don't have enough of a reason to leave my home. This is my home. I'm not going to Norway."

"Why?" He fought the desperation in his voice, knowing if he kept this up, he might lose her, and the possibility she might already be lost made him dizzy. "Whatever I've done… What *have* I done? I don't get it."

Her eyes said his transgressions were too numerous to recount.

"So this was why you invited Wolf? You were going to spring this on me, and he would be the buffer. I would control my anger, wouldn't I? That's what you counted on." Rage surged through him. Humiliating him in front of Wolf must have been part of her plan too. "Are you still trying to punish me for not wanting the baby as much as you did?" She glared at him, her arms crossed over her chest, but she didn't pull back. He went on. "I *didn't* want the baby as much as you. There, you're right. But now, more than anything, I want you to be happy. Things are different. We'll go the fertility doctor route, OK? If that doesn't work, we'll adopt. I want a child too."

"You don't want a baby. You don't want the inconvenience of a family. All you want is the freedom to devote everything to your work."

"What have I been doing all spring but caring for you? My work? What work?" He tried not to shout. "I've done *nothing* but my best for you. And let me tell you, it has not been one goddamn bit convenient."

"See! You do keep score. And let's get straight what you've been doing all spring, as you so modestly put it. After the miscarriage, you

122

were so grateful, so goddamn blatantly relieved there wasn't going to be a baby, you became a model husband. I knew that couldn't last. And it hasn't. It's been only three and a half months, and already it's *your* work, *your* sabbatical," she spat. "What about what I might want? Why should I quit my job, leave my friends, my mother? I like it here in the boonies, although you seem to think you're too good… Why should I tag along with you to the Norwegian tundra? To be your *little hausfrau*? Forget it."

She stood, knocking over her chair, and took a swing at his leg with her bare foot, then stalked to the sink. Water rushed onto the stacked pans. She cut off the stream to fill a glass and turned back to him. "What's your work about anyway? Boys' fantasies, that's what. Man and nature? The quest? Good god, who are you fooling? These canoes of yours, all you've done is take something that is beautiful because it is useful, that has a real function, and you strip away its utility, hoping what you've mangled can bear the weight of the trumped-up symbolism you call ART."

Blood throbbed in his ears. He couldn't speak.

"I'll tell you what happened," she hissed. "You got scared. You looked around at adulthood, at responsibilities, and you retreated. Your so-called art is about escaping."

Shoving back his chair, Rolly stood, knocking the overhead lamp. She tensed like a prizefighter, her arms up, as if she really expected him to come swinging. And she was delighted.

"You've never understood my work."

"I do understand. I understand how lame it is."

He could crush her. Her arms would snap like wishbones. He lurched toward the back door, jamming his elbow into the screen.

"Bitch."

9

Alice stared at the table, at her white napkin draped over its edge, certain any movement would bring everything down, napkin, table, chairs. She'd said unforgivable things, but she couldn't reconstruct exactly who had said what first or what exactly had happened. She had wanted him gone, he was gone, and now she was terrified.

* * *

Sunlight fell on her shoulder. It was morning. She was in bed and she was alone. She reached for Rolly's cool pillow, then remembered their fight. Opening her eyes, she looked around their bedroom for some sign that she wasn't a vile person, that she hadn't gone too far, that she'd been justified, and noticed the postcard of the Virgin tucked into the frame of her mirror that reflected Rolly's shirt hooked on the closet doorknob. Where had he spent the night? What story had he told to whomever's doorbell he'd rung? Mortified by what he might have said, eager to get out of the house, she dressed quickly. She could hang out at the office. No one would be there on Saturday. If only she could cancel her afternoon gym date with Patricia — Patricia and Rolly had become such devoted pals — but if she did cancel, Rolly might weigh in before Alice could explain to her mother.

With her gym bag, she hurried down the stairs and jerked to a stop, seeing Rolly asleep on the living room couch. She grabbed the newel post and held her breath, but he didn't stir. No movement from him. He hadn't heard her. His shoes rested beside the coffee table. When had he returned? Why hadn't she heard him? And why, even asleep, did he intimidate her? She should yell at him to get the hell out, but she tiptoed down the last two stairs, through the hall, into the kitchen, and out the back door.

At the *Herald*, she unlocked the front door and stepped into the cool, familiar mustiness and felt safe. She clicked off the desk lamp Fritzie had left on and turned off the alarm system. Alice Becotte, star reporter. Here she was in charge, not in charge of everything, but she knew what to do.

What she didn't know was what she should do if Rolly was still there when she returned. Where had he been last night? Wolf's or that dumpy motel by the VFW? Maybe he'd only come back to get some things and would be gone when she got home.

Upstairs smelled of the carpet Barry had installed after rewiring for the new computers, which the software guy guaranteed were fully Y2K-compliant. She doubted it. Nothing worked out as promised. Nothing was certain. She hadn't known for certain that she wasn't going to Norway until she realized that she didn't even want to spend another evening with Rolly enthusing about the good times ahead, but she hadn't thought about practical matters, like, how soon would he leave on his sabbatical? And where would he stay until then? But these were questions he had to solve, not she.

She turned on her monitor and scanned the news feeds, finding a perfect *Herald* item: an item about lightning strikes in soil creating nitrogen. She padded the two sentences into eight graphs, "Lightning: Electric Fertilizer," then edited Ken Saffold's sermon on "Save a Life, Your Own" for the Christian Thoughts column that no one read.

Around ten, Barry came in. "What are you doing here on a perfect Saturday morning?" he asked.

"Catching up. What are you doing here?"

"I'm on my way to the links. And I'm here to pick up my new golf club."

Shipped to the office. His wife wasn't supposed to know that he'd spent a grand on a new wedge.

He tore open the box. "As long as you're here, could you call the hospital and find out about the kid the cops picked up last night? He was strolling down the middle of the interstate."

"On it, boss."

Barry saluted as he headed downstairs with his new club.

Val Sorreno, who worked intake and was Bettina's cousin, said that the kid, name unknown, age unknown, had vomited up knotted condoms and was being treated for an overdose, adding that he had a fresh tattoo lettered on his chest: "Beam me up, Scottie." Alice wrote a quick draft, leading with anonymous kid in peril on the highway, a graph on the growing drug problem in the county, another with stats on Indiana's drug enforcement. Then she rechecked the news feeds. In Calcutta, a twenty-six-year-old bridegroom had set his seventeen-year-old wife on fire. They'd been married five months. She'd burned his *naan*. No arrest was made. The police were still investigating. Could the prophecies about the world coming to an end be right? Last week, a man had tossed his young bride off their balcony, and there'd been another involving fire. Sickened, Alice turned off her monitor. That she felt inconsequential to Rolly, that he treated her like an appendage, that his interests, his plans, his dreams eclipsed hers, these facts were trivial in comparison to what went on in these bride-burning stories — she shouldn't even think of them at the same moment — but her unhappiness was deep and real. That she felt banal only seemed to make it worse.

***

Patricia was waiting in the lobby of the health club.

"Are you OK?" Patricia said, nodding to the clerk as she showed her card. "You look like you're coming down with something."

"Allergies," Alice lied, wishing she hadn't let Patricia persuade her into a gym membership.

"Something's wrong," Patricia said, leading the way to the women's locker room. "So tell me?"

"I'm fine." She'd tell her about her decision after they'd worked out, when Patricia's endorphins would be flowing. "But I came from the paper where I read a wire story about another dowry murder in Calcutta. He lit her afire."

"India's one place I never want to go. The squalor, everyone washing and drinking from the Ganges, and setting the dead adrift. Warren said we should take a Mississippi cruise—"

"He tossed kerosene at her and chucked her off the balcony." Alice shoved open the locker room door. "And I don't want to hear about Warren right now."

"I think you're coming down with something," Patricia said, following her in.

"It's just that I can't stand how men can think their wives are so negligible that they can be 'disposed of'."

"Let's talk about something nice." Her mother pulled a blue-green leotard from her gym bag and dangled it in front of Alice. "New." Alice scowled and Patricia put it down. "These things in India are awful, but you're getting carried away." She patted Alice's arm.

In the aerobics room, a dozen women milled around while Ang, the sleek Vietnamese instructor, fiddled with the volume of the techno-Motown. She and Patricia found their customary places in the middle row, right.

"Everybody, march, knees up." Ang did an about-face, his waist-length black ponytail whipping over his shoulder. "Take a deep breath." He raised his hands above his head. "And again, chests high, abs in."

The pounding beat, Ang's barked commands, the effort and the sweat were just what Alice needed. Afterward, she hurried to the locker room, while Patricia lingered with a couple of women.

She would remind her mother that she, Alice, was an adult, and that she did not welcome Patricia's advice. She would say that this news was bound to disturb Patricia, that she was sorry about this, but this was something she had to do.

In the shower Alice let the spray pummel her face. She wanted the next half hour behind her.

"Are you OK?" It was Patricia.

"Let me finish here, will you?" Alice kept her face in the spray.

When she'd toweled off, she returned to the locker area and found Patricia sitting on the bench in front of her open locker.

Alice sat down. "I'm not going to Norway with Rolly. I told him last night." Keeping her eyes on the edge of the locker door just behind Patricia, she explained about not wanting to leave her home, her job, the life she loved, to follow him to some arctic land where she didn't speak the language, had no job, no reason for being there, while he would be busy all the time, "happy as a pig in shit."

"I don't get it." Patricia fiddled with her gold necklace.

"I need to be on my own for a time." This sounded as lame as a country and western song. What she felt was a cliché, but that did not undermine its depth. She reached into her own locker and pulled out the bag with her clean clothes. A couple of women carrying wet bathing suits sauntered by.

Patricia rested her hand on Alice's arm. "Dear, what you've wanted for so long is a baby. Are you sure this isn't...?"

"I don't know." She wanted to lift off Patricia's too-hot hand. "Can't you be on my side?"

"I *am* on your side. A miscarriage can be as bad as a death. My dearest friend Gracie...well, we don't have to talk about Gracie. You still want a baby; I know that. How does sending your husband away square with that?"

Alice looked at the bank of mirrors reflecting the confusion of lockers. How could she explain? How could she explain the claustrophobia she felt with Rolly, when what she'd said was that she'd be left on her own with nothing to do in Norway? It wasn't logical. How could she say that thinking about trying to have a baby was too painful? How could she say anything except excuses, excuses that didn't add up to what she was feeling?

"What you're talking about is a separation," Patricia said, finally lifting her hand from Alice's arm.

Separation. She'd thought about being alone, not about a state of being that had a legal definition.

Patricia was asking, "But why? What's gone wrong?"

"All I know for certain," that word again, "certain" had no meaning, "is that right now, I need to be on my own for a while. Then we'll see."

Patricia's face sagged. Alice felt ashamed but she said, "If you want to argue with me, go ahead. It won't change anything."

"I'm not going to argue with you, but I do want to talk to you and Rolly, together. Soon. Now."

"I don't know where he is." Was she going to have to endure a talking-to from her mother?

"I'll call your house. We'll make it an early dinner."

At the front desk, Patricia asked to use the phone. She reached Rolly — he was still at the house — and Alice was trapped.

With Patricia following in her own car, Alice stopped at a fish shack by the river, and they waited, swatting mosquitoes, not talking, until their order was ready.

At the house Patricia pulled in alongside Alice's car, next to Rolly's studio. Through the kitchen window, Alice saw him in the kitchen, standing by the refrigerator.

Patricia reached for the bag of fish. "I'll carry this. You go ahead."

Alice pushed open the gate and strode through the grass that Rolly had neglected to mow.

"We're here," she said, opening the screen door.

He leaned against counter, feigning ease, though she could see his jaw tense beneath his beard.

"Listen," she said. "Patricia's waiting by the gate for the all clear. Let's try to keep this civil."

"Civil? I can do civil." He brushed past Alice to call through the screen. "It's OK to come in, Patricia." He held the door for her and said, "So she told you?" He kissed Patricia and took the sack of fish.

"She did," Patricia answered.

She? *She* was right here. Alice turned to the refrigerator. "Anyone like a beer?" She rattled the bottles noisily, pleased by the racket, and turned to see Rolly and Patricia putting the food on the table. Alice set the beer bottles on the table.

"Listen. I've made up my mind. I'm not going. This isn't part of some big scheme. I'm not talking about a 'separation,' Patricia's word."

Rolly's face was expressionless. Patricia folded the empty fish sack into a tight square. Even in their silence they were allied against her.

"Give that to me, Patricia," Alice said, tossing the paper toward the sink, where it fell short.

"Do you think I still want you to come?" Rolly said, his eyebrow twitching.

"Please, kids, let's sit and talk this through."

"What I am saying is I want to be alone for a while. Why don't you get it?"

"Notice I'm not arguing with you," Rolly said. "You want to stay here, stay."

Patricia patted the air, her eyes darting from Alice to Rolly. "Kids, Alice, sit down."

"I refuse to be a parasite for a year," Alice said.

"Parasitic wife of a third-rate artist?" Rolly responded.

Patricia scraped her chair loudly on the floor.

Alice, ashamed that she was acting like a teenager and furious at being caught in this impossible situation, sat down, as Rolly pulled out the third chair. Patricia picked up a piece of fish and nudged the platter toward Alice. Disgusting fish. Disgusting French fries. Rolly rose to get the salt and pepper. Alice repressed her urge to hold her breath — breathe deeply — but she couldn't. Her chest was as tight as a fist.

When their plates were loaded, Patricia put her hand next to Alice's plate and said, "Dear, I've been thinking, couldn't you develop some writing projects? Travel stories maybe? Remember Fran Danhoff from my old bridge group? She's now an editor of a family magazine now, in Chicago…"

"Not interested, are you?" Rolly inserted.

Travel pieces? Why had this never occurred to her? Alice hadn't even considered lining up freelance or spec work. Was this because she'd known all along she wasn't going? Stung by the possibility that some unacknowledged part of her had held out on Rolly from the beginning, she looked down at her plate. "I don't want to go. What will it take to get you two to listen?"

Patricia slammed her hands on the table. "I *am* listening. What I'm hearing is nonsense, coming from you, my darling daughter. And you Rolly are doing nothing to get out of this mess that Alice has dragged you both into. Alice," she held up her hand, "don't interrupt me. What you've said, Alice, is that you want to stay here, but you don't want a separation. Right?"

Alice saw Rolly's fingers tense against the table's edge. She nodded.

Patricia sighed. "This doesn't have to be irrevocable."

Alice refused to meet her gaze. This was a set-up.

Her mother went on. "Alice, could you visit Rolly after he's settled? A trip. A few weeks. After you've had your time to yourself." Without waiting for an answer, Patricia turned to Rolly. "Can you consider having Alice visit?"

From the corner of her eye, Alice saw movement, Rolly nodding. They had trapped her.

"OK," she said, to end this.

Rolly's eyes softened. Relief or triumph? And her mother and executioner reached across the table for their hands, her grip inflexible. Alice pictured the Indian bride tumbling from the balcony.

"Kids," Patricia said, "it's worth it; believe me, it's worth it."

***

Rolly set his departure date for the end of July. When they were together in the house, she tried to think of him as a foreign exchange student, one she resented, but who would soon leave. She could muster politeness for the remaining few weeks. They ate some dinners together, and they slept in the same bed, she clinging to her side. In the morning she would be in the same position, and he would be gone. He

132

worked long hours in his home studio and often at the college. Shippers came and picked up crates from his studio. When he asked when she might come to Bergen, she said she had to wait and see, regretting that she'd agreed. But she wouldn't renege and get blamed for that too.

***

Things slowed down at the *Herald*. By mid-June, when the graduation features, honor roll lists, and wedding stories were over, few editions ran thicker than the free *Savvy Shopper*. The drought dominated the front page: the drought's effect on crops, on livestock, on futures and financing. The drought was the topic spoken of at the diner, around the gas pumps at the self-serve, at the bank, and in the sunbaked square where Fourth of July bunting was hung on the bandstand. What had seemed a local scourge last year, now afflicted the entire heartland. The drought had taken on mythic proportions.

"Fill the inside with what the people want," Barry insisted, and she stitched together features with ancient Peruvian and Egyptian calendars and iffy stories from history, but she wondered, as Rolly prepared to leave and she spun drivel, if she was any better than the tabloid writer who concocted wild theories for the lunatic fringe. At the drugstore lunch counter, she heard outlandish tales of cults out in the county, stories that couldn't be pinned down. The confluence of these stories with the recent appearance of tent churches along the Wabansee River, and the drought, were enough to make her think, "Where there's smoke, there's fire." Clichés might be lame, but they were usually true, as she'd discovered to her shame. Had Heidi been a part of this madness?

***

Once she woke up in the middle of the night to find Rolly sitting in the chair facing the bed, his face hidden in shadows. She sat up and pulled the sheet to her shoulders.

133

"Are you angry with me?" she asked.

The chair creaked as he shifted. "I have been. Now I don't know how I feel. I want things to be different, but there doesn't seem to be any way I can change them. You don't want them to change, do you?" The fingers of his right hand played a scale on his leg.

"I don't want you to determine the cast of everything. That's what the past few years have been, all about you. I want to figure out what I want."

"Is there any chance that you'll want me?"

"I don't know."

"You do realize that this, what's between us now, is intolerable."

"Yes."

"And?"

"It will change when you go. Then we'll see."

He stood. "I'm going for a walk."

She listened to the front door shut behind him and felt the emptiness of the house close in on her. She was glad he hadn't seen her cry.

✳✳✳

Friends came over to say goodbye. Herman and Irenia stopped by with a thermos of gimlets, not trusting Rolly and Alice to stock gin, and gave Rolly a leather-bound journal. Patricia brought him a pocket-size English-Norwegian dictionary and a conversational tape. Wolf came for dinner and took away a crate with a small sculpture of Rolly's that he would ship to California in September. Rolly didn't want to burden Alice, he said. She was relieved that she wouldn't have to enter his studio, ashamed that she'd denigrated his work, and guessed that he probably didn't trust her to act on his behalf.

The night before his flight, at dinner, she gave him a set of Japanese brushes in an ivory silk case that she'd ordered from a museum store.

Ink, a dry black brick that needed to be wetted for use, was stored in a smoky porcelain box fitted in the center of the bottom tray. The length of padded silk with pockets for the brushes wound around the long box and tied.

"For sketching," she said.

"This is very beautiful." He kissed her tentatively on the cheek.

Glad that he liked it, glad that she had made the gesture, she took his cheeks in her hands, stroked his beard, then kissed him on the lips.

Surprised, he held her close, neither one of them saying anything.

✳✳✳

As Alice searched for her keys to drive Rolly to Indianapolis for his flight to New York, the UPS man delivered a last-minute package.

"Something came for you, Rolly."

He trotted downstairs and unwrapped it. Nestled in a shoebox was a handsome, antique ship's compass. A brass ring, burnished from use and incised with curlicued characters, surrounded a small glass dome that was cloudy, making it hard to see the wavering needle. A smile of pleasure spread across his face.

Alice picked up the wrapping. "Who's it from?" No name, no return address.

He riffled through the packing left in the box. "Here's a card: 'To guide you on your journey.' No signature." Thoughts raced behind his eyes, and she couldn't tell whether he'd figured out who'd sent it. He took the wrapping from her. "To hell with it. I'll just get rid of this," and walked into the kitchen.

She stared at the compass he'd left on the table. It had to be from a woman. She tipped the compass off the card, not recognizing the angular, neat script. To Rolly she said, "We have to leave. The traffic around Indianapolis could be heavy."

She waited while he raced upstairs to get his bags. When she heard him behind her, she glanced into the front hall. The compass was gone from the table. He was taking it with him.

"No idea who sent that?" she asked.

"No idea."

"It's quite a gift to give anonymously."

"Yes. A real gift, in a way, given from the heart, making no claims."

Given from the heart, but definitely staking a claim. Alice dug out her sunglasses and slipped them on, not wanting Rolly to see her eyes.

"Let's go then."

He offered to drive.

"Just get in." She got into the driver's seat, turned the air-conditioning to high to throw a wall of sound between them, then backed into the alley with unusual caution. The potential for an accident seemed very high. The airport was almost two hours away, all interstate. She kept her eyes ahead, trying to puzzle out who was the gift-giver. A lover? Someone she knew?

At the airport they stood at the gate, waiting for the announcement to board. She held herself rigid, careful not to brush against him. Would his lover join him in Norway? Was that why he hadn't pressed Alice to make definite plans? Why had he even pretended he wanted her to come?

When the stewardess unlocked the door, passengers shuffled forward.

"I'll email you when I get there," Rolly said.

"No personal email," she reminded him. Barry's rule. Neither she nor Rolly had wanted a computer at home.

"This doesn't qualify for an exception?" he said.

"When we first met, you phoned. That's fine. No, I don't want that either. No phone. Write me letters. That's what I want: long, carefully

136

written, beautiful letters. Woo me as if I were your lover." The knot of spite in her throat almost choked her.

"Rows twenty-eight through ten, now boarding."

"You are my lover, Alice." He put his arm around her and kissed her.

She pretended he was the foreign exchange student again and patted his back. She didn't want him to know she was on to him.

He pulled away. "Well, then…"

An older couple pushed past them, hurrying to the Jetway.

"Well, then," she echoed.

✳✳✳

On the interstate, she rolled down her window and thought about what she would do first when she got home. Change the sheets and towels so there was no Rolly smell. Toss out the blueberry jelly that only he liked. But who would help her if she cut herself badly on a kitchen knife? Or had a flat tire? Or fell from the ladder cleaning the gutters in October? And what if the lawn mower broke? Where was the key to the safe deposit box?

✳✳✳

In Ang's class, Patricia asked how she was doing.

"It's like having a cast taken off. A huge relief, but I feel a little shaky."

"I don't think you'll find single life is all that much fun."

"I'm willing to give it a try."

"Obviously," Patricia said, her smile the one that had galled Alice in her teenage years. "By the way," her mother went on, "tonight Warren's taking me out to Salvatore's. Why don't you come with us?"

"I'm looking forward to being alone. Maybe next week," Alice answered, wondering what Patricia would say if she told her about Rolly's anonymous gift. She would say it was a student with a crush. She would say Alice was blowing things out of proportion. Maybe this was true.

Maybe he didn't have a lover. It could have come from someone who had Rolly in her sights. That was possible. Was it possible? She no longer knew what was possible with Rolly. What she did know was that the mystery at his core, which had once charmed and attracted her, might be sufficient to hide his desire for another woman.

He ignored her request that he not email her at work.

From: rdbecotte@hotmail.com
To: a_becotte@HHWeekly.org
Sent: July 21, 10:45 p.m.

Your anger at the airport told me that it finally hit you that I was leaving. I'm writing to you quickly, before anything intervenes, to try to convince you that we belong together. So no well-penned letter on stationery that will arrive two weeks later, but an urgent email to say I want to begin again. Please, Alice. Write immediately to say you read this. Write anything.

She printed this out and mulled it over at home, vacillating. He wouldn't bother to write such a warm note if he weren't sincere. Maybe she was wrong. Maybe the compass wasn't from a lover. Possibly a student with a crush, one he'd noticed watching him across the classroom but hadn't encouraged, some eager and terrified girl. Like she had once been.

✳✳✳

On Sunday in early August, she sat on a blanket in her backyard, reading the *Indianapolis Star* when the gate creaked open, and Wolf wheeled his bike in, propping it against the corner of Rolly's studio. She tugged down her shorts and folded the paper.

"Wolf, how nice."

"Hello, Alice."

He unwound his red headband and wiped the sweat from his neck. She watched him peel his sticky T-shirt from his chest and pull it free of the waist of his many-pocketed khaki shorts. His arms were rippled with muscles, and his legs were long and thin with sharply defined calves under a haze of soft hair. A bumpy vein ran from the inside of one knee into a too-heavy sock that fell over the top of his hiking boots. She'd never seen his legs before.

"Wolf, have you been working out? You didn't used to have muscles, did you?" she asked, as he settled cross-legged beside her on the blanket.

"Work out? You Americans. My muscles are pure testosterone."

"Have some strawberries." She pointed to the nearby basket. "They're from the pick-your-own place, but I didn't do the picking. A friend picked too many." Why was she rattling on? "Would you like a beer?"

"Ah. A beer and strawberries, perfection. Yes, please, a beer would be nice, but water first, if this is not too much trouble." He sat on the grass next to the blanket and noticed something in the *Star*'s arts section.

"Look at this." He swatted the newspaper and Alice paused to see the target of his outrage: an article about an exhibition at the Indianapolis Museum of Art, accompanied by a picture of what looked like a fedora next to a half-dug grave.

"They call Beuys the 'voice of the German conscience in the era following post-War expressionism.' He is a fool. He puts Luftwaffe uniforms, suits, into glass boxes, smears them with dirt and this fraud works. That is what is stunning."

Grinning, Alice wiped grass clippings from her feet. She enjoyed how Wolf and Rolly dissected the shortcomings of what they considered the competition. "Write a letter to the editor. I'm sure they'd love to hear from you. And I'll be right back."

"You are right to flee, Alice, woman of wisdom, from the prevarications of art critics who are no better here than in New York or Berlin. I never should have uttered—even by quoting art critic nonsense—such lies in the hearing of a woman of your delicacy and good sense."

"Stuff it, Wolf."

When she returned with a tray, Wolf was lying on his back.

"Was there a reason you stopped by?" She handed him a glass of water.

"Reason?"

"Did Rolly ask you to keep an eye on me?"

He looked at her with amusement, accepting the water. "I biked along the canal through the woods and was on my way home. I thought you might offer me a cold drink." He drained the glass and gave it back to her. "Thank you."

"Does that mean yes or no?"

"It means no."

"Good." She sat on the blanket, the *Star* scattered between them. "I don't want to be watched. I would like to be invisible."

"From everyone or just Rolly?" he asked and reached for the beer bottle on the tray. He rolled it over his throat, then uncapped it, and took a long swallow.

"From everyone, I guess, but just now I meant Rolly. And I don't want to be watched by you."

"You are denying me much pleasure then."

"Wolf, I can never tell when you are serious or when you are joking."

"It is very simple. Let me explain. I am always joking seriously." He put his empty bottle on the tray, picked it up, noted the damp ring, then set the bottle down, and lifted it, again and again, creating a series of linked dark circles. "I must go." He stood.

"Wait," she said. "Your shoe is untied. Let me show you this new knot I learned. It was supposedly invented by an ingenious mother of eight, tired of retying children's shoes all day. She wanted a sturdy knot that wouldn't come undone, but could be untied easily, unlike a double knot."

She felt his gaze on her neck as she took the loose laces in her hands. "See, here, instead of yanking it tight through, you take this loop and thread it back through the central knot." She pulled slowly on the two loops of the bow until the knot was secure, sensing a charge between them. Not wanting him to see her smile, she kept her head down. "There, let's see how that holds."

Wolf stepped back, shaking his feet. "Thank you. I hope I can get this boot off later. And thank you for the beer." He wheeled his bike out the gate and waved.

When he disappeared, she flopped back on the blanket and stared into the honey locust's leaf cover. It had only been a tiny moment, a little flirting, but she liked feeling transgressive, a silly, art-world word she'd learned from Rolly. She liked it a lot.

10

From: rdbecotte@hotmail.com
To: a_becotte@HHWeekly.org
Sent: July 23, 11:33 a.m.
Subject: Hello

Dear Alice,

Sorry again for breaking your NO EMAIL rule, but I want to let you know I've arrived. It feels strange to be here without you.

Love, Rolly

July 29
Dear Alice,

(Here is a proper letter, not the wooing kind, but the pen pal kind, which seems like what you asked for.) It's been a week and I've hardly slept. The endless days or endless sun you've heard of. I think of you on the other side of the world, the same sun beating down on you. (Letter writing brings out an unexpected antiquarian side of me. This may drive you to reconsider your ban on email. Internet cafés are everywhere. I await your go-ahead.)

You would like it here. Oslo is beautiful, fine old buildings, lots of parks, judicious new buildings, a huge, modern harbor, cranes everywhere, but the water is as blue as the swimming pool in Schmidt Park.

You would like the gardens. Colors more intense than anything in the Midwest. Except for geraniums and petunias, I don't know what they are, but you would. The parks are full of sculptures of mermaids, fierce sailors, heavy, kindly women with small boys and girls. Would you like this "useless" public sculpture? You might not be able to stop yourself.

A fellow from the University called the first night, said he was coming this way, to Oslo, and offered to show me the sights. A nice guy, Per Harveldt, in his fifties, studied in New York with Louise Nevelson some time in the late sixties. He jabbed at passing sights as we hurdled around Oslo in his buggy-size car, and I tried to keep a sense of direction for finding my way later in the rental car. In the morning, I head for a couple of excavation sites where Viking boats were found.

Pictures in books did not prepare me for the Viking Ship Museum. The boats are stunning. The important ones each have a room to itself, vaulted, whitewashed rooms, and filled with light, reverent as chapels.

It's exciting on my own, but I miss you too, in spite of how things were when I left. I have to admit that I'm surprised by how much I miss you. I want to show you Oslo. "Things Alice will like" is the heading on a list I'm compiling, for when you come.

I called you a couple of hours ago, 8 a.m. your time, but you must have already left for work, and the machine wasn't on. It's been two weeks and I'm not sure I remember your voice.

Love, Rolly

From: rdbecotte@hotmail.com
To: Wlemmen@maildrop.wcindiana.edu
Sent: July 30, 5:45 p.m.

Wolf,

A week here. It's great spending my time on my own work
and not working on syllabuses. In the morning I leave Oslo,
heading to some excavations. I remember telling you about
not being sure I had any real interest in researching Viking
ships. That's changed. After my first day in the Viking Ship
Museum, I could barely sleep. Check this out: www.khm.
uio.no/vikingskipshuset. The boats exhibited there were
dredged from harbors or unearthed from farm fields. The
important ones are displayed singly, in their own rooms,
clerestory windows. Even after their time spent sunk in
the sea or the ground, the care and skill of the builders is
what you see, not the deterioration. The abstraction and efficiency of design is exceptional and fine. Nothing in our
culture matches the unequivocalness of spirit I see in them.
My own work seems overdetermined and overwrought. If I
could handle wood with a fraction of the understanding and
knowledge evident in these boats, I would be a happy man.

The curators were gratifyingly impressed with my letter of
introduction and gave me the run of the place. Associate
Professor must mean something here.

Met a sculptor, another woodworker, Per Harveldt, who'd
studied in NYC but is now ensconced at the University in
Bergen. He told me that at the university I will share his studio, which is a quarter of a barn at the edge of the campus.

Sounds perfect.

Write and tell me how everyone is doing.

From: rdbecotte@hotmail.com
To: Msaffold@maildrop.wcindiana.edu
Sent: August 3, 10:45 p.m.

Dear Meg,

It's been six months and it's either fitting or ironic—you decide—that now that it's over between us—it is over between
us—I approach you by email, which I couldn't risk when I
was home. Nothing was private from Wolf on our shared
office computer.

The family I'm staying with is asleep. I'm writing on their
computer. I brought your compass with me. I shouldn't
have, but it's on the table beside me.

Part of me misses you. All we had was a few weeks, but every
moment is still alive in me. The way your freckles float on the
surface of your skin, the jut of your hip, the way you move
as if you can hear music no one else can. With you, I was
buoyed up, yet steadier than I ever remember being. Weeks
of dreaming, that's what we had, or I had. Then I woke up.
The miscarriage did that. Awake, I know that my life was, is,
with Alice. I wish I were capable of living two lives at once
but I can't. Having to turn away from you kills me. This is
what I tried to say to you that afternoon in February. This is
what I've been repeating to myself ever since.

As you must have heard, Alice didn't come with me. She says

she needs to be alone. I think time apart will be good for us. Her grief about the miscarriage is focused on me, transformed into anger. And I admit to you, I resent her for not appreciating what I've given up for her, that is, giving up you. That's why I'm actually grateful she didn't come with me. I need time away from her too.

It's late. Across the keyboard, the compass shoots shards of light. It reminds me of you. Too many things remind me of you. You are inside me. I want impossible things, I want it all, but that's not what life offers.

August 10
Oseberg, Norway

Dear Patricia,

I hope you got the postcards I sent from Oslo. The most remarkable thing here is that the people are so un-neurotic that something seems missing.

Now I'm staying with a farm family near Oseberg, where one of the Viking ships was found. Historians say this ship might have served as a grave for a woman, probably a queen. Before this ship—it's about seventy feet long—was excavated at the turn of the last century, it had remained hidden for about a thousand years. Old photographs show a farmhouse in the background, still here, and cows grazing near the site where men dressed in suits and hats lean on shovels around the unearthed ship skeleton. They might have been breathing air trapped for a thousand years and exhaled by Vikings. Now these diggers are ghosts too. Today, at the site, I was alone. From a quarter of a mile away, I could hear the sea.

How is Alice? You do know that she insists she and I communicate only by letter, for now, which means I haven't heard from her, since I haven't reached my fixed address at the University of Bergen.

It's been two weeks and I'm beginning to feel strange writing letters and not hearing from anyone, except emails from students asking for various favors. I feel like a telegraph operator in the Old West, confidently sending out messages, not knowing whether the lines have been cut.

Love, Rolly

He wrote to Alice:

It's three and a half weeks since I saw you.

I've rented something that's called a Ford, an imposter with hints of Italian lineage in its snug body and honest-to-god Albanian mechanics. It's so loud, it frightens the cows in the fields as I drive by on my way east to Stockholm. I'm hoping to find an inn or a resort and spend some time sketching from nature, using the brushes you gave me. Once I get to Stockholm, I'll meet with the curators that Jacqueline arranged. A show may be in the works. After that I'll return to Oslo and follow the coastal roads to Bergen. Traveling the interior of Norway is not recommended, too mountainous with few roads. Good skiing later.

Every cottage, town, person, trash barrel, highway sign, stone I've seen has been pretty. That's the only word for it. I'll send you some pictures.

Is this the right way to write to you? Is this really what you want? Week-old tourist letters? I feel as if a wall has sprung up in the middle of the Atlantic, separating us. Each time I've phoned, I've gotten the damn machine. When I get to Bergen at the end of the month, I hope to find an avalanche of letters from you.

From: rdbecotte@hotmail.com
To: Wlemmen@maildrop.wcindiana.edu
Sent: August 22, 3:40 p.m.

Wolf,

For you school starts in five days—right?—and I'm sitting by an open door in an Internet café in the old town of Stockholm. Above car fumes, I smell the sea. On the sidewalk in front of me, young women dressed in summery dresses stroll by with their children. Just now, one stopped and bent to her baby in a stroller, her blond hair swung forward, shining, covering her face, rippling like sunlit water. They are all so beautiful, these young mothers. I've never noticed before how really sexy young mothers are. (And they aren't all long-limbed, blond Swedes.) These women possess an easiness in their bodies and a heart-stopping power that's got to spring from knowing they can, and have, produced new beings. What these women exude is so much better than what you see in the adolescent beauties who are supposed to be the ideal. Watching this parade, I can see that young mothers are the sexiest women in the world.

I'm waiting for Agatha Ngoni, not from what I know a mother, but a dreamsicle anyway, from Zimbabwe. She's a textile artist. I met her a couple of days ago at one of the galleries Jacqueline set up for me. I'm giving her a ride to Oslo. Are you imagining something more? Yeah, you are. I know you. But don't. I'm in monk mode.

You were right, it's great to have unfettered time to work. Before I got to Stockholm, I stopped for three days at Lake Vajtotern and sketched. Where the water met the shore, I reduxed Dürer: grasses, silt, small insects, percolating tidal pools, currents, shreds of orange and white wrappers, a perfect brown rabbit nosing a plastic motor oil jug. I drew what I saw, not what I could imagine. I needed to observe directly, short-circuiting my expectations, my sense of form, my insistent tendency to aestheticize. It was almost as good as being a student again, unburdened by what I've already done, cleansed. If my appointments with galleries here hadn't been scheduled, I would have remained sketching until I'd run into the void drawing always has brought me to, but as it stands, I'm excited to get back to it.

After dropping Agatha off in Oslo, I plan to drive up the coast to Bergen and stop whenever I like again, since no one needs me to be anywhere.

＊＊＊

At the edge of the large, modern campus of the University of Bergen, past a couple of low garages storing the university's snow plows and landscaping equipment, at the end of a service road, stood two former dairy barns that the art department had converted into faculty studios. The painters and printmakers used the long one; the other was for sculptors. It was here that he was given a studio.

The sculpture building was divided into three rooms, a large studio at each end, separated by a communal space in the middle, with couches, a couple of long tables, sink, coffee pot, lockers, and extra storage. The stonecutters — Eric Thorval, who worked in a variety of stones, and Elise Wahloo, who worked mostly in marble and granite — occupied the north studio. Rolly moved into the south studio with Per

Harveldt, who'd prepared for his arrival by moving his finished work off to one side. Per — ruddy-faced, bristling red hair, and with a belly that hung over his belt — seemed glad for Rolly's company. After Per helped Rolly uncrate his boxes, he introduced him to a lumber dealer near the harbor who specialized in fine woods.

✳✳✳

August 30

Alice dear,

I hope you accept the apology I left on the machine. (Both calls, me being pissed, me apologizing, were made from the art department's phone. The Lund's cottage has no phone. Which is why you can't call me back.) Let me explain. After settling in the Lund's cottage, I drove to the university and introduced myself at the art department. After some confusion, they figured out who I was, gave me keys, and sent me off to the personnel office. Before I left the secretary handed me a bundle of mail, with nothing from you. NOTHING. Why, Alice? I don't get it.

Love, Rolly

✳✳✳

The Lund's cottage with its flower boxes and slanting roof looked exactly like the photograph he'd left at home for Alice. What wasn't visible was the path that descended to the road or the dense surrounding forest. Inside, spartan furniture, mostly upholstered in greens and browns, an orange rug in front of a woodstove, a loft bedroom, a porch off the kitchen, a hand-operated coffee grinder.

✳✳✳

During his first few days at the university, the stonecutters' din was overwhelming; and he thought he'd have to limit his work to nights, but the racket faded or he got used to it. Sharing a studio was harder to get used to. Per's presence was a distraction. Rolly worried that he was encroaching on Per's space, and he felt watched. If he guessed that Per was about to launch into conversation, he would move to the communal room with his sketching materials.

Each day he walked downhill from the Lund's cottage to the bus stop. Twelve, fourteen hours later, he came home. On the weekends he worked alone, with no music from Elise and Eric and no interruptions from Per. When he took a break, he would open the windows so that he could hear the distant hum of traffic and not feel cut off. On his days alone, not having to give voice to his thoughts gave him the freedom to think without edges or limits. He didn't have to make sense to anyone else. Every perception was heightened. A twig bouncing off the studio's roof, the smell of metal on metal, the different colors of rain. Nothing was muted. Being with another person dimmed the world. Alone, he felt buoyant and alive.

But he missed Alice, even though her silence frustrated him. When he sat down to a meal, he thought of her, the old Alice, and wished she were here; and when he woke in the night, he reached for her. If only Meg's gift hadn't arrived when it did, too late for him to reset things with Alice. He'd assumed Alice would think it had come from a student, like the notes from girls he'd shown her in the past, some slipped under his office door, some in email. Alice understood girls got crushes on male faculty. He'd hoped Alice would see the compass in the same light, especially if he didn't point it out. Now he could see that he'd botched that with his 'gift of the heart' comment.

Each day he stopped at the art department to check his mail. Two weeks after he began receiving mail at the university, which was six weeks after he left home, Alice's first letter came, in a business envelope, mailed from the *Herald*, not her nice stationery.

"Dear Rolly," she wrote. "Little news to report. Muriel Swenke is dying."

Muriel, in her nineties, lived on their block, on the other side of the street, near the corner.

"Her daughter has put the house on the market."

Why the hell was she starting with this? She wrote about how Paul and Bettina were appalled by the ludicrous listing price "that greedy California girl" was asking, but they hoped the house fetched that inflated sum since it would boost everyone else's home values. Had he heard that Patricia had sprained her ankle? He hadn't. The tomatoes were producing a bumper crop. She was canning. She hoped he was enjoying himself and that his work was going well.

Nothing about the anonymous gift. No comment about the letters he'd written to her. No questions about his life. Nothing about when she would come to see him.

From: rdbecotte@hotmail.com
To: a_becotte@HHWeekly.org
Sent: Sept. 12, 10:13 a.m.

Alice, oh Alice,

You said no email, but I tried to reach you last night at what I think was 1:30 your time and got no answer. Your first letter arrived, more than six weeks after I left, and it's all about Muriel Swenke (???), the Faraccis, and Patricia, but nothing about you. Canning? Really? What's going on?

Except for your silence, everything is exactly right here.

I can see you, but I feel as if I've gone deaf, not hearing from you. The silence is crushing. Please.

11

A lice clicked on "compose" and began to write:

From: a_becotte@HHWeekly.org
To: rdbecotte@hotmail.com
Sent: September 13, 1:37 p.m.

Dear Rolly,

I am sorry I wrote what I did. When I was a kid, Patricia would lecture me on the difference between an excuse and a reason. I tried not to listen, but I remember that a reason is a reasonable explanation for a wrong action, while an excuse is a cowardly explanation used to scoot out of responsibility. I wrote my get-out-of-my-face letter because your near-constant communications feel like an assault. Is this a reason or an excuse? Either way, I'm sorry.

You apologize. I apologize. A cycle of apologies is no help.

You've been gone two months and my anger xxxxxxxxxxxxx

She deleted the xxxs. Her anger had...what? Expanded? Shrunk? Spread? Shifted? Sometimes softened, sometimes hardened? Morphed into a tangle she couldn't tease apart but that included repugnance, the wish to hit him again and again, and remorse, which angered her even more. Why should she feel remorse? But as the weeks passed, she wasn't sure of anything. She wasn't even sure he had cheated on her. The compass might have come from someone who had a crush on him. He might suspect who it was from but not know for sure. His letters seemed sincere, but how could she know? She wasn't even sure she cared.

She deleted her last two words and typed:

> and I'm still finding my way. I'll come at Christmas. After three months apart, you and I should know how we feel. Until then, I'll write weekly and you'll write back, weekly. Not more often. I'm glad you've settled in and are working well. Per Harveldt sounds like a good friend. I'll write you a real letter tonight. Please, no more emails and no more phone calls.
> Alice

***

Marriage took more time than she'd realized. Without Rolly, she had too much free time. She stayed busy at the paper, working more hours than Barry expected or paid for. Running around the county chasing down stories and hanging around the office was better than being at home. Before Rolly had left, she'd never noticed how the rooms echoed. The garden was a mess. She was tired of tomatoes. She let the fruit rot on the vine. Later, she'd turn everything under to compost. She was alone too much. She accepted the dinner invitations that friends extended. She slept badly and woke at the slightest sound. A rash of petty, kid's crimes in the neighborhood — like stolen bikes, basement break-ins, tagging garages a few blocks away — disturbed her. Downtown Haslett was hit by a string of fires, most set in the trashcans behind the shops on the square. Jet told her the police were taking these crimes seriously, but no one was caught. Classes began at the high school. School officials were on high alert because of the horrific school shooting out west, but there was no money for metal detectors, as some people demanded in letters to the *Herald*. After Labor Day, a bunch of teenagers, names withheld, were arrested in a drug bust near the town swimming pool, which had closed for the season. In mid-September, five mink jackets were stolen from the vault at Bobbie's Bridal and Fur Salon on the Square. Valued at $4,500, according to Bobbie Rohrbach, the owner, a figure Alice headlined. Fritzie joked that no one would dare wear a mink to church anytime soon, but it was too hot anyway. By the end of September, three farms had gone into foreclosure, the first in the county in more than thirty years. Alice attended the auctions. "Worst times since the Depression." "With the new millennium, who knows what's coming?" "The smart money's laying in supplies, in case the system breaks down." These clichés made it into her copy.

When she'd wrung what she could from the local news, she spent more hours than necessary writing features on outsize squashes, old-fashioned remedies for bagworm and voles, and the "What's Doing" calendar. September was the month for block parties and corn mazes.

She worked out a lot at the gym. She noticed attractive men.

After Ang's class, she asked Bettina, whom she'd persuaded to join at the low September rate, if Bettina thought Asian men had any body hair. They were drying off after showering.

"I don't think I've ever seen a naked Asian man, not in real life. Maybe not even in a movie. I'm thirty-four and I may die without ever seeing one." Pouting, she looked at Alice. "I'll probably never get to

Paris either. But I think I've seen armpit hair. I'm sure I have."

"Can you imagine what sex would be like with a man as smooth and muscular as Ang?" Alice asked, picturing Ang's black ponytail.

Rolly was the only man she'd ever had sex with, not counting heavy petting with Dix Friedlander and Tim Sturmer. She'd graduated from high school as a virgin. In college, there'd been that gorgeous Peruvian guy, whose name she'd forgotten, whom she'd met at a house party and gotten seriously drunk with and petted and licked — it was all thrilling — but when she woke up alone on a couch in the shabby upstairs den, half-dressed and sore between her legs, she decided not to count on her private sexual scoreboard what she couldn't remember, so she was still a virgin. Then she met Rolly.

Bettina said, "Ang would definitely have the moves." She wiggled her eyebrows like a bad actor leering. "By the way, how long has Rolly been gone?"

"Oh, please. Ten weeks and it's not about missing Rolly. I'm just curious. If I were really free — and I'm not talking about not being married, but free as in free-spirit…"

"Forget about it." Bettina pulled on her shirt. "You're not 'free.' You're a grown woman."

"I'm just saying that I can see how incredibly sexy all men are, not just the good-looking ones. Yesterday — I couldn't believe it — when I was at the bank, I stared at the man who goes into the vault. Do you know who I mean? Sixty, or sixty-five, slicked-back hair, and a belly that is almost a perfect sphere, pants pulled up right to the equator. Humpty Dumpty. How would you fit yourself around that belly?" Alice curved her spine as if she had a beach ball on her lap and reached forward with her arms, struggling to hug the air.

"Are you crazy?"

156

"I'm not going to have sex with him," Alice laughed, tugging her sandals from her gym bag. "But haven't you ever had a more or less abstract but intense interest?"

"Not since I got married." Bettina replied, stuffing her gym clothes into her bag.

Alice grinned. "That's too bad."

"That's not what I meant." Bettina flicked a hand at Alice, pretending to be miffed.

"No need for abstract with Paul," Alice said. "Your husband is a hunk."

"So's Rolly. Let me tell you, Rolly's one of the good ones."

Alice tried to think of Rolly as desirable. "Don't worry, Bettina. I haven't forgotten I'm married to Rolly."

***

That night, she stood in the upstairs hall, staring at a gouge in the nursery door that Rolly had overlooked while repairing the damage she'd caused. Patricia had been right: The anguish did recede. Spring and summer, the end of September, and what had happened no longer underscored every moment of every day. She pressed her finger into the gouge. The baby would now be eight weeks old.

She wished she could talk to Rolly. She didn't want to say anything, just wanted to hear his voice, but she wasn't yet ready to breach the barrier she'd erected. She turned off the hall light and stood in the half-dark, listening to the night sounds. Through the bedroom's open windows came the roar of cicadas and far off music from someone's backyard radio. She wished she wasn't so alone.

***

One unseasonably warm afternoon in early October, she drove country roads back to the office after attending the official reopening of a restored covered bridge. Because of the drought, the fields were full of tall, parched corn. Ahead, on a low hill, was an odd, bent sign-post. As she got closer, she saw it was a cyclist walking his bicycle and swung to the left to give him a wide berth. It was Wolf.

After cresting the hill, she slowed and pulled over onto the shoulder of the embankment. Since he'd wheeled his bike into her backyard a couple of months ago, she had wondered when she might see him again. That he hadn't been around told her that he hadn't been acting as Rolly's spy. In the rearview mirror, she watched him appear over the ridge, one hand guiding the bike.

The roar of flapping cornstalks hit her when she stepped from the car. Waiting for Wolf to recognize her, she leaned against the hot fender, shielding her eyes from the sun. Unlike last time, he was dressed for serious cycling: cleats, black shorts, yellow bike shirt. His arms were corded with veins and he looked exhausted. He stopped, balanced the bike against his hip, and pulled the goggles away from his eyes, wiping his forehead with the back of his hand.

"I was afraid you were a mirage," he said.

"A puncture?" she asked. The sun shone through his right ear, making it glow red.

He knelt beside the bike's front tire to probe a gash in the rubber. The nape of his neck was sunburnt. She imagined touching him there, in the hollow between the two ridges of muscles.

"This I can't fix with the patch kit," he said. "I will need a new tire."

"Throw it in the trunk, and I'll drive you to town."

He rocked back on his heels, wiped sweat from his face with his forearm, then detached the wheels from the bike's frame as she opened the trunk.

When they got to town, she'd ask if he wanted to get something cold to drink. "How long will it take them to replace it?" she asked.

158

"I do it myself."

Disappointed — no chance of a drink together — she opened the driver's door.

Wolf held up his hand. "I think I hear water." He closed the trunk quietly. "But I have this slight ringing in my ears all the time. I don't know what you call it in English."

"Tinnitus."

"It is only bad when there are no other noises. That is why I bike out here. The noise of the wind drowns out the ringing. But I am sure I hear something." He walked toward where the road's shoulder fell off into brush.

She peered down through the prairie grass and wild raspberries and saw a rim of concrete. "We're standing over a culvert."

His shadow fell over her. He was closer than he would be if they weren't alone, as close as she'd been when she'd tied his bootlace. Fighting breathlessness, she said, "The ringing in your ears must be awful. What do you do?"

"I live with it. Let's see what's there."

She half tumbled behind him, lost her footing, and he helped her up, brushing off the grass that clung to her skirt. They stood on a track wide enough to drive a tractor along the cornfield that extended in both directions as far as she could see. Behind them, the road level was at least four feet above their heads. On their right, in the shade of the embankment, a culvert, four feet across, expelled coolness so welcoming, it seemed enchanted. Water trickled over the metal lip into a muddy pool bordered by a truck retread and bent-over weeds. The air smelled tangy, like minerals and crushed grass and something else. Wolf's sweat? She took a deep breath, her skin rising in goose bumps.

"This is good, no?" he said, peeling off his sweaty bike shirt with its laden back pocket and dipped its front into the water burbling inside the pipe.

His back was pale, without a freckle or a mole. She imagined her hand gliding over the slick plane of his shoulder blade and wished he were someone she didn't know, someone she could have sex with and who would disappear afterward. She took off her sandals and eased her toes into the pool. Eddies of tobacco-colored silt funneled up between toes. Deep inside her, desire unfurled, making her hips heavy. She knelt to cup water in her hand and dribbled it in the open collar of her dress, liking the chill rivulets that curved around her breasts, then warmed.

"This is good," he mumbled.

She looked up to see that he was wiping his neck with his dripping shirt, his eyes on her. Excitement fizzed in her. She smiled, knowing her smile was an invitation. He stood, slung his wet shirt over his shoulders, and stepped across the small pool that separated them to touch her cheek.

"What are you meaning?"

She touched his chest.

"Do you want this?" he said.

"Yes." She could barely hear her voice above the flapping corn and the pounding inside her.

The muscles along his jaw clenched, then relaxed. He lifted her chin and kissed her mouth. She was shocked, shocked by the smoothness of his skin, no prickly beard like Rolly's, shocked by the strangeness of kissing some other man, shocked by the electric jolt that traveled through her. They pressed together. He was nothing like Rolly. His body was lighter, silken, except for the bones of his pelvis and his shoulders, and his penis was startling. She'd never seen an uncircumcised penis. She hid her embarrassment by kissing his chest, and he pulled away — recoiling from her naiveté? — and fumbled for his shirt, unzipping

160

the back pocket. From his wallet, he produced a foil square, a condom. This was real. They were going to have sex. She took the packet from him and tore it open with her teeth.

Afterward, they fell asleep on the grass, legs entwined.

A droning mosquito woke her. She sat up, careful not to wake him. What had she done? Wolf was now her lover. Lover? No. What had just happened didn't mean that they now had a relationship. This was a blip. It was wonderful and nothing, like breath on glass.

She had never noticed that his eyelashes were white, almost transparent. Did he always carry condoms in his wallet? Was he always on the lookout for chance encounters? The business with Irenia Laasche was a joke, but how many women had he had sex with? Dozens, she hoped, multitudes. She wanted to be one of many, and inconsequential. He was inconsequential to her. Not a lover.

He was too thin. His pelvis jutted like stone ridges from his flat abdomen. She glanced at her own belly to see if he'd ground bruises into her skin and was surprised that he had left no marks. She studied his body from the red blister on his left little toe, to his ears, which hugged his near-shaven scalp. Next to his Adam's apple was a sickle-shaped scar.

How strange that she'd just made love with him. Tenderness washed through her, not the gentle stirring of love. Attraction: yes. Physical desire: yes. Yearning: no. She had no feelings, or no deep feelings for him, although she wished that he wasn't Rolly's friend. She leaned away from him and snapped off a feathery weed. Rolly would never have to know. No one would ever have to know.

"Shh, Wolf, we have to get up." She tickled his forehead with the weed. "The bugs are out."

He jerked, frowned, then smiled, seeing her, and sat up, his expression now serious. Afraid he might make a declaration; she turned away to reach for her clothes. He put his hand on her ankle.

"Alice, you are wonderful. But this can't fit into my life, or yours."

She held her dress against her chest. "OK."

His eyes narrowed.

Was he disappointed? She reached for his hand. "You're right. We don't fit into each other's lives. That would be a mess. But you're leaving in December, aren't you? Returning to Germany? Why don't we, for two months, know each other? I could. I would like to unzip my regular life, like a tent, and slip out to be with you. It doesn't have to be part of my real life, and not part of yours."

He shook his head, suggesting that she was a child to think this was possible. "Rolly's being away, it's even more wrong. This can't work."

"This has nothing to do with Rolly. I want...just this." She trailed the tips of her fingers up his arm and watched his penis jump. "This, your body, mine. Simple. Not complex."

He reached for his shorts. She thought, or hoped, she saw an argument behind his eyes. He stood, dressed, cleats in hand, and stared off as a gust of wind set off a roar among the cornstalks. The moment held, like a water drop on a faucet about to fall. When it did, her life would change, one way or the other.

"OK," he said, as if already regretting it.

She hid her delight. She knew she could make it work.

＊＊＊

During the next week, she was tossed between exhilaration, shame, and aching desire to be with him. When he called to ask if she wanted to go biking, she claimed she was too busy, and knew that he took this as a brush-off. She was glad. This was best. She'd been crazy to think she could pull off a no-strings affair with him. The following Thursday, she called him. It was after ten o'clock; she'd written a breezy letter to

Rolly, about their block party where she'd taken his family's bean salad, about the unusually warm October weather, and about the new curtains she'd made for the pantry — and she felt like a fraud. She wanted to be with someone who knew almost nothing about her, who found her desirable.

Wolf lived on the third floor of an old limestone mansion that had been divided long ago into student apartments. Worried about being seen, she parked two blocks away in a strip mall parking lot and walked past formerly grand homes with fraternity flags hanging in windows. In the house where Wolf lived, third-floor rear — she and Rolly had dropped him off once — someone was practicing the flute. At the base of the external staircase that led to his apartment, she hesitated — one time could be dismissed as trivial, but twice was definitely something — then saw Wolf lean over the railing and her heart lifted. Under the house's high security light, his dark, short hair shone. He'd showered for her. With a courtly gesture, he ushered her into his dimly lit kitchen.

Nervous, guessing he was too, she turned quickly to hug him.

He whispered her name. "I was unsure if I should call you again."

"I wasn't sure either."

Locking his hands behind her, he looked down at her. "Simple. As you said, simple."

＊＊＊

Several times a week, she went to his apartment, always late at night, and left before dawn. She never invited him to her house. He didn't have lots of women, she learned. Carrying condoms was a habit from his youth. His leaving for Germany in mid-December meant they had a built-in limit. He was as grateful for this as she. She felt as if she were performing a tight-wire act, especially when she wrote her weekly letter to Rolly. A few days after Wolf left for Germany, she would fly to Oslo.

The weekend before Halloween, a call came into the *Herald* about a disturbance at a farm on the edge of the county. Fritzie handed Alice the note when she returned from a quick trip across the square to Weiland's to see their new and dismal selection of winter boots.

"Landwehr's farm. The Landwehrs, whose son was valedictorian last June?"

"The same. Kid's the only one with brains. Last night someone took a tractor — one they found in the barn — and cut a swath out of corn that should have been harvested already."

Alice didn't know the farm, but the road number suggested it was near the Fenders'. She hadn't seen Heidi since April when the girl had rebuffed her, but she'd thought about her often in the summer, before Rolly left, and when school started, she wondered if Heidi was in town, but she hadn't pursued this, not really wanting any news about the girl. Heidi was part of what was over. The baby, the hopes, the plans, the girl, the Virgin — all of it was behind Alice now. To think of any of it pained her.

"I'll get the camera," she said, pocketing Fritzie's note, "and head out after I check in with Barry."

"Don't bother him. He's upstairs with the accountant."

"Then it's lucky I didn't put the camera away where it belongs." She lifted the camera kit out of the USPS bin on the back worktable.

***

The Landwehrs' place was more forlorn than the Fenders', which Alice had gone out of her way not to pass. Since she'd started seeing Wolf, any stray thought of Heidi brought on the certainty that if she were to run into her, the girl would know about Wolf and be disappointed in Alice. The Landwehrs' porch roof had been torn off years ago, judging by the water damage on the aluminum siding, and the barn needed a coat of paint. A squad car was parked by a rickety rabbit hutch and near the front steps. Jet Bower stood talking to a red-faced, thick-bodied man in overalls who had to be Ben Landwehr. Jet was trying to calm him down, but he wasn't about to be calmed.

"Hi, Jet," she called out, stepping from her car.

Landwehr twisted his neck to look at her without easing his belligerent stance toward Jet.

"Goddamn time the *Herald* sent someone. I lost me five thousand dollars, a week before harvest, and this guy's saying..." Landwehr reared back his head to glare at Jet. "What horseshit were you saying?"

Jet ignored him and shook Alice's hand. "From the air, the state copter reported that the word 'Repent' had been mowed right across Ben's back four acres, in script — which is a skilled display of tractor driving, you'd got to admit — and no, Ben, I'm not making light of any of this. Got insurance?"

"Crazies." Landwehr jerked his head in the direction of the Fenders' farm. "That girl stirred 'em up. People trampling over my fields, askin' if the Virgin had lighted down on my land too. Halloween coming. They're back. The millennium, all that nonsense. You publish that shit in your paper, don't you?" He tipped his head toward Alice.

Alice stared at the white stubble on Landwehr's chin. Jerks like him had scared Heidi. "We publish the news. You're the news now."

Jet said to Ben, "I'm not ruling out crazies, what with Day One of the new millennium coming in two months, for whatever the hell that means, but I'm thinking your tractor, your getting some flack for not bringing in your corn, I'm thinking this could be personal." Jet lowered his eyes to his hat that he held in front of him, at buckle-level.

"I have got not an enemy in the world," Landwehr said. "My corn has not been giving cover to any coyotes. And if the word 'Repent' means jack to you, let me translate: The Jesus creeps have come out of the woodwork. What about those snake handlers down by the river?" He turned from Jet to Alice, a strand of spit trembling between his upper and lower lips. "If the *Herald* hadn't run that shit about the Fender girl. Woo woo." He wiggled his fingers at his temples. "Jeeeesus H. Christ, you gave every loony that breathes all kind of ideas." He jabbed a finger in Alice's direction. "And, you missy reporter, I hold *you* personally responsible and that asswipe paper of yours."

Adrenaline sizzled on the surface of Alice's skin. He might have terrified Heidi into silence, but he wasn't going to silence Alice.

"Don't you threaten me," she growled, "unless you want me to write that up."

"Wait a minute here, Ben." Jet held up his hand.

Alice stepped around him, to stand within a foot of Landwehr. "Here's my headline: Drunk farmer Ben Landwehr threatens reporter. The lead: Ben Landwehr, drunk good-for-nothing farmer who can't plant a straight row believes that Christians who venerate the Virgin Mary vandalized his crop." Jet moved his bulk between them as she singsonged, "Officials say that the word 'Repent' was clearly visible from the air. Many believe that Ben Landwehr should heed that advice."

Landwehr tried to jostle around Jet's elbows. "You get her out of here. You get the hell off my property, you whoring, lying slut."

Jazzed and frightened, she skipped backward to her car, keeping Landwehr in sight as she roared out of his driveway. She'd shown him. She thumped her fist on the car's ceiling.

When she stopped half a mile away to take pictures of the crop damage, his words, "whore" and "slut," came back to her, and she dropped her forehead to the steering wheel. Was her affair with Wolf common knowledge?

166

A stinging sensation coiled in her jaw. It couldn't be common knowledge. She squeezed the steering wheel. Some friend would have asked her about it, or Fritzie, who was in on all the gossip, would have acted differently. That SOB Landwehr was insulting her the way men like him insulted women, and she'd been a fool to provoke him, and unprofessional. In front of Jet too. Was her high-wire act with Wolf undoing her? She wanted to cry, the urge burning in her chest, but not breaking free.

* * *

The cops didn't catch whoever had vandalized the Landwehr place, or after Halloween, whoever started a fire under the water tower that caused $13,000 in damage. Everything seemed to be falling apart. Maybe the crazies were right.

Alone at night she strained at every sound, expecting a prowler. On the nights when she couldn't quiet her fears, she would go to Wolf, her anxiety receding as she drove through the quiet streets. She didn't love him, he didn't love her, but she needed to be treated with tenderness.

She was fraying. She liked having a secret life, one that would shock Rolly and Patricia, but as the weeks went by, the deception and rule-breaking seemed to degrade everything in her normal life. When Wolf left, she would return to her real life. Slip back into the tent.

12

For the first time since he'd left home, Rolly was lonely. He sketched Alice, not from the photograph he'd brought, but from memory. Shading under her wide cheekbones and tracing the slight asymmetry of her upper lip, he felt close to her, close enough to touch. The next day he mailed her the drawing, hoping that this portrait would thaw her as his words hadn't.

Per invited him to family dinners a couple of times, and Elise, who worked in the metal workshop, took him hunting for mushrooms twice. On weekends he had the entire studio building to himself; the others, having families, seldom came in. When he was lonely, he wrote letters. When he needed to talk about his work, there was Per and Wolf.

From: rdbecotte@hotmail.com
To: Wlemmen@maildrop.wcindiana.edu
Sent: Oct. 10, 10:27 p.m.
Subject: greetings

Wolf,

You're halfway through the semester and wading through committee work. Just thinking about being trapped with Herman and Chloe makes me even more grateful to be here.

You'll leave Wesley College soon, right? Two months? Herman throwing you a party?

Work is good here. I got the new woods I ordered, and I've been thinking about the Oseberg ship. Did I mention that a female skeleton was discovered on the foredeck? Possibly a queen, Queen Asa, of the sagas. Along with the body was a wagon, four sleds, cooking utensils, pots, jewelry. Some ritual stuff, some everyday. I began sketching things that might be buried today—a Walkman, a corkscrew, keys, an Elvis clock—wanting to understand the function of burial objects. What might the dead want or need? That's what I'm thinking about now.

I never told you this. Last winter I had a brief affair with Meg Saffold (red hair, the dean's office). Really brief, a few weeks in February. Alice knows nothing about it. After it ended with Meg, I thought I was going to suffocate. Even that is over now. Here in Bergen I'm not even anchored by what I miss.

Why am I telling you this now, six months after it ended? Maybe it's because I don't talk to anyone here. Maybe it's because I'm concerned about Alice—you can connect the dots: deception, betrayal, restitution—and her letters don't tell me anything. Could you look her up and see how she's doing? Don't let her know I asked.

***

Two days later a letter from Alice waited for him in the mailroom. Had Wolf ratted on him? Panicking, he shoved the envelope in his bag. There was no way Wolf could have talked to Alice and for this letter to travel across the ocean and get here so quickly. He hurried to the university lounge to find a private spot in the hubbub of indifferent students jabbering in a language he couldn't understand and pulled out Alice's letter. The postmark read: Haslett, IN, October 7, which was four days before he'd written Wolf. Exhaling, Rolly slit open the envelope.

It's been really hot here, way too hot for October, more like August, but I'm keeping to my regular schedule at the gym, and Bettina comes with me most Saturdays. I've lost five pounds.

Another of her shitty, impersonal letters. He leaned against the hard plastic chair and skimmed the rest. The water heater guy had come out and said they needed a new one. What did Rolly think? The bike she hadn't ridden in years, she decided to take in for repairs. Rolly looked up from her familiar handwriting. She didn't even like cycling. Was this part of her staying in shape or a sign that she, too, was looking for ways to fill her days? She didn't say. And she didn't mention her portrait. She didn't write that she was making travel plans for her visit. She closed by saying she missed him.

It didn't sound like it. He stared at her signature, her check-writing signature, not her sailboat A. From his bag, he pulled out a sketchpad and tore off a sheet.

October 13

Dear Alice,

My being here, you in Haslett, this seems to fuel our troubles. Come now. Don't wait for Christmas. A long weekend. I've checked the airfares; we can afford it. Or should I come home for a few days? Don't wait a week to write back. Don't pull away, Alice, and don't push me away.

I love you,
Rolly

***

Ten days later he hadn't heard back. The cottage had no phone, which for the first time annoyed him. He stayed late at the studio to call her at 6 p.m. Haslett time.

"Finally, Alice in person. This is Rolly." He sat on a stool, fixing his gaze on the coffee pot that Elise had said she'd empty, but hadn't.

"Oh, hi." She sounded on guard. Under her voice, he could hear something, like another, faint conversation.

"Did I wake you?"

"No. I just got your letter yesterday."

"Yesterday? Really? I'm calling to make plans."

She said nothing. Under the heavy silence, which should be filled with her enthusiastic response, he caught indecipherable wisps of distant talk.

"What the hell is going on with you, Alice?"

"Nothing's going on. You're right: It's not that I don't have the time to write, but that I have a thousand things crowding in and confusing me. And I don't have anything to say."

"What things?" He stood, wary, and carried the blackened coffee pot to the nearby sink, listening to the other, muddled conversation.

She sighed. "I can't explain, Rolly. It's too hard."

"What's hard is that we're apart. Come to Bergen, Alice. How can we fix what's wrong if we're not in the same room?" He put down the coffee pot and pressed his fingers into the corners of his eyes, trying to quiet his distress, hoping she wouldn't hear desperation. "Do you want me to come to Haslett?"

"No," she answered quickly. "I'll come there."

"When?"

"Christmas, like we said."

"Come on. That's more than six weeks. I don't want to wait that long."

"Maybe before Christmas. Maybe in early December. I'll ask Barry. But you have to promise not to write unless I write you. That was the deal, but now you're writing twice a week. God, Rolly, your letters make me feel guilty."

"That's great."

"I'm sorry… Promise me?"

"Promise. Good-bye."

After she hung up, he listened to the ghost conversation until it broke off. Had it been another conversation, or was it only he and Alice echoing in the vast space between them? He turned off the lights in the studio and began the four-mile walk to the cottage. Something had changed between them, but he didn't know what. The next day he sent her a postcard.

THIS IS A GUILT-FREE POSTCARD.

Whenever you come, I'll meet you in Oslo and show you some of what's on the "Things Alice will like" list. Then we'll drive here. Get at least two weeks, if you can. I won't ask again about when you're coming. You'll tell me.

* * *

He settled into a steady, but less-driven rhythm in the studio. He worked on his new shallow-hulled boats in a kind of trace that drove out thought. What passed through his mind where thoughts might be were more like grunts: this, not that, no, yes. His concentration was exceptional. He didn't hear Per come or go. He didn't hear Elise or Eric stop by to ask if he wanted to go for lunch. They understood. Per would leave an apple or a slice of his wife's cake on Rolly's workstation. Sometimes, he and Per would take a break at the same time and go for a beer together. Afterward, Per would go home and Rolly would return to the studio.

As promised, Alice wrote once a week, chatty letters that avoided

172

the only thing that mattered to him, which was how she felt about him. Instead, she gave him an account of her daily life. Patricia was still involved with Warren. They'd come over for Sunday dinner, and Alice had served roasted chicken, second-crop of peas from Fritzie's garden, and Silver Queen corn from Behm's farm stand. Her description of the meal filled a page. No wonder Barry assigned her so many food stories. Another letter covered the visit of her college friend Judith and an argument with the farmer she'd gotten into while covering crop vandalism on his farm. Luckily, Jet Bower was there to intervene. Nothing bad came of it, but she'd lost her professional cool and regretted it. This admission seemed significant — she'd expressed regret about nothing for as long as he could remember — but then she shifted back into her "What's Happening in Haslett" voice. The revivalist tents along the Wabansee River had folded up for the season. Barry had to hire a new delivery guy since the old guy, Dave, was retiring to Florida.

Disheartened, he wrote back in the same impersonal way, unsure if this was childish tit for tat or whether it was best to let her set the tone. He wrote about his daily routine, how he woke in darkness, filled the wood stove, made breakfast of toast, coffee, and herring. He told her about running the tap water until the rust cleared, about simplifying his chores, flipping back his duvet on the bed as soon as he got up, and how he put his washed plate and silver on the table after breakfast, ready for his evening meal. He thought but didn't write that these were bachelor skills.

He was resigned to being in a kind of stasis with her until her visit. Sometimes at night, when he was exhausted, he wrote imaginary letters, calling her a "bitch," a "tease," a "ballbuster."

In the studio he never thought about her. He was producing the best work of his life. He'd started six new boats, each twenty feet long, loosely abstracted on the shallow-hulled Oseberg ship. These six, in varying stages of completion, would be triumphal vessels returning from either a successful war or exploration. He would decide later. They bore scars of hardship and trial. They might carry booty or the dead.

He got a call from Helsinki, a curator whom Per knew, who wanted to see Rolly's work. Rolly thanked Per for recommending him. On a sleety Monday, Anders Toivanen arrived at the studio, a squat man in his sixties, with an impassive face that looked vaguely Eskimo. He spoke English with a British accent but said little as he studied Rolly's boats and leafed through his sketches. He refused the offer of coffee and left within an hour. The next day he called to offer Rolly a show and asked what other work he had in America. Could Rolly send slides or jpegs?

Elated, Rolly broke his promise to Alice and emailed her, giving the details of the exhibition. At the end, he added:

I've said before that I missed you, but after almost four months, I've discovered what missing really is. It's a physical tipping toward you, but you're not here.

***

He didn't hear from her. Was there not even a ghost of the old Alice left? It was the middle of November, and she was due to arrive in Oslo on either December 15 or 16, a detail she hadn't firmed up. He phoned and left messages on her machine. He thought about, and rejected, contacting Patricia. What the hell is going on with your daughter was a question too humiliating to ask your mother-in-law.

When two more days went by with nothing from Alice, he emailed her.

I give up. What's going on with you? The answering machine still says, "I'll get back to you right away." Not to me, you haven't. Nothing. Nada. Zippo. You're supposed to be here in less than a month, but you haven't said when. Why the hell are you playing games?

174

13

From: a_becotte@HHWeekly.org
To: rdbecotte@hotmail.com
Sent: November 19, 5:34 p.m.
Subject: mea culpa

Dear Rolly,

I'm sorry for creating confusion. I had written to you about your exhibition good news, but that letter, addressed and stamped, got mislaid under a pile on my desk. It's on its way now—mailed as originally sealed—and you'll get a second envelope with my detailed flight info (SAS, Dec. 17, arrive 11:30 a.m.). Your phone messages, "Hey, what's going on? I miss you," didn't alert me to the communication breakdown.

I think I miss you too. Married life is steadying, I realize. In these past months, I've made a million mistakes, like my misplaced letter. Like putting my checkbook with the utility bills in the freezer. Like forgetting appointments. Like hitting "discard" instead of "send." Like getting into it with that farmer I was supposed to interview. It's as if too much of my brain is somewhere else, probably trying to figure out what I want. Will being with you in picture-postcard land at Christmastime make things clear? Sounds like a set-up, but I will be glad to see you.

She wasn't lying. She did miss him. And she saw little of Wolf. He was wrapping up this semester at Wesley and completing the last paintings to send his New York dealer before he left for Germany, which would be three days before she was flying to Oslo. They didn't speak of this being the end. He invited her to visit him in Bremen. "I can't see how I can," she said, hoping his offer wasn't sincere. She was glad a natural conclusion was coming so she, a coward, a chickenshit coward and a betrayer, wouldn't have to break off what she never should have begun. That she had embarked on a purely sexual relationship seemed more like arrested development than an assertion of rightful freedom. That he was a close friend of Rolly's exposed an unexpected vengeful streak in her character that shamed her. That she'd started something with an artist — another artist? — was bonehead stupid. In every way possible, she should have known better.

The sex between them was good, but she wanted him gone.

***

With Thanksgiving approaching and advertisements swelling the pages of the *Herald*, Alice was kept busy producing more copy. In addition to her regular What's Happening in Haslett column, she wrote a multi-week feature on Thanksgiving traditions, without repeating any anecdotes from previous years — this was a triumph — interviewed an old-timer with stories about wild turkey shoots during the Depression, and profiled Bella Duchene whose carved and painted duck decoys sold for several hundred dollars at the antiques mall.

She had barely any time alone. Friends, overly concerned about her being alone, invited her over for dinner too often, Bettina and Paul at least once a week. When the Baileys, whose garage faced Rolly's studio, phoned to invite her for a chili dinner on Sunday after Thanksgiving, she wondered if she was giving off pathetic signals and said she'd loved to come, vowing this would be the last. But she was curious about the inside of their house, which she'd never seen. As she jotted down the time on the kitchen calendar, she noticed the absence of her little five-pointed star on November's grid. This star she drew on the calendar to keep track of her menstrual cycle. She flipped back to October. There was her star on the second to last Thursday. She counted forward ten days. Today she was ten days late. Fluttering in her chest made it hard to breathe. Was this her normal irregular or another sign of the stress that had made her mistake prone? Or she could be pregnant? Without recalling any of the steps that got her to the not-clean restroom in the drugstore on the outskirts of town, tearing open a home pregnancy test kit, she read the instructions. Accurate only when administered first thing in the morning.

✳✳✳

The next morning, in her own bathroom, she stared at the green lines. She *was* pregnant. How was this possible?

Stunned and elated, thinking about Wolf's condoms and the few times they hadn't bothered, she pushed open the bathroom window to steady herself with the pre-dawn cold. How could this have happened inadvertently after so many years of effort with Rolly? Only the careless had unplanned pregnancies. She and Wolf had been careful, mostly careful. She hadn't thought, not once, that she could become pregnant. Not using condoms. Not with Wolf. Wolf was not part of her real life. But those green lines meant that, against the odds, she was pregnant. The last time the lines lined up was last January, less than a year ago, eleven months ago. Only eleven? It seemed much longer ago than that, in a different life. She leaned against the sink and picked up the test wand. She might be pregnant or she might be in the inaccurate two percent. She touched the little plastic window above the indicator lines. Or she might be pregnant and lose this one too. She put the wand back in the packaging, tossed it in the wastebasket, and splashed water on her face.

The sun hadn't risen yet. At three o'clock she was due at Patricia's for Thanksgiving dinner, but right now she had to get away from this room and this house. She dressed quickly and hurried through the dark backyard to her car. Overnight a dusting of snow had collected under the shrubs. The season was changing. Everything was changing.

When she reached the edge of town, the sun broke through the clouds to the east. She stuck to two-lane roads, mostly heading north, but without a destination. In some of the farmhouses she passed, lighted windows presented miniature scenes: a old woman in a robe standing with a mug, an empty dining room, a blue glow behind a curtain. The lives sheltered in these homes were mysteries to her. Her own life was a mystery to her. She tried to think about what might come next or what she should do, but her mind skittered away, so she focused on the road and her speedometer, which she kept at sixty. There was nothing she wanted more than a baby. Crossing the bridge into Illinois, she wondered if she was trying to outrun disaster.

Having a child with Wolf was unimaginable. He was a remote loner. He was German. They didn't know the same pop songs, didn't get the same references, didn't despise the same politicians, laugh at the same jokes, or think at all alike. In the two years he'd lived in Haslett, he'd avoided close connections. The only friends he'd made were she and Rolly and a couple of retired German guys he hung out with at Brecht's Tap. What she valued most were close connections. Wolf did not want a family and he disliked children. Beyond all else, she didn't love him. She wasn't even sure she liked him.

178

Two hours later, at Ecklenberg, Illinois, population 1754, she filled her gas tank at a truck stop.

"I'm going to have a baby," she told the wrinkle-eyed woman behind the cash register.

"Congratulations." The woman jiggled the tub of cigarette lighters. "Will there be anything else?"

***

A little after three, she arrived at Patricia's with a couple of pies she'd bought at the supermarket and transferred into her own pie pans, hoping to fool Patricia. Warren opened the door, grinning, wearing a cranberry sport coat that made him look like a timeshare salesman. He took the pies, saying that he had strict instructions not to let anyone into the kitchen.

"I'll be out as soon as I've finished basting," Patricia called, and Warren ushered Alice into the living room where a dozen of Patricia's friends had gathered around the TV. Everyone said hi and the white-haired couple from down the hall, whose name Alice had forgotten, said the party could begin now that she was here. Arlene, Warren's sister, stood up and gave Alice a quick hug. Arlene's sullen teenage son, intent on the half-time show on the TV, ignored Alice's entrance, and Patricia's upstairs neighbor Esther waved for Alice to join her on the couch.

"Isn't it bitter cold outside?" Esther said.

Alice agreed and everyone went back to arguing football strategy. No one noticed that she was electrified.

Esther passed her a bowl of cashews, "I brought these," and Warren offered her a glass of champagne or wine, and she asked for ginger ale, wishing everyone would disappear. She needed to talk to her mother, but she'd have to wait until the dinner was served, eaten, and everyone left, which would be hours from now. With her drink in hand, she couldn't follow the conversation or the action on the TV. At half-time, fireworks exploded and the band played "The Age of Aquarius." Patricia's white-haired neighbors said they never thought they'd live so long as to see the dawning of the new millennium, and Arlene's son gave them a flat-eyed sneer.

Alice should have realized that she'd be stuck like this. She should have arrived just in time to serve the pies. She could have claimed there'd been an emergency story to cover, but one of Patricia's guests might have called Harry at the radio station to check. She could have not come at all, phoned to say she had car trouble, but Patricia would have sent Warren out to help. Esther leaned close and said something. Alice smiled and nodded. On the TV the game resumed. She tried to pay attention, but all she could think about was what might be happening inside her body.

Patricia called for Warren and Alice stood up. He patted the air. "You've been working too hard, your mother says. You're to stay where you are and take it easy."

* * *

After Patricia's friends left with most of the leftovers and the dishes had been washed and put away, Warren drove Arlene and her son home, leaving Alice at last alone with her mother. She dried her hands, nervous about how to begin.

"I need a cigarette," Patricia said. "Step outside with me?" Patricia, forever trying to quit, didn't allow herself to smoke inside.

The air was sharp, the sky blue-black. Standing on the narrow back porch, Patricia lit a cigarette. "Something's up. So tell me."

Looking at the house across the alley, Alice leaned against the railing. "I might be pregnant."

Patricia took a drag on her cigarette, then exhaled. "That means what exactly?"

"That I took the test this morning and it said I was pregnant." She felt as if she might throw up.

"So 'might…'"

"Means I probably am. Unless I'm a statistical anomaly. Which I could be."

Patricia clutched her glass ashtray, refusing to look at Alice. The silence expanded. Alice searched for something to say to interrupt the spreading cloud of trouble.

The mother stubbed out her cigarette. "Whose child is it?"

"That's beside the point. I'm going to have a baby, that's what I care about."

"I think whose it is *is* exactly the point. Because it sure isn't your husband's, right? God, what a mess. Did you do this out of spite?"

"Of course not."

"Don't they pass out condoms in high school these days? How the hell did this happen?"

"Condoms fail," Alice answered, furious that Patricia wasn't focusing on what was important, furious that she wouldn't even look at her.

"Is that all you've got to say about this, 'condoms fail'?"

"I don't have to explain myself, Patricia. But I hoped you'd be happy for me, knowing what this means to me."

"Happy? My daughter does her best to destroy her marriage, and I'm supposed to be happy? Alice, did you really think I'd be pleased with this in any way?"

"See it from…"

"Does he want to marry you?"

Marry Wolf? Alice wished she didn't have to see him again. This evening he was at Herman and Irenia's combination Thanksgiving dinner and farewell party for him. He would leave in two and a half weeks.

"No."

"Oh my god, is he married too?"

"Patricia, please, no, he's not married. You're making this worse."

"Worse?" Under the porch light, her face looked pebbly and gray. "What are you and he planning to do?"

"I don't know yet."

"And what about Rolly?"

She didn't know. She said nothing.

Patricia patted her pocket to locate her cigarettes, pulled out the pack, then slipped it back. Crossing her arms, she turned to look directly at Alice.

"Well then Miss I-Don't-Know, you better start to know. Let me give you a piece of advice. Go to Norway as soon as you can, and don't ever tell Rolly the baby isn't his."

There was a shuffling sound behind them from the kitchen. Alice stiffened and Patricia turned. Warren was back. He smiled at them through the diamond-shaped window, then opened the door.

"Hi, ladies. Taking a little breather after all that cleaning?" He looked from Patricia to Alice, bafflement spreading across his broad, stupid face.

"I'm leaving," Alice said, trembling. She snagged her dress on the doorknob as she brushed past him. A small ripping sound chased her into the kitchen.

"I didn't mean to interrupt," Alice heard him say, and her mother say, "Let her go."

Coat in hand, Alice reached the front door, when Patricia called out, "You think about what I said. That is the only way."

Alice carefully closed Patricia's front door to dissipate the melodrama of her stalking out, but in the parking lot, she slammed over the speed bump and screamed. It wasn't fair. Through the dark and empty streets, she sped, glad the cop usually parked at Miner and Elm wasn't on duty. At the corner where she usually turned, she changed her mind and headed towards Wolf's. She parked in front of the fortress-like house where the lighted windows on the first floor suggested that Wolf's landlady had guests. From the front Wolf's windows weren't visible. Unless Alice got out of the car and walked around to the back, she wouldn't be able to see whether he was back from Herman and Irenia's. She imagined telling him she was pregnant, seeing a look of horror spreading by degrees over his face, seeing his tea-colored eyes going flat. Would he deny he was the father? No, he wouldn't retreat that far, but he would hate her.

She put the car in gear and yanked away from the curb. Out of nowhere a car behind her honked; she jammed on the brake as the car she hadn't seen swerved around her, its horn blaring. When her heart quit knocking, she restarted the engine and drove away, not caring where she ended up.

At the edge of town, she began to speed until her headlights caught an iridescent sign with a black arrow, the turnoff to the Fenders' farm, and she realized that this was why she'd come this way. She wanted to go to the place where the Virgin had appeared.

At the edge of the Fenders' farm, she saw the sign Heidi's father had posted last winter: "Visit the Holy Site," with blue arrows pointing into the black field. Switching to her parking lights—she didn't want to alert anyone at the Fender house on the horizon—she bounced her car along the road's shoulder rutted by the curious before interest died down. She turned off the engine and waited for her eyes to adjust to the dark and her jangling nerves to quiet. Lightheaded and almost nauseous, she stepped from the car, shut the door quietly, and walked on shaky legs into the field. The almost full moon lit the ground well enough for her to walk easily.

Ahead appeared the shabby enclosure Fender had built to prevent anyone from getting a free glimpse. As she got closer, she began to mutter words from movies she'd seen, "Mother of God, come to me, protect me, help me, tell me what I must do."

Two ordinary Madonna statues from the garden store flanked the entry to the enclosure. Inside was much darker than outside, even though it was open to the sky. Alice felt as if water were rising around her. She fought to steady her breath. She could just make out, ten feet on, the cluster of the trees where Heidi had seen the Virgin. Their branches disappeared into the slate-black sky.

"Mother of God, help me, tell me what to do," she whispered or thought as her eyes adjusted to the new level of darkness inside. Something large and square was at the base of the trees. She walked forward. An altar. Roger Fender had built an altar. He was a real Hoosier huckster, a regular Barnum, as Barry said.

She touched the altar's top, which, even in the cold, had a sticky, furry texture, and her fingers found a strip of curling paper, probably a newspaper clipping, thumbtacked to its surface, some coins, and a limp ribbon. She picked up the coins, two of them, larger than quarters, cold and wet. These she nestled in the palm of her hand. Then she prayed out loud for her baby to survive, to emerge whole and pure, radiant with life, her words echoing around the enclosure and vaulting into the dark sky, as something like pain, but not pain, shot through her and words she couldn't understand, not her words, rained down. Warmth enveloped her. The Virgin was present, Alice knew, and this baby would live. Certainty surged through her, driving out fear. Deep within, she felt the baby's infinitesimal cells multiplying.

Filled with happiness, she dropped the coins onto the altar. "It's my baby, mine alone," she said, in answer to Patricia's question. This child would be hers alone. She would not tell Wolf. She would never tell anyone who was the father.

***

"Patricia, it's me. I'm sorry I shocked you." Alice's bedside clock read eight twenty-eight. She'd overslept, her first good night's sleep in months.

"Shocked isn't the word," Patricia said.

"Use any word you want. For now, I don't want any advice. I'll figure this out alone."

"Are you going to Rolly?"

"I have the tickets."

"That's no answer."

"That's my answer this morning. I don't know if I'm going."

"Oh, please, Alice."

"You want me to trick Rolly into fatherhood? Fatherhood isn't what he wants. You want me to deceive—"

"You're already done that."

"You're right. There's nothing else I want to say to you about this right now, and there's nothing I want to hear from you. So, for a while, let's not talk."

"Won't you at least—"

"No. Whatever you're going to say, no. I'll call you when I'm ready."

***

After Thanksgiving weekend, Alice worked extra hours to cover for Fritzie, who was babysitting for her grandnephew, and she didn't return Patricia's calls, at home or the paper. Wolf phoned in the middle of the week, but she didn't pick up, afraid he might sense a change in her. She decided to put off making an appointment with Dr. Petrillo until after Christmas, being in no hurry to enter the medical arena that had failed her before. If Dr. Petrillo mentioned Rolly, and he was bound to, she didn't know what she would say. She watched the TV in the evenings, kept busy at the paper, and refused all the holiday invitations by saying they would interfere with her travel plans to see Rolly. Outside of work, she saw no one. Holding her new state, her happiness, close and private felt essential. She regretted that she'd told Patricia.

Wolf called again, twice more. If she avoided him much longer, he might become concerned, and she didn't want that. He might come to the house. To prevent that and to forestall his becoming curious about why she acted differently, she called him late four days before his departure date and offered to help pack. He seemed relieved.

She used work as her excuse.

"The paper, it's been crazy," she said, walking into his kitchen that was cluttered with boxes, bubble wrap, sloppy stacks of newspaper. He closed the door behind her and took her in his arms, his eyes narrowed.

"I thought you might be angry with me, now that the end is almost here."

"Just swamped." She kissed him lightly, then more deeply, feeling his reserve soften. "Now I'm here to pack. Afterward, we can relax."

"First, I must give you something." He walked into his bedroom and returned with two large canvases. "For you, a gift."

A gift like Rolly's compass? Dismayed, she watched him prop one painting against the refrigerator, the other against the stove. Painted entirely in battleship gray, with tiny strokes that changed directions, it was hard to tell if they depicted geometric shapes, maybe bowls, bottles, or abstracted fruit. Only by looking very intently could she see anything other than boring gray.

"Wolf, they're amazing." That he devoted his time to painting pictures like these showed how detached he was from adult reality. "But I can't take them."

"Rolly, he will not mind." He moved the paintings off to the side, a thought making him pause. "If you like, I will write and tell him that they are for both of you."

She shook her head. "If you want to give them to Rolly, leave them in your office."

"But they are for you." He drew her close and touched his forehead to hers. "I see the problem. I will leave them for Rolly, but you must remember that they are yours."

She mumbled her thanks.

He kissed the top of her head and put the paintings away in a closet, saying he'd take them to the college, then handed her a roll of packing tape and pointed to a pile of flat, ready-for-construction cardboard boxes.

"Those shelves, they must be packed, and bubble wrap is here." He lifted a shopping bag from behind the couch. "I will finish in the bedroom."

Listening to him open drawers in the next room, she studied his shelves that she'd seen often and never really looked at: hardcover books with German titles, heaps of art magazines, a boom box, CDs — there was the Fantcha disk she'd given him the night he'd prepared an elaborate Senegalese dinner—and some white paper models of multi-point stars, tetrahedrons, interconnected cubes, none of which would survive shipping. Surely he didn't want them packed.

How little he owned. The weightlessness of his life saddened her. Once he was gone, his landlady would rent this meager apartment with the worn-out furniture to another transient loner, and there'd be no sign of Wolf in these rooms, or at the college, no sign that he'd ever been here, except for those dull gray paintings he might leave behind.

Or he might change his mind, since she wouldn't take them. Someday he would probably learn about her having a baby — "Yes, I know Alice Becotte," he might say — but she doubted he would think it had anything to do with him. If he bothered to consider the baby's, or the child's, age, he might wonder, then put away the thought, feeling lucky not to have gotten involved in a mess.

She picked up a handful of CDs and mentally measured the smallest packing box. As soon as he left, she would figure out how to tell Rolly, but she couldn't concentrate on her future until Wolf had left.

＊＊＊

Wolf decided to take a bus to New York so he could see the American landscape. Alice offered to drive him to the bus stop at the Stop-N-Go minimart on the edge of town. It was still dark when she picked him up. He swung his knapsack into the trunk — he'd already shipped his boxes — and slid into the passenger seat, reaching over to kiss her.

"I wish you would come with me."

"I wish I could," she lied, guessing that he was lying too.

After Wolf bought his ticket, they waited under the high metal canopy that covered the gas pumps, holding cups of burnt coffee, their breath fogging the air.

"Regrets?" Wolf said. She shook her head. He went on, "It is hard to know until the end, if something was the right thing or the wrong thing. For me, you have been everything I could want. For you, I don't know if this has been right."

She looked down at the coffee she held, at the reflections of the overhead fluorescents. The baby was now about six weeks old, not as big as her thumb, but she could feel it, as she hadn't the first time.

"Don't worry, Wolf." She looked up at him and smiled. In the air between them, she mimed opening a tent zipper. "Outside of our real lives, remember? Private. Just between you and me."

Wolf stroked her hair with his gloved hand. "Ah, Alice, you are so good." He lifted his gaze in the direction the bus would come from, then turned back to her. "Rolly, I have wronged. I will not see him again. He's written, asking me to visit, but I can't."

She hid her relief by nodding solemnly. They finished their coffee, and he carried the empty cups to the trash, returned, and draped his arm over her shoulder. She wished the bus would arrive. Together, they stared down the road to the west. Just as the sky was lightening, a silver coach appeared. The door sighed open and the bus driver stepped down, massaging his kidneys as he limped into the mini-mart.

Wolf took her face in his hands. "I will always remember you like this."

"With a red nose?"

"You are lovely."

"And I'll remember your tweaky eyebrows," she said.

Wolf leaned down and brushed his lips against hers. "Good-bye, Alice."

She tucked the end of his scarf into his jacket. "I'm going to miss you."

The driver came out. Wolf picked up his knapsack and climbed onto the bus behind him. Moments later, toward the back of the bus, a hand wiped a clear circle in a fogged window, and Wolf's face appeared, ghostly, already half gone. She waved, surprised by how small and abandoned she felt. When the bus pulled away, belching exhaust fumes, she remained on the center island, watching its red taillights recede until it disappeared around the bend.

14

Rolly cleaned the cottage in preparation for Alice's arrival. He stashed his sketchpads and art magazines under the bed, refreshed the stack of logs outside the back door, then sat at the kitchen table under the window with a second pot of coffee, watching the snow-mist that obscured the woods. Eager as he was, he was also filled with trepidation.

In the night he'd awakened with an insight, possibly he'd dreamed of her, but he understood that a baby was for her what his work was for him. Equating the importance of his work to a human life was something he could never say to her. It would confirm her worst ideas about him, that he was a narcissist, self-indulgent, and selfish. He recoiled remembering what she'd said about his work. He would never admit to her, or to anyone, that he couldn't see how a baby could ever be as absorbing or as interesting as his work. He stared at a pine bough half-hidden in the mist. Maybe what they both wanted was to live beyond their own confining limits.

He wished he'd figured this out last spring. These next few weeks wouldn't return them to the state he wanted, she'd said as much in her last letters; but if they approached each other with care, this might lead to where he wanted to go.

He washed the coffee pot and mug, checked his backpack to make sure he had what he needed, and sat at the bench by the back door to pull on his boots. Tomorrow he would leave for Oslo, two days early to call at Toivanen's gallery, and visit a rare wood dealer. This would be his last day in the studio until she left, unless he could persuade her to stay. He wasn't sure he wanted her to. She'd have to return to Haslett, in any case, to close up their house and make some sort of arrangement with Barry.

* * *

At the university the path to the studio building had been swept clear of snow, but it was slick. He unlocked the outer door to the communal space, a techno bass from the stonecutter's studio announcing that he wasn't alone. Either Elise or Eric was already at work, and Per's coat lay on one of the red couches. Rolly hung up his wet parka, set his boots near the radiator, poured a cup of coffee, and logged onto the computer. There was, as he expected, a last-minute email from Alice.

> Dear Rolly,
> Things have changed. Everything has changed. I am pregnant.

The letter vanished and up popped a different email, in Norwegian, a memo from the university. He clicked back to Alice's letter. This had to be a prank.

> Dear Rolly,
> Things have changed. Everything has changed. I am pregnant.
> The baby is due July 1.

A baby? July 1? How could that be? This wasn't real. This wasn't from Alice. He scrolled to the top and saw her email address at the *Herald*. Had someone hacked into her account? He read the letter again. How could a baby come in July when February, ten months ago, was the last time they'd made love?

The air grew cold. Pressure squeezed his chest. The techno beat from the other side of the wall pounded. He tried to breathe. July 1. It wasn't his.

As you can guess, I am very happy. Nothing about this has been intended to hurt you, although I know it must. This baby will be mine alone. There is no "father." I'm not involved with anyone. As I just said, this baby is mine alone. This time I'm convinced I will carry this baby to term, but whether I do or not, our marriage is over.
Alice

He reached for the skein of twine next to the computer — he couldn't think — and twisted a loose strand of twine into a figure eight. He'd bought this to make netting for the stones he would lash to its sides of his lead funeral boat. He planned to attach a length of rope to its prow, the other end to an animal, a life-size ox or a narwhal.

Something fell, a clump of snow from the roof. He stood, shaky. Beneath the throbbing techno coming from the stonecutter's studio, he heard a saw whine.

It would be narwhal, not an ox. It would lay a pool of blood, the rope from the animal's neck to the boat's prow would be taut above the blood or, better, slack, the narwhal dead, the boat stranded.

Warmth spread from the crown of Rolly's head and he felt dizzy. He jerked, hearing a sound. Per behind him.

"I thought I heard you. Are you all right?" Per's thick hand landed on Rolly's shoulder, its weight crushing, and Per began to cough. "Inhaled some dust when I took off my mask. Wait." He hacked, pummeled his chest, then wheezed, "Are you sick?"

Rolly pointed to the computer screen. "Read it."

"What?" Per leaned forward.

"A letter from my wife. Look."

Per straightened. "I don't read such things."

"I want your goddamn opinion." Rolly tipped back in his chair. He was somewhere on the ceiling watching himself drop the twine back on the counter, watching Per turn away, disgusted, watching the draft from the door Per had left open rustle the tracing paper sketches someone had left on the couch.

"Alice is pregnant," Rolly said. "Alice, my wife. I come here, and she gets pregnant."

At the sink Per poured a glass of water. "This is good news." He gulped down the water, then turned to Rolly, his brows pinched. His cheeks trembled slightly as comprehension came over him. He put down the glass and stared at Rolly. "Dear god, I'm sorry…"

Rolly stood, shoved his feet into his boots, grabbed his jacket, and stalked out.

Downtown, he sat in a coffee shop. Midmorning shoppers came and went and were replaced by the lunch crowd. The hubbub was a relief, until two teenage boys in oversize jackets claimed a nearby table, blocking his view of the street, and began to posture and argue using words he couldn't understand. He stood, his legs were shaky, threw too much money on the table, and walked out. The snow-mist came in gusts as he wandered toward the harbor, into a warehouse district, and beyond. As the faint daylight dimmed, he walked into neighborhoods he'd not known existed. Young women with shopping baskets were the only people out. The streetlights came on and he kept walking, his feet numb with cold, until he paused to let two men stumble out of a bar, and he decided to go in. Beer, a sandwich, another beer. He was glad he couldn't understand the conversations around him. When it was late enough to call Haslett, he left to find a phone in a quiet place. In an empty Laundromat, snow pelting the plate glass windows, he dialed Patricia's number.

"Rolly, thank god." The line crackled. "She's ruining her life and she has no idea."

Her anxiety appeased him. "She emailed me today. When did you know?"

"She... I guess almost two weeks ago. It was Thanksgiving, of all things. She won't listen to reason."

"And you didn't tell me?" He pulled a smear of pine resin from his jacket sleeve. From cutting logs for Alice's visit.

"I thought she should tell you first."

"How long's it been going on?"

"In the summer I saw a lot of her. Everything was fine, then fall came and she was always busy. Too much to do, in a hurry, the paper, yada yada. But now I know..." She stopped.

Outside the Laundromat's steamy window, lights funneled through the mist, a city bus pulling up.

"Rolly, you've got to do something. There has to be... I don't know, surely, there's a way out of this mess."

He pressed the phone to his ear as if he might hear something that would change everything, but all he could hear was Patricia's breath.

"What can I do?"

"Come home."

What could he do at home? He missed the next thing she said.

" ...and pick you up."

"I'll arrange something," and promised to call her with his flight information as fresh resentment surged through him. A dealer from

Berlin was coming next Monday. Rolly had planned to introduce Alice. He would have to cancel.

At midnight he dialed Alice again. It was six o'clock in Haslett. She should be home from work. His hand hurt from gripping the phone as he willed her to answer.

"So you got my email."

Her sharpness — no remorse, no shame — unnerved him. He didn't know how to reach the speech he planned in which he would say that he was coming home to talk things over.

"Why the hell did you do this to me?" he spit into the phone.

"I'm hanging up if you rant."

"I'm your goddamn husband, Alice. Have you forgotten that?" He touched his forehead to the cold windowpane. "I'm coming home."

"Your coming home won't change anything. I've thought all this through. I said what I wanted to say in the letter. Stay there. Work. That's what you want."

"Don't tell me what I want. You have no idea what I want." He stopped. The bus pulled away, leaving the street outside in darkness. "You send me an email saying you're having someone else's baby. I think you *owe* me answers, face-to-face."

She didn't answer.

He said, "I've been gone five months. When I write, you don't answer."

"I answered."

"Empty letters. When I call, I get the damn machine. You keep me in the dark. Then, wham, 'I'm having a baby.' Why did you do this to me?"

"This isn't about you, Rolly. This is about me. It has nothing to do with you."

"Say that again," he shouted.

"If that's how you're going to be, I'm hanging up. And if you come, I won't see you."

"I'm coming." He listened to her breathe, then heard a rustle.

"You're right," she said. "Come. We should talk."

∗∗∗

Because of the Christmas holidays, the first flight he could book was five days later. With a delay in New York, his plane was late arriving at Indianapolis. He'd turned down Patricia's offer to pick him up, not wanting to talk to her, or to anyone, before seeing Alice. He rented a car and when he reached Haslett, it was almost 11 p.m., and the streets were empty, except in front of The Pit Stop. He paused to let a small blue sedan pull out and recognized the car: Meg's. His heart lurched. Through the neon sign's reflections on the windshield, he saw a boy's profile, with a hat worn backward. Not Meg. Not her husband. The guy rolled down his window and shouted to a friend, and Rolly remembered Meg beside him on the dusty couch in his studio, her toes resting on his ankles as she lay in his arms. Less than a year ago. No one had been hurt by what they'd done. Not Ken. Not Alice. Only he and Meg had suffered.

He drove on.

Christmas lights decorated the houses on both sides of their block. The Faraccis had installed their demented Santa and sleigh on their roof, as always, and Alice had hung a wreath on their door, but no lights were draped over their shrubs. That was his job. He parked at the curb and looked at their house. Since getting her letter, he'd been propelled forward. Now he wished he hadn't come. He retrieved his bag from the backseat.

Alice stood at their open front door. Light from the kitchen silhouetted her.

"Rolly."

He stepped into the hall and closed the door behind him. Her face seemed fuller, and her cheekbones more pronounced, more Slavic. She'd grown out her extreme short haircut of last summer, so that her hair was the way he had liked it, loose, curling at her neck. She was taller—but she couldn't be—and dressed in jeans and a coppery tunic he hadn't seen before. She was careful not to touch him when she took his coat. He explained about the delay in New York, reluctant to say anything but the superficial before he got his bearings. Her tunic was loose, but from what he could see, her belly seemed flat. A thought came, that this was a ruse designed to hurt him, but then he realized that Alice wouldn't make up a pregnancy. When she reached for his coat, her wedding band caught the light. He was surprised she was still wearing it. For an instant he was relieved, then suspicious and angry.

"It's late. Have you eaten?" she asked as if he were a guest, as if she had done nothing wrong.

"I'm not hungry."

"Would you like something to drink?" she asked, with an infuriating hostess smile, and turned away before he could answer, to adjust one of the candles burning on a tray in front of a small, traveling altar — Mexican? — with a beaming Madonna. This wasn't one of their Christmas decorations. This was a signal meant to say that things had changed.

"I'm tired," he said. "Too tired to be thirsty. Let's talk in the morning."

"If that's what you want."

"For the past six days, I've thought of little else but what you said, but now I just want to go to sleep. OK?"

Her lower lip tensed in irritation. She'd girded herself for battle, that was clear, and now she was disappointed. She said, "I've made up the guest room for you."

With the lights out, still dressed, he lay on the bed that had been his parents. As a boy, he'd traced with his fingers the wheat sheaves carved in the headboard, but he had never slept in this bed. The light beneath the closed door vanished. Alice had switched off the hall sconce. He waited for something to tell him that he was in his own home as he listened to her across the hall in their bedroom, trying not to think of her with her lover, but trying to remember the force that had brought him here, but it was gone. Jet lag? Or had returning to his home — so much of him was in this house — diminished his sense of injury, made it seem, not exactly unimportant, but not as important as if had seemed when he was far away?

The next morning he found Alice standing at the kitchen sink, staring at the Faraccis' yard. Two placemats, Patricia's gift a few years ago, sat on the table with a fat, red, unlit Christmas candle. The scene was both familiar and strange. He walked to the back door and looked out. Beneath a sweatshirt-gray sky, the yard looked forlorn, and his studio abandoned.

"Did you sleep well?" Alice asked.

He turned to glance at the clock above the stove: 11:20. He'd slept for ten hours. "I didn't fall asleep quickly, but once I did, I didn't stir."

"Breakfast?" She set a mug at his accustomed place at the table, nodding for him to sit down. Despite her indifferent expression, she seemed stiff and wary — a sign, he hoped, that her resolve might not be as fixed as when they'd spoken on the phone.

"Just coffee." He moved his chair sideways to avoid the glare from the back window, and she sat down opposite. Her hands on her mug were chapped. She always forgot to wear gloves.

"I don't want to rehash the past," he began. "What I did wrong according to you, what you did wrong according to me, that's finished."

198

He sipped his coffee, scorching his tongue. The sideways light from the window gave her gray, speckled eyes an eerie dimension, making it seem as if she wasn't looking at him, but through him. He went on, "Would you answer some questions for me, clear things up, before we discuss what comes next? OK?" He leaned slightly forward, relieved that she didn't withdraw.

"It depends."

"Well, let's try. Do you love this man?"

Her eyes widened, dismissing the possibility so quickly it unnerved him.

"No, but that's got nothing to do with it. I'm going to raise this baby myself."

"So I take it that you don't plan to divorce me and marry him?"

"I want a divorce, but I don't plan to marry anyone else. As I said, this baby will be mine alone."

The word divorce tore through him. The phone rang.

"It's on the machine. Patricia, probably."

Four rings. They listened.

When he heard the click, he said, "I will never ask you who the father is, but I want to know why you did this?"

"Do I owe you an answer?" She looked away, shaking her head. "I don't know. Curiosity? Anger at you? Old-fashioned lust?"

"Was it to have a baby? Because if it was, I understand. While I've been gone, I've come to realize something that had never gotten through to me, about your wanting a baby. I thought that having a baby was the next thing to do. First you get married, then you have kids."

Her lip curled. He was losing her. He'd reduced her to a cliché. Trying to recoup, he hurried on. "But I see now that a baby is how you want to extend your life."

She kept her eyes on the window above the sink. "That's your way of looking at things. Not mine. I want to love a baby, that's all. You make it sound so egotistical."

"I don't mean…"

"Getting pregnant was a gift. Unexpected. Unplanned."

A gift? The bomb ripping apart their marriage was a gift from some gift-giving fucker? "I understand how much you want a child."

"Brilliant."

"I want to have a child too. I want to stay married to you."

"Are you saying you want to be a father to this child?"

"I'm saying I want a baby with you."

"I'm talking about this baby."

"Are you sure you're pregnant?"

"What do you mean?"

"Mistakes can be made, especially in the first months."

"There's no mistake."

He leaned close. She was looking at him now, puzzled. She thought he didn't get it, was refusing to understand. He reached for her hand.

"If you have this baby, if you're pregnant, it will stare at you with the face of some guy you say you don't love, some guy you say you don't want to marry. But you do want to stare at his face for the rest of your life? I know you, Alice. That's not you. Let's start again, have our own baby, yours and mine."

"Stop." She wrenched her wrist from his grasp.

"Alice, I'm not asking you to do this for the hell of it. This is the hardest thing…after what you've, we've, been through. But I'm asking you to have a family with me."

"I intend to have a family."

Her jaw was set. She would trample him but she would flourish. She was that strong. Night feedings, sickness, squalling in the supermarket, she wouldn't need him. He admired her and he hated her.

"What about us?" he said.

"There is no *us* anymore."

He stared at her across the table barely able to say, "All I am, my very best, is not good enough for you?"

"It's not about *you*. You think you're the center. One minute you're the problem, the next you're the solution."

"Don't you love me at all?"

"You, you, you." Her features pinched together as she spat the words at him. "This baby is mine, do you hear? I'm having it without you, without anyone."

Without. He was nothing to her. He pushed out of his chair. "You're going to have to drag this squalid mess of yours through the public streets of hell to get a divorce from me. You don't care about me or our marriage, but I'm not going to make it easy for you to get out." The room was swaying. He saw his shadow stumble on the floor as he lunged for the back door. Down the steps, into the yard. The keys to the rental car were upstairs—he wasn't going back inside—so he kept running past his old studio, into the alley, and toward downtown. In front of Weiland's, he called Patricia from the pay phone and asked her to pick him up. She said she'd see him in ten minutes. Shivering without his coat, he waited on the sidewalk, his thoughts racing and incoherent. When Patricia tapped his arm, he didn't recognize her.

"Where's your car?" he asked.

"Later." She led him to Holloway's, where the hot, perfumed air assaulted him.

"You look frozen," she said, touching his cheek with one hand while loosening her scarf with the other. "You need something hot to drink."

At the back of the store, behind the makeup displays and twirling card racks, the lunch counter was empty except for an off-duty waitress smoking over a cup of coffee, talking to her on-duty friend. Patricia slid into one of the wooden booths that had survived remodeling, and he sat down opposite and let her order coffee for both of them.

When the waitress left, he said, "Get out, that's what she said. Our marriage is over."

Patricia clasped her throat, a stagy gesture, but one, he recognized, as genuine distress.

"You can't," she said. "There's got to be a way. You've got to make her see reason."

He told her about what he'd said, what Alice had said, and about what he'd suggested. Patricia looked appalled but what else could he have done? He couldn't raise someone else's kid. He told her about Alice insisting on a divorce. Patricia's blue eyes reddened and her chin trembled.

Unable to face her anguish, he shifted and looked over the top of the booth at a couple of teenage girls at the lipstick display. The one with hacked-off, cherry-colored hair rouged the cheeks of her blond friend, then spun her toward the mirror. The blonde with rouged cheeks giggled, and a laugh rattled inside him, at these girls' lovely, innocent self-regard. The blonde noticed him and whispered to her friend. They both lifted their eyebrows and glared at him: *Perv.* Embarrassed, he turned to Patricia. The deep lines around her mouth made him sad. He reached for her hand.

"I can't fight her, Patricia. She's too much for me."

"Why?" she asked, the skin above her cheekbones pinched and pale.

He stood and slipped into Patricia's side of the booth and put his arm around her narrow shoulders. "I'm sorry," he muttered. Her bony hip dug into his thigh. She curved into him, her crackling silver hair scratching his neck, and she began to cry.

202

"It's OK, Patricia. It'll be OK."

He heard a rustle to his right, and someone tweaked his hair, one of the girls. A shuffle of feet, a bark of laughter as they rushed by, setting the card carousel spinning. It creaked to a stop. Once, Alice had been like these girls. What had happened? What changed fun-loving girls into hard, remorseless women?

"Drive me home, will you? I'll tell her, I'll give her the divorce."

15

Friday, December 31, 1999, New Year's Eve. Alice peered through her kitchen window at the Faraccis' house. Every window, even the girls' bedroom, blazed with light. This year's New Year's Eve party was an even bigger deal because of the millennium. "Come dressed as who you want to be in the new age," Bettina had said, before backpedaling when Alice made a face. "OK, if a costume is a deal-breaker, don't worry about it." For a second, Alice had thought about wearing a maternity outfit, even though she wasn't telling anyone she was pregnant, not until after the first trimester, not even Bettina. Alice had promised to show up at Bettina's party, knowing she wouldn't. She wasn't ready for questions about where Rolly was and why wasn't she in Norway. She'd told Bettina that she'd postponed her plans until after the new year, and Bettina — wrapped up in Christmas, the girls, her huge deal party — hadn't pressed.

Alice shifted her viewing angle to peer at Rolly's studio. What was going to happen with all his stuff? She and he hadn't begun to talk about any of the details of their divorce. Somehow they'd have to figure things out by email. He'd taken his suitcase and moved to Patricia's for a few days, leaving on Christmas Eve, Patricia had said, to stay with friends in Milwaukee. Who?

Movement at the Faraccis' house. She ducked behind the curtain and watched their kitchen door slide open as a guy in a football uniform, minus the helmet, stepped onto their deck and reached under his shoulder pads for something. A pack of cigarettes.

ON THE EVE OF THE MILLENNIUM
WOMAN HIDES IN DARK KITCHEN

Oh, hell. She turned to the small TV she'd bought to keep her company during her solitary dinners. Fireworks were exploding over London, again, and the crowd roared, again. Quick cut to a woman in sparkly eyeglasses that spelled out 2000, her eyes blinking behind the center zeros.

In less than an hour, the big moment would arrive in Haslett, and she wished she'd figured out how to mark this once-every-thousand-years moment in some meaningful way. She wasn't a nutcase, she wasn't waiting for the End of Days, she didn't expect the fields to rupture or the seas to rise, but the lunacy in town and the Internet chatter and Y2K frenzy said that there was at least the possibility that something could happen, and should something happen, she didn't want to be in her kitchen when people poured out of the Faraccis' waving noisemakers and banging pans and Bettina came pounding on her back door, insisting Alice join the fun. She wanted to be somewhere significant, someplace important to her, and the only place she could think of besides here at home was Roger Fender's tacky shrine in the middle of a frozen field. She abhorred Fender's exploitation of what Heidi had experienced, and she doubted that heavenly beings made themselves present on Earth, but she knew that a mystical force had visited her on Thanksgiving, a force she knew was real.

She grabbed her jacket and purse. Someday her child might ask, "Where were you when the millennium came?" and she would say, "Where the Virgin told me you were coming."

Without turning on the porch light, in case anyone at the Faraccis' was looking, she hurried down her back steps, made her way through her yard, past Rolly's studio, and pushed aside the gate she'd broken on Christmas Day, rushing to that miserable brunch with Patricia and Frog-face Warren. At least the day ended better, with tacos at home and old movies. In her new life as a single woman and a single mom, she would make her own traditions. She could choose. She could choose tacos for Christmas dinner and choose to spend the last moments of 1999 and the first moments of the new millennium alone in a frigid cornfield.

Her car smelled of last week's Thai takeout. As she sped through town and out into the county, sporadic fireworks exploded on the horizon, so far away they looked like birthday cake sparklers. No one was out on the roads. Everyone was watching clocks tick down.

She approached the shrine from the same direction as last time, the night she'd driven from Patricia's, but her headlights didn't pick out Fender's lurid "Visit the Holy Site" sign, or the arrows that had pointed toward the enclosure. Had vandals taken them down? Or that ass Landwehr? Surely not Roger Fender, who was intent on milking every cent he could out of Heidi's visions.

She parked on the side of the road, certain she'd come to the right spot even though she couldn't see Fender's signs, turned off the engine, and hesitated. It was dark—she could barely see anything—and it was cold, too cold for snakes, but there could be coyotes. She could trip and seriously hurt the baby. She might get lost. But the Fenders' yard light in the distance could be her landmark. She was being silly. Nothing had happened last time.

Faint stars dotted the black sky, and the waning moon gave off little light. She dug out a flashlight from the trunk and started off. The beam barely illuminated the uneven ground, but she found her way because of the faint snow outlining the path's edges. The enclosure should be no more than a hundred yards ahead. When she'd walked at least that far, and her eyes had adjusted to the dark, she still couldn't see anything but field. She turned in a circle. The Fenders' barn and house, the smudgy line of trees against the sky, but no high-walled enclosure. Had Fender dismantled his cash cow? In the past month? She swung her flashlight back and forth. Ahead and to the right the path widened into a large tamped-down area that might have been the interior of the enclosure, and beyond stood a clump of trees, which had to be where the Virgin had first appeared to Heidi. But the enclosure was gone, and the altar, too. A shallow, rectangular trough in the center of the smoothed ground was probably where the altar had been. She took a deep breath to get her bearings. She was glad Fender's exploitation had failed, but things changing so quickly unnerved her.

The wind whistled over the broken ground. She inhaled cold air, then followed the flashlight's beam toward the trees, imagining that the rest of the world had fallen away, Haslett, the Faraccis' stupid party, the Rolly mess, Patricia's disapproval, all of it, leaving her alone with the eternal: the sky, the stars, the earth beneath her feet.

She heard a sound and froze. Aiming her flashlight at the trees twenty feet ahead, she caught something red. Another sound, snuffling, and maybe a giggle. Kids. Dangerous? Adrenaline corkscrewed through her arms.

"Who's there?" The wind tore at her words. Her left hand dug in her pocket, found her keys, and slid their pointed tips to jut out between her fingers, as she walked forward, scared.

The red was a sleeping bag that moved. A blond head popped out—Heidi's? No—then a second, matted brown hair. Not Heidi either. Alice backed up a couple of paces and smelled something acrid, not pot, and lifted the flashlight as both kids struggled out of the sleeping bag, brown hair first, a boy with bad chin acne, then the blonde, a girl with frazzled braids and pale skin. Blinded by the light, they turned away, giggling, and tugged up their gray long johns to meet their flannel shirts. This pair was too stoned to hurt her. She pulled out her fist bristling with keys.

"What're you doing here?" she demanded.

Brown hair lifted a tattooed hand to shield his eyes, unable, she guessed, to see her. "No shit. What're *you* doing here?"

From somewhere near the kids came a faint, high-pitched crying. A tricked-out baby doll? A cat? A Halloween CD? She dropped the beam to where the sound came from, near the sleeping bag, and the mewling waffled into a whimper, then soared into keening. The boy said something, then he was running away, with the girl stumbling behind, the sound of their feet lost under the awful wailing that climbed the scale, slipped, and rose again. Panic thundered through her. Why were the kids running? She spun around. How stupid was she not to realize that this spot would be a magnet for crazies? She swung the flashlight in wide sweeps. They, the kids, other crazies could sneak up behind her. She turned in a circle, searching with the flashlight, but she could see nothing but frozen ground and hear only the high-pitched cries, which hiccuped, then began again.

She waited, her pulse pounding, then walked toward the awful sound. A puppy, ululating, strained against a plastic rope tethering it to one of the trees. Next to the sleeping bag were two other puppies, not moving. Dead? She stepped back and the yelping animal leapt at her. She set down the flashlight and grabbed for the dog. The smell she hadn't been able to place was dog shit, soured by terror. Trying not to gag, she wrestled with the surprisingly strong little beast, who did not understand she was doing her damn best to help, and forced her fingers under the noose as it twisted and nipped and growled. With her free hand, she dug out her keys on the chain with a tiny Swiss Army knife. The flashlight's beam skimmed the unmoving chest of the nearest puppy and shot off into the night. This was a nightmare. She was in a freezing, pitch-dark field with an out-of-control animal. She flipped open the knife, cut her finger, sucked it, then sawed through the plastic rope, releasing the noose, and pressed the little beast against her thigh until it quit yowling. She heard no sound from the kids. No car starting or driving away. In the distance the Fenders' yard light was the only sign of life. She wanted to cry. Inside her jacket she was shaking. The puppy trembled, its torso in spasms. She held it close as wind rattled the branches above and stung her face. After a time, the puppy calmed.

She knew nothing about dogs. This one was a girl. It had a body about the size of a submarine sandwich with a longish tail, a classic dog head, its coat the same beigy-brown shade as Fritzie's dye job. The flashlight's beam raked over the other two: probably littermates, definitely dead, maybe tortured. Sickened, she sipped air, shrugged out of her jacket, and wrapped it around the puppy. She would take this one home. Later, she'd figure out what to do. For the dead ones there was nothing she could do. Frozen ground and no tools to dig with. Crows would come, or coyotes. She wasn't coming back.

Shivering, she balanced the bundled-up puppy on her hip and fumbled the flashlight in the direction of her wristwatch: 12:20. It was past midnight. She had missed the big moment, but there'd been no glorious opening of the millennium, just ugly, meaningless, almost routine, cruelty, like the cattle mutilations, like Mrs. Gruenke's dog. Could the brown-haired boy be Mrs. Gruenke's neighbor? Or was the world full of sadistic monsters? Or had these stoned kids come seeking something meaningful, as she had, and found these puppies already abandoned, two dead, and left this one to suffer? No dawning of a new era, no sign from the heavens. Just savagery.

She touched one hand to her belly, praying for her baby, and, clutching the wrapped-up little beast, started across the field, the flashlight all but useless. She lost the path. Afraid to stumble, she went slowly, keeping the Fenders' light behind her until she found her car.

In the trunk she found a cardboard box for the tiny dog and tossed aside Rolly's old gloves, wondering what he would think about her bringing home a puppy. But he wasn't at home and what he thought didn't matter. He could be in Milwaukee, New York, or back in Bergen. She'd always known where he was, even during the last six months when he was thousands of miles away. Not knowing now shouldn't matter but it did. She felt unmoored.

Her headlights cut into the dark, and the puppy in the box on the seat beside her made no sound. It was 12:43. The millennium had arrived and there was no one who cared about what had happened to her tonight.

* * *

The airplane's cabin lights dimmed, leaving only a few reading lights on in the rows ahead, for the other insomniacs. Rolly's personal monitor had gone dark after takeoff from JFK, so he couldn't follow the plane inching over the map, the one pleasure of international flights. They were probably over Greenland or the vast tracks of the Atlantic. The heavyset man beside him had turned his screen off before falling asleep, as had the woman across the aisle. Outside, sooty clouds below and black above, no stars. The view hadn't changed since the plane broke through the cloud cover over New York, and except for the engine's roar, there was no evidence that they were moving. He'd imagined this flight would be, exactly that, a flight from Alice and all that had become claustrophobic in his overprogrammed life, and a flight into a new chapter in which he'd set his own rules, not a temporary break, not just his half-over sabbatical, but a new arc. But staring at the blank screen of his personal monitor, unable to watch his little yellow airplane struggle its way heroically over the sublimely indifferent ocean left him uneasy and despondent.

In the last announcement before lights out, the stewardess had joked that passengers on this plane had entered a glitch in the space-time continuum since they'd taken off from New York before midnight, and midnight had come and gone where they were now, so they'd missed the dawning of the new millennium. Shouts of "So we didn't fall out of the sky?" "Were there any crashes?" "Does that mean I won't get a year older?" "Time stopped, has it?" led to calls for champagne, which the stewardess quieted by telling them they could find the drinks list on the card in the seat pockets. No millennial moment: how disappointed Alice would have been.

He didn't want to think about her. For years he'd let her needs overshadow his own desires. For what? For her to tear apart what they'd made together? His stomach clenched. After too many days of talk with Patricia, and more with Jerome and Mary in Milwaukee, going over the same damn ground, the miscarriage, her grief that distorted everything, blah blah blah, he understood what had happened no better than before. Every explanation seemed beside the point. He was tired of what others had to say, and he was tired of his own thoughts. He twisted against his seat belt and fought his urge to shove the fat guy who'd begun to snore.

The flight attendant glided past, and Rolly stopped her. "Do you have a spare blanket?"

"I'll be right back."

The snoring guy stirred and resettled.

Rolly lowered his window shade. He had to get back to the studio. Work was the one thing that could always bring him back to where he wanted to be. Work drove out worry, work drove out thinking. He'd get an idea — OK, an idea is a thought — but after that first instant, once he began sketching or playing with materials, what would come couldn't be called thinking. Phrases would float into his head, "too long," "too vague," "lumpen," but soon what he was doing was more like grunting. Hmm, mm mm, hmmh, not words, but impulses. Alice was the queen of words, but he didn't trust words. In the studio, that's where he needed to be: working, not thinking. If he thought about her, if he thought about her deception, if he thought about her betrayal, if he thought about how she'd treated him like the fucking bad guy, he would be riven by fury. And that would be the end of work, the one absolutely reliable thing in his life. Before everything with Alice had exploded, his work had been going well, and his career. Had his new-found productivity in Bergen sprung from being away from her? Or from teaching? Either way, the past six months offered a foretaste of what was to come: his work and his career gaining traction. A couple more dealers were coming for studio visits in January, and he had to make slides for Toivanen, the curator Per had sent his way.

"Sir."

He took the blanket from the flight attendant and tucked it over his shoulders, pushing aside the snorer who'd slumped again.

If he never had to return to the U.S., he would be happy. He could stay in Norway, learn the language, and build a new base. Or somewhere else. London. Berlin. The European art scene was entirely different from that in the U.S., and he was already doing pretty well. Jacqueline pretended she was pleased, but she wasn't entirely happy with the opportunities flowing his way without any help from her. She got her percent. If he stayed in Europe, he'd find another rep.

His contract with Wesley said that he had to return to the college for one full academic year after his sabbatical, but would they insist? He'd never known anyone not to return from a sabbatical. If he had to go back to Haslett for a year, where would he live? The house was as much his as Alice's, but he didn't need a high-priced lawyer to tell him that there was no way he would get the house. His studio? All the renovations he'd made turning that leaky garage into a decent studio had been paid for by his sales. Not a dime from Alice. His art paid for the studio. It was his.

He leaned back, elbowed the snorer, then closed his eyes, envisioning a black clot that the waves of sound from the engines broke apart and dissipated. The black clot was Alice. Hollowed out and aching, he wondered what would fill the space that Alice had occupied.

He woke to whispers, a commotion in the row ahead of him. A different flight attendant was blocking the aisle, leaning over the passenger in the seat in front of the snorer, and next to her, looking down, too, stood the curly-haired man in a Manchester United shirt, who'd stepped aside for Rolly during boarding, and whose expression now said something was wrong with the passenger Rolly couldn't see.

"Can you squeeze my finger?" the man in the soccer shirt said.

The stewardess noticing Rolly, bent to whisper, "We might need your help."

"What's going on?"

"The gentleman…we may need help getting him to the bulkhead row, where he can lie down."

Soccer shirt straightened, nodded to the stewardess, and the two of them hoisted the man to his feet. Huge belly, trousers sagging, head wobbling. The stewardess gave Rolly a look, and he stepped over the snorer, feeling a rush of pride and worried that he wasn't up to what might be asked of him. Even in the dim light, he could see sweat gloss the slumping guy's pasty face, and he smelled sour, like vinegar. The stewardess shifted the man's weight onto Rolly — "follow me" — as Soccer shirt — "I'm a doctor" — reached around to grab the man's belt. Rolly wedged his shoulder under the sick man's armpit, hoping he wouldn't make a fool of himself. Next to where the sick man had sat, an Indian in a turban folded his hands over his seat belt and closed his eyes. This was not his problem. Was this sick guy traveling alone? No one nearby seemed to have tuned into this drama.

Rolly and Soccer shirt, with the all-but-inert guy between them, stumbled slowly to where the flight attendant stood at the vacated bulkhead row. She'd spread a blanket on the carpet. Rolly helped stretch out the guy as the woman stepped away. Fighting a spurt of alarm—what if Soccer shirt wasn't really a doctor? What if the stewardess didn't come back?—Rolly removed the guy's shoes, uncertain if this was the right thing to do while Soccer shirt probed the man's neck. Moments later, the woman returned with a black nylon bag, which she handed to Soccer shirt, who pulled out the stethoscope and began to listen intently.

The stewardess knelt next to Rolly. "Thank you. But now I must ask you to return to your seat."

"Will he be OK?" Rolly asked.

She lifted her eyebrows and turned her face toward the rear of the plane. That was the only answer Rolly was going to get.

Back at his seat, he struggled over the snorer and sat. A stroke? Heart attack? The poor guy could die on this airplane, in, literally, the

214

middle of nowhere, but he hadn't started this journey thinking this might happen. If he lived, he wasn't going to disembark to the future he had expected.

Rolly closed his eyes and slept. He dreamed of a river; he was the river, a river flush and full, rushing through canyons, around bends, picking up speed, thundering through curves and loops, until the canyon walls vanished, then he, the river, charged forward over flat land strewn with rocks, the rocks breaking him into streams, then smaller streams that slowed and meandered into pools and rivulets before seeping away. Alice had broken him into smallness. The job, the house, the regular husband — all of it had diverted his course.

Dinging bells and sudden light woke him. A different stewardess handed him a glass of water over the head of the snorer. The seat in front was still empty. Rolly half stood to see the bulkhead row, but the rolling cart blocked his view. He hoped the guy was alive. Even if he was, the best that would happen was that he would be carried off the plane into a medical circus. In a moment, what was good in a life could be over. Rolly had no more time to waste. A divorce as soon as possible was what he wanted: no delays, no wrangling, no wasted emotion. What had been was over. He would move on.

16

From: rdbecotte@hotmail.com
To: a_becotte@HHWeekly.org
Sent: February 8, 11:05 p.m.
Subject: Again. Moving forward

Alice.

What's with the silence? Ten days since my last email and you haven't responded. I'd like to begin this process ASAP, you too, right? and wrap it up before your baby is born. When's the date? If that's not possible, we can try to reach an agreement on issues, like the house.

I got some lawyer recommendations from friends at the college, and I'll settle on one soon. Send me the name of your lawyer, so you and I can turn this over to our appointed stand-ins and cut down on our direct communication.
Rolly

Bettina glanced up from the email that Alice had printed out and brought home. "You haven't answered this? It's dated a week ago."

"I need to think." Alice reached for the coffee pot, annoyed that Bettina seemed to think she was being unfair. "First, I had to get beyond the first trimester. So ta-da! Not that I was worried, but even if it didn't… I'd still want a divorce."

Bettina waved away coffee pot. "So you're…"

"Out of the woods; that's what Dr. Petrillo says. Where does that expression come from: Robert Frost? I'm fourteen weeks and safe." She rapped her knuckles on the table. "Now I can think about what comes next." She stood and turned sideways to show off her belly.

"Looks like you stuffed a pie plate into your jeans," Bettina laughed. Despite the misgivings she'd expressed about Alice going into motherhood alone, lately she'd been doing her best to hide them, and she'd agreed to be Alice's birth coach. "If you're asking if I know any divorce lawyers, I don't, but I can ask around." She glanced over Alice's shoulder at the stove clock. "Where are those girls?"

"At the animal shelter?"

Ariana and Gia had gone to the animal shelter with Alice when she realized she couldn't keep the puppy. Since then, they volunteered once a month, playing with the dogs in the shelter's yard.

"They're supposed to be home by lunchtime."

"Come upstairs and see what I've done to the baby's room."

"Next time. I've got to chase down the girls."

From her back steps, Alice waved good-bye, wishing Bettina had stayed, wishing someone would admire the new nursery, wishing someone would say she doing a great job all on her own.

She had hired a painter for the baby's room, which was now a soft tangerine with crisp white trim, and cheery even on gray February days. She'd made curtains of white eyelet and lined the drawers of the old bureau with fresh paper. Even Patricia hadn't bothered to stop by in the past two weeks, "too busy" with her new immigrant clients and with Warren. You'd think she'd be excited about having a grandchild.

At work, Alice kept quiet about painting the baby's room, since she hadn't mentioned her pregnancy. Fritzie, whose eagle eye wasn't as sharp as usual, hadn't noticed any changes. At three months, maybe it wasn't that noticeable. Belly and boobs a little bigger, and she hadn't been sick at all. Next week, she would tell Fritzie, who would take up the ugly duck blanket she'd hidden after the miscarriage. Alice wanted to ask Fritzie's advice about how to tell Barry. Surely he would agree to a maternity leave. And Alice had to figure out childcare. She wanted everything settled as soon as possible, but some things would have to wait until May or June. Patricia would help. Her coolness was bound to change once the baby arrived.

From outside she heard Bettina scolding and a child protest. The girls had come home. Later in the afternoon, Alice would invite them over for cookies and a look at the nursery.

✳✳✳

To Alice's surprise, Bettina came up with a lawyer: Ned Reimus, specialty in family law, whose office was in Rockton. Over the phone Alice explained to him the bare bones. Divorce, "a sad business," he offered, but much less painful when you knew what the law required and you had someone in your corner. He could see her in two weeks.

His well-appointed office, overlooking the square and the county courthouse, had all the traditional touches: bookcases crammed with leather-bound books, brass lamps, Oriental rug, and an immense, orderly desk. He was taller than she'd expected, freckled, big features, gelled blond hair, and shoulders that said he'd played football in college. When he shook her hand, he held hers between his thick, well-manicured paws for a few seconds longer than customary. This was a man who would take care of her. This was a man she would be glad to have in her corner, especially since her corner seemed a little understaffed.

She explained again her circumstances, and he took notes on a yellow pad. This would not be a contested divorce, she told him again, as she had on the phone. She and her husband wanted the divorce. She explained that she and Rolly both had earned incomes. His was greater than hers, but she did not want alimony. They had a savings account, separate checking accounts — she could produce photocopies — and they owned a house together, with a $75,000 mortgage. In an email her husband had said that the house would be "an issue," but she wanted to keep the house. And she was pregnant. She hadn't mentioned this on the phone, it had seemed too complicated to get into. Her husband wasn't the father. She wanted the divorce to be completed, if possible, before the baby was born. August, that's right. August seventh.

Reimus tossed down his pen.

"Mrs. Becotte, it's not that simple. The court must consider the well-being and maintenance of the child. You may claim that you do not want your husband to be held responsible for the child, but in the eyes of the law, he is responsible, unless proven otherwise. Two parents accountable, that's what the court seeks. Will this other man, the father, accept responsibility?"

"That is not going to happen. In this case, there is only one parent responsible, and I'm it. She." Why did she have to defend this? "The news is full of single mothers who don't have fathers for their children. What about them?"

"First, that is a situation that is considered to be unfortunate, if not tragic. And, second, these women are single. They are not married, denying their husband is the father, and seeking divorce." He pushed his glasses onto his forehead to rub his eyes.

"The husband," she made quote signs with her fingers, "will deny he's the father, because he's not the father. I have not come here to be lectured. My pregnancy is not a tragedy. It's a blessing. Do you want to represent me or not?"

He sighed, resettled his glasses on his nose, and picked up his pen. "There is no other man whom you wish to declare as the father?"

"No one. The actual biological *donor* is out of the picture. He doesn't know about the baby, and if he should ever learn about it, and suspect, I will deny that it's his. Is this clear enough?"

"Mrs. Becotte, I'm on your side here. That's what you're hiring me for, if you hire me. I'm here to give you the best advice I can and to protect your interests, as best I can, and your child's."

He returned to his notepad, then looked up. "Alice—can I call you Alice?—the court must be convinced that what you have in mind is best for you and your child. That is what the court will be most concerned with. It's not just what you and your husband agree to."

"I don't see why I can't be regarded as capable of deciding what's best for my child."

He leaned back in his chair and smiled, as if taking her point, then rocked forward. "No father to help carry the responsibility and the financial burden of raising a child? This is a long-term commitment, Alice. I don't have to tell you — the expenses over eighteen years, and then there might be college — these expenses can be considerable. You're a reporter. That doesn't pay a lot, does it?" Alice said no. "Do you have an independent source of income?" She shook her head. "Not many do." He sighed. She was scoring poorly on his test. "You've informed me most clearly and forcibly of your wishes, and I will do my best for you. Now I need to look into some matters."

They should meet again in a month. In the interval he would look into the questions she raised and seek precedents where the mother, not the father, denied paternity.

On her way out, she took his card to send his information to Rolly. Ned Reimus might be in her corner, but he wouldn't be her best buddy.

* * *

Dr. Petrillo said she was doing well. The ultrasound looked "on target" for seventeen weeks. He was amused that she didn't want to know if it was a boy or a girl. Her diet? She was constantly hungry, but if she ate more than a few bites, she felt nauseous. Not to worry. She was putting on weight nicely. Taking her vitamins? Yes. Exercising? Not really. Not at the gym. Working out seemed risky. He nodded sympathetically and said she mustn't worry. She was doing fine. No gym was perfectly acceptable as long as she stayed active at work and at home.

Her body was changing, but not quickly enough to satisfy her need to have her new, wondrous state announced wherever she went. She just looked fat. But the tingly breasts, thickening middle, and back twinges pleased her. Someone else was controlling her body. This was thrilling. "Just wait," Bettina said, and Patricia seemed uninterested.

With the baby's room ready and Rolly's things boxed in the basement, Alice took on the rest of the house, beginning in the attic and working her way down. She organized, cleaned, and divided the junk they'd accumulated into two groups, throw out and sell-for-cheap. Before the baby came, she wanted the house emptied of her life with Rolly.

Returning from work she ran into Bettina in the alley and asked if she wanted to go in on a "multifamily" garage sale.

Bettina dropped her trash sack in the garbage can. "Are you selling the house without telling me?" She banged down the lid.

"How could you think that? No." Alice bent to pick up a flattened spaghetti box. Since the snow had melted, every ugly, overlooked thing had been revealed. "Come on, Bettina. This is where I live. I'm counting on Ariana and Gia babysitting in a few years."

"You will tell me first."

"Of course, but it's not going to happen."

Watching her stride away with barely a nod. Alice wondered if Bettina felt that having a single mom next door threatened the Faraccis' honorable Noah's ark two-by-two status. Or was it that Bettina feared that Alice might ask too much of her and Paul? Maybe it had been a mistake to ask her to be her birth coach.

✳✳✳

From: rdbecotte@hotmail.com
To: a_becotte@HHWeekly.org
Sent: March 23, 9:07 p.m.

Alice:

I'll be in NYC in mid-April to plan an exhibition. I may need to make a quick trip to Haslett. While I'm there, I think you and I should meet. My lawyer says if he and your lawyer have to duke it out over every detail, it will cost us both a fortune.

I'll phone you from NYC.
R

✳✳✳

She suggested Jethro's, a roadhouse where nobody she knew went.

The pine-paneled room was less than half-filled at lunchtime, a sure sign of lousy food, but a relief. She was nervous about how Rolly would react to seeing her obviously pregnant, but they would be monitored by the bartender, the father/son duo at the bar, and three women in green polo shirts who must be on lunch hour from the mall. Was that Rolly in a back booth? He'd shaved off his beard — he'd had it as long as she'd known him — and his skin was pale as skim milk.

222

She sat down opposite him. "You look good without the beard," which wasn't true. Vertical lines she'd never seen framed his mouth. He looked monkish and hard.

"And you look large," he said, as his eyes flicked over her torso.

"Thank you," she said, hurt, though she'd expected something like this, and pretended he meant this as a compliment. "I'm halfway there, four and a half months."

His eyes moved with pointed slowness to the TV. He was telegraphing that he found her grotesque.

"How long are you in town?" she asked.

"Through Monday," he said, eyes on the TV.

"And you're here for?" He was going to make this a real struggle.

"To send some pieces to New York that I'd left in my studio at the college. With Wolf gone, there's no one I could rely on to handle this."

Wolf. She looked away, at the TV. She'd worried Wolf's name would come up, but she wasn't prepared. "Have you been in touch with him?" She hoped her voice didn't give her away.

TV noise. The bartender sloshed glasses in the sink. Finally, Rolly said, "I thought I'd visit him, but probably not. He's *ocupado*. You know Wolf."

Probably not? *Ocupado*? She could hear the distress under Rolly's words. She turned from the TV back to him and made her face communicate that she understood how much this must pain him. His eyes softened. He was glad she understood. She glanced down, stung by shame, at pretending sympathy for his loss—no, she did feel sorry about that—but for everything about her affair with Wolf, and she was ashamed she was relieved that he knew nothing about it. And she was grateful, giddy with gratitude, that Wolf had the good sense, or the guilt, to pull back from the friendship. She began talking too much, about the Swenke house selling for nearly the asking price; the Baileys putting on an addition; and Bettina and Paul sending their regards. Finally, the waitress arrived.

Rolly ordered a beer, iced tea for her, and two hamburgers.

He understood their lawyers had spoken.

"That's what I heard too," Alice said. "My lawyer also said there's no sense in starting until after the baby is born, and your guy agreed. Judges always continue cases with pregnancies, until after the birth. That's why I really haven't taken it very far, if you were wondering."

"I was. Wondering. My lawyer, Jim Singer, said the more we agree on, the faster this will go. When's your due date?"

"August seventh."

His face stiffened, as if she were playing a trick on him. She wasn't going to explain that it was pure chance, her becoming pregnant almost exactly a year after her first — their — pregnancy. "I haven't been stalling, if that's what you're worried about."

"Why would I worry? It's all yours. But I would think you'd want to conclude the you and me chapter." He leaned forward, shoving aside their drinks. "There's the house and the matter of 'child support'. " He curdled the phrase. "I'm sure your lawyer mentioned that."

The baby kicked her diaphragm. "My guy did say that was something the judge would require—"

"You're not going to try to hit me up for child support, are you?"

"You're *not* the father." Was it the due date that had uncapped this sudden spitefulness? "I told my lawyer I'm responsible, no one else. Who do you think I am?"

"I haven't been sure who you really are for a long time." His nostrils flared as he downed half his beer. "We divide our savings fifty-fifty. With the house, we calculate the value of my studio—I get that—and the remainder we divide fifty-fifty. Fair."

224

"Sell the house? I want to keep it." Had he no residual feelings of fairness from their years together? She said, "I'll figure out something, some sort of buyout."

"I'm not prepared to—"

"I don't want to take advantage of you."

"What the hell do you think your fucking some guy…"

"That's not what… I'm sorry."

"I'm not. I am as un-sorry as I can be. I am so fucking glad that this strangling marriage is over."

She tried to shove back from the table, but there was no room to move. "We can spend every goddamn dime we have on lawyers, if it comes to that." She maneuvered awkwardly out of the booth.

He leaned back, his eyes flat, smirking. "If that's how you want it."

"That is how I want it."

She picked up her water glass, held it high over the table, and tipped it over, delighted as water streamed down, spattering her dress, ice cubes bouncing, the puddle spreading to soak the placemats and spill over the edge. Rolly jerked. She slammed down the empty glass and stalked away, the shock on his face buoying her out the bar and into the parking lot. Inside her car she began to shake and struggled to insert her key in the ignition. She had to get away before Rolly came out.

∗∗∗

"Patricia, he wants me to sell the house."

"I can't talk now. I'm with a client."

"Should I call back for an appointment?" Alice set down the phone with the kind of precision that was the opposite of slamming, hoping her mother could hear her rage. Why had Alice been so stupid to think her mother would be a help? Patricia had been in full retreat since Alice became pregnant.

She dialed Reimus's number. He said "perhaps" it had been "unwise" to meet with her husband. He didn't have to be so goddamn patronizing.

"Could I be forced to sell the house?"

"In all likelihood" blah blah blah, and told her not to worry.

"You will fight this, won't you? You are working for me."

"Of course I am. In the future, it might be better to let me and Jim Singer handle these matters."

She gave him the finger, glad he couldn't see her, and hung up.

No one listened to her, no one cared. She grabbed her coat, the buttons tugging over her belly — "you look large" — and headed into the backyard.

"And you look like a bastard," she should have responded.

In spite of the April sun, the air was bracingly cold and the rake was where she'd left it last fall. Dragging it to the arborvitae, she dislodged the dried needles underneath, but couldn't find the heart-shaped rock she'd hidden when she and Rolly were still a couple. Not under the big arborvitae, nor under the two smaller ones. She dropped the rake and pressed her hands into the small of her aching back, disappointed. But it had to be that the missing stone was one more sign, as if she needed it, that the past was over. All her doubts about Rolly and their life together were magically confirmed. Not that she believed in magic, but still.

She retrieved the rake and carried it to the lilacs to clear the matted leaves that had collected during the winter. Beneath were beautiful clusters of fresh white crocuses. Kneeling awkwardly — her belly large enough to throw her off balance — she sniffed for the flowers' scent, but could detect only dank earth. Their cupped petals gleamed in the sunlight. She touched one. It was cold and soft. She rocked back on her heels, letting the sun wash over her face too. It was spring. Things would work out. The world was cycling into light and warmth, and in

226

less than five months, she would have a baby.

Straightening, she stared at Rolly's studio. She could rent it out and use the monthly income to buy him out over time. She'd heard old-timers at the courthouse talk about setups like this, but maybe only in connection to farms. Land contract sales they might be called. Real estate layaway.

INNOVATIVE FINANCING IN THE NEW MILLENNIUM
Pressed by a cruel and greedy soon-to-be ex-husband, a single mom in Haslett has applied an old financing strategy…

Rolly wouldn't agree to anything that would suit her. She might as well take a torch to his studio. The image of flames against a night sky flashed, then faded. She'd get caught. She always got caught.

✳ ✳ ✳

Ned Reimus would discuss her idea about the garage/studio with Jim Singer, but it was "pre-mature." The whole divorce business had stalled. "These things always take longer than people want," Reimus intoned.

Week by week, the baby grew, a constant presence. It, her intimate, arched and flipped, turned and pressed against her lungs, and tugged hard against the small of her back, but each twinge, each thrust against her heart made her happy. She hadn't expected it, but she wished she had someone to share this with.

The late-season tulips bloomed and faded, and the grass greened as spring gave way to summer, and the high school kids exchanged their parkas for shorts and flip-flops. In the square opposite the *Herald*, bunting swagged across the War Memorial for Memorial Day.

She parked in front of the office, envying those who had cars with movable steering wheels. Two more months to go and she felt like a beached porpoise, without the grace. From the car, she could see Fritzie had taped her Back-in-Ten-Minutes sign to the inside of the glass door. Alice used her keys and relocked the door behind her — she didn't want to deal with someone wandering in — and glared at her downstairs desk. When she'd begun wearing maternity clothes, Barry had decided she shouldn't climb the stairs anymore. "I do at home," she'd protested.

"Anyone here?" she called up the stairs. No response.

On her desk were notes. The Purple Heart Veterans had called about a used clothes pickup; Barry wanted an introduction to some recipes headlined "Salads for Summer: Eating Light" — he wouldn't ask John Weideroe, her maternity leave replacement, to handle this kind of stuff — and another note asking her to cut three graphs from her piece titled "How to Improve and Retain Your Memory."

Kicking off her shoes to ease her swollen feet, she logged onto her computer, then heard keys rattle in the door: Fritzie with, surprisingly, Patricia.

"Look who I found," Fritzie said.

"How nice." Alice rose from her chair. Patricia had canceled their last two dates. The last time, backing out of a shopping trip she'd proposed to buy a crib, she'd told Alice to go on her own; she would reimburse her. Alice hid her wariness, admiring how, in spite of the heat, Patricia looked stylish and pretty, as always, like she'd just come from the hair salon. "New haircut?" Alice asked.

"Last week. I was just passing." She shot Fritzie, who remained at the door, a puzzling glance, then walked toward Alice.

Fritzie jiggled her keys. "I'm going to the hardware store. Back in a few."

"What's that about?" Alice asked Patricia as she drew up a chair.

"I ran into her coming out of Waggoner's."

"The travel agent? Are you planning a trip?"

Patricia shrugged. "One thing lead to another, and she thought I should come in and talk to you."

"About?"

"I was going to stop by tonight."

Misgiving flooded Alice. "About?"

Patricia's eyes refused to meet hers. "I know this is sudden." She pulled a Kleenex from her purse and wiped a flush of sweat from her lip. "Warren and I are flying to the Bahamas in a week."

"How nice," Alice said, not bothering to hide her sarcasm. "That should be lovely."

"We're getting married."

"You're not."

"We're getting married in Miami, at his younger sister's, then flying to the Bahamas for a honeymoon, a place called Harbour Island."

"Marry Warren? Why?"

"Well, we've been talking about it for some time. With all your troubles..."

"Troubles? Everything's fine with me."

"I didn't want to give you anything else to worry about."

"What are you talking about? *This* worries me. Why on earth do you want to marry him? He's a drunk. He's going to bleed—"

"Stop right there."

"I'm sorry, Patricia, but marriage?" She grabbed her mother's hand. "He's got a drinking problem, Mom, you know that. He's a lush. You want to be harnessed to that?"

"Sure, he likes his old-fashioneds, but he doesn't have a 'drinking problem.' " She pulled away from Alice's grip. "You've never gotten to know him. He makes me happy. I love him and he loves me."

"And how long do you think that will last?" Alice struggled to speak calmly.

"You don't know the first thing about making a marriage last, my dear. I knew this would be hard, talking to you, that's why I put it off. I'm not usually such a coward, but I just couldn't face you acting the way you're acting. You resent my having a life of my own. Warren's wonderful. He's kind and fun and steady, and I'm tired of being alone."

"What about me, Patricia?" She was the one who would be alone.

Around her mother's eyes, the wrinkles pinched together. "I'm not ready to retire into being a grandmother. Not exclusively." She patted Alice's hand. "You look miserable. Don't worry. I'll, we'll, be back in two weeks, by mid-June, long before the baby comes."

"It's not that."

"I'm still your mother, dear, and I love you, but I get my own life."

Was she throwing Alice's words back at her? "I know you do."

"Well, then," Patricia smiled at her, a smile that said it didn't matter what Alice said, flicked her Kleenex into the wastebasket, and stood. "I've got to run. Come over for lunch on Saturday, and pretend you're happy for us."

Alice walked with her mother to the door and unlocked it. The outside light was blinding. Holding the door open, Alice tried not to cry.

"Saturday, one o'clock," Patricia waved, sun flashing off her silvery hair.

***

On Saturday Alice brought a cake with roses and congratulated Warren. With his round, bald head sweating with delight, he acted like he couldn't believe his luck in snagging such a lovely woman as her mother. His happiness was sickening. Everyone was jolly. Alice asked lots of questions about their trip. They had decided against a cruise.

OLD HONEYMOONERS MAKE FOOLS OF THEMSELVES

Midwestern oldsters, seeking the Fountain of Youth, try to turn back the clock by journeying to the sparkling waters of Bermuda, and on to Disneyworld, where they plan to spin in the Tea Cups and addle what's left of their demented brains.

She gave them a stained glass window ornament, "Time Flies, Only Love Endures," her smiling face aching with deceit as she handed her mother the gift. She couldn't risk losing Patricia.

"Thank you, dear," Patricia beamed.

∗ ∗ ∗

After they were gone, about a week before the summer solstice, Bettina asked if they were back yet. Alice said not yet. They'd decided to stay an extra week.

"Guess who *is* back?"

Alice said nothing. From Bettina's expression she knew she meant Rolly.

"I saw him at the KwikTrip."

"Did you talk to him?"

"He was driving away. He's ditched the beard. He looks…"

"Harsh?"

"I was going to say 'different, but good'. "

Had Bettina gone to the other side too? "Just don't invite him over for a backyard barbeque without warning me. I do *not* want to see him."

"I thought you should know he's in town. Change of topic." So she'd realized her news had upset Alice. She hurried on. "Want to come over on Monday to meet my mothers' group? You'll want to meet Christine, who's having a baby this summer too. You'll like her. We meet at ten o'clock, now that school's out."

Bettina had promised for weeks to invite Alice to her mother's group. "Sure. Great," she lied. She couldn't go; she was still working. Her leave didn't begin for a month. Did nothing of her reality register for Bettina?

"Listen, I've got to run," Alice said. Inside her, the baby flipped, making it hard to breathe.

17

Rolly drove his rental car under the ironwork arch that spelled out "Wesley College." Home a week, his first time on campus, and the place was even more lifeless than he remembered. "Embalmed" would be the word: no one walking between the oppressive stone buildings, no groundskeeper mowing, no kids smoking outside the Union, not a squirrel, not even a student poster flapping on tree or signboard. One year, that was all he was going to give this place, and he'd be out of here. He followed the drive to the art building and parked next to the loading dock. On the third landing of the fire escape sat a withered houseplant, and the grimy windows hadn't been washed either. He got out of his car, sighed, and leaned against its door. Nothing had changed.

One thing had: Meg was gone. He'd driven by the Methodist church and seen Ken's name missing from the notice board, replaced by The Reverend Caroline Hulge-Carley. Meg had told him that Methodist ministers moved every three years, but he hadn't expected her to disappear, not without telling him. She had his address.

In the church office, he encountered a woman who looked like Mrs. Santa Claus, who told him that Ken had been reassigned to a church in Walnut Creek, California, and had left less than a month ago. Rolly asked for the new address.

She smiled. "I don't recall seeing you at church."

"A friend of the family," he said.

She beamed and handed him a printed card.

When he first held the compass Meg had sent, he'd assumed she'd chosen it because of his canoes and his love of old things, but staring at her new address, he wondered if what she might have meant was that he was so lost, he needed a navigational device. And that was a year ago.

Thanking Mrs. Claus, he dropped the card in his shirt pocket. If that's what Meg had thought then, she would judge him as even more lost now. Uncertainty clouded every aspect of his future. He couldn't contact her.

She was gone and nothing held him in Haslett, but so far nothing beckoned him elsewhere either. Until the divorce was final, until he could see a way forward, he would wait. He didn't want to jump into a wrong decision and end up full of regrets. Something would come to him. It always did.

A car horn tooted. Rolly jumped as Herman Laashe's Mercedes pulled into the parking space marked "Chairman."

"How does it feel to be back?" Herman asked, limping past Rolly, his hip no better, not bothering to wait for an answer as he led the way up the stairs into the shipping area.

He'd aged. Under the July sun, his scalp shone through his sandy hair.

Rolly followed him inside and down the corridor to the back door of the art department's office suite. The same lousy student work hung above the file cabinets, and the Venetian blinds near the secretary's desk still sagged at half-mast. He was being sucked backward in time.

Herman made his way around the secretary's desk, into the small cubbyhole that held the fax machine, the network printer, and the faculty mailboxes, and grabbed the overflowing stack in Rolly's box. "Welcome back."

"Thanks." Rolly took the pile and dumped it in the wastebasket.

Herman raised an eyebrow and, with his foot, nudged a package on the floor. "What's this?"

Rolly's name was printed in bold on the label.

Rolly bent to look. "Stuff connected to my show in Helsinki. Probably copies of the catalogue."

"Let me have one, will you? I'll show it to the dean." He smiled his calculating chairman's smile and put his own mail down on a ledge. "So what else have you got going on?"

"The Whitney is talking about a solo exhibit, something they'll put together with the Dallas Art, to travel to a couple of other cities. It's still at the talk stage. Nothing's signed. Jacqueline, my rep, visited me last winter and went into high gear after seeing what I was doing. A couple of curators flew over, and by spring Jacqueline had promises in her pocket."

Herman clasped his shoulder. "Great. That's what a sabbatical is all about. The dean will love this." He smoothed his hair, his thoughts elsewhere, probably trying to figure how to finagle maximum advantage for the department out of Rolly's productivity. His eyes reconnected with Rolly. "What work of yours is it, by the way?"

As if he was interested. For Herman the least interesting aspect of Rolly's success was the work behind it, but Rolly told him about the fifteen new pieces he'd started in Bergen and the drawings that would be exhibited in Stockholm next spring.

"Great. Great. Good." He scanned the mailboxes. "And how's Alice?"

Rolly bent to the wastebasket, pretending to reconsider a large envelope he'd dumped, then shoved it back. Had Herman really not heard anything, or was he trying to knife him for his professional success?

"We're getting a divorce." He was pleased to see Herman blanch. "My sabbatical was a kind of trial separation, and we both found that we were happier living apart."

"I'm sorry to hear that. Alice is such a delightful girl. I always liked her. If there's anything…"

"At this point, I just want things settled," Rolly said, more curt than he intended.

Herman lifted his eyebrows in a gesture as close to sympathy as Rolly had ever seen before heading for his office.

Behind Rolly the fax machine began to hum, and a sheet of paper fell to the floor. He ignored it. Once Alice had said, "The only way out is through," and he'd accused her of talking like the White Rabbit. But she was right. The year ahead would be hell, but the only way out was through. He lifted the box from the Helsinki printer and carried it to his office. A note was taped to the door. "Patricia Jenks" and a phone number. It took him a few beats to recognize Patricia's married name. He'd spoken to her when he first got back. Juggling the package, he unlocked his office door.

The room smelled of dust and heat. The cleaning crew must not have been in since Wolf vacated six months ago. Mailing tubes were piled in front of the bookcase, and a computer missing its plastic housing sat under the window. Who'd decided his office should be the junk storage room? He kicked the door shut, dropped the carton of catalogues on a chair, and stared at Wolf's desk. Gone were the perfect black German rulers, the immaculate steel tray that was Wolf's "in" box, and the architectural rendering of the Jewish Museum in Berlin. One by one, Rolly opened Wolf's desk drawers, empty except for the lower right, which held Rolly's Elvis clock. Wolf had kept his promise. Rolly shut the drawer, missing him, still wounded. Wolf hadn't given any reason for pulling away, but he made it clear that his friendship with Rolly had been part of his American phase and that was over.

Rolly picked up the slip with Patricia's number. If he'd gone straight to his studio, he could have claimed, rightly, that he hadn't gotten it.

"Hi, Patricia. New number, I see."

"Where've you been? I've been trying to reach you all morning." Her voice rushed at him, high-pitched, upset.

He exhaled slowly. "Errands. I'm at the college now."

"Thank God, I've got you. I'm at the hospital and Alice's in labor. It's not going well. She's in something called 'back labor' I've never heard of. You've got to come."

"Patricia, that's crazy."

"Bettina's here too. It's been at least fourteen hours—no, sixteen hours now. They're saying she might need a C-section, but she wants everything to be natural. You've got to come."

"Isn't she due in August?"

"It's a couple weeks early."

"Listen, Patricia, this has nothing to do with me." He sat in the chair that had been Wolf's, propping his feet on the desk, on the desk-pad calendar: December 1999, and pictured the snowy landscape outside the Lund's kitchen window.

"Just come. Come now." Patricia's voice sounded taut.

"Oh, please." He closed his eyes, trying to hold onto the calm white scene with the strokes of pine green.

"Rolly, I'm telling you, you have to come."

He opened his eyes, fixing on Wolf's disconnected lamp. "Why?"

"Because she needs you."

"I'm not coming."

"You have to."

"Has she asked for me?"

"No."

"Then why the hell…?"

"How many years, eight, ten, right? Enough years not to banish."

"What makes you think she'd want me?"

Muffled voices. Patricia had covered the mouthpiece. When she came back, she sounded scared. "Please come."

Alice's face on the night of the miscarriage came to him, her sobbing when the nurse tried to wrench off her wedding ring, her terror as they wheeled her away. "OK."

In the car he wanted to scream, "This is your doing. You've brought this on yourself." Why the hell had he agreed to this?

Patricia was waiting in the lobby by the elevators, her hair flattened on one side, her face colorless with exhaustion.

"What's happening?" he asked.

She stabbed the elevator button, keeping her eyes on the lighted floor numbers above — to avoid looking at him? — until the doors opened. "I don't know what's going on." They got on and the doors closed. "Alice's midwife, Hillary, isn't here. Son was in a bad car accident. Instead her partner comes, someone Alice has seen only once. A midwife? What was she thinking? Why has she latched onto this 'natural' nonsense?" They stepped from the elevator into the soft hum of fluorescent lights. "Alice's upset Hillary isn't here. Nothing's going the way it's supposed to."

Patricia guided him through double doors and nodded toward a tall man in a green smock upbraiding a short woman in a floral smock. "Supervising doctor," Patricia whispered, "and Hillary's partner." The partner-midwife, graying blond hair in a braid, crossed her arms, holding her ground.

Where was that jerk Petrillo?

The doctor glanced at Rolly, then asked the midwife, "Is this the father?"

Patricia stepped in. "This is Alice's husband."

The doctor glared at Rolly. "What kept you?" Without waiting for a reply, he turned to the midwife. "Either you get a signature for a C-section or you get a waiver. Explain it to him," he nodded at Rolly. "I'll hear from you in less than an hour." He walked away.

Angry at being dismissed — why the hell had he come? — Rolly watched the arrogant jackass disappear around the corner as Patricia introduced the partner-midwife, Nan Greenspan. The woman's heavy-lidded eyes reassured him.

"Come this way." She touched his elbow. "But first, do you know what to expect in here? I know Bettina's been trained as her coach."

"Alice and I are estranged. We haven't lived together in a year, but Patricia called me."

The midwife blinked in slow motion. "Alice doesn't need any more complications."

Wishing he could escape, but not wanting to be shoved aside, Rolly tensed, and Patricia intervened, grasping his hand. "Stay." To the midwife, she said, "I asked him to come. I think it would help Alice."

The midwife looked from Patricia to Rolly. "I'll ask her."

He and Patricia waited in the hall, opposite a mural of multiracial babies lolling on a cloud, their cheery faces mocking his uneasiness and Patricia's distress. At some signal he missed, she led him into Alice's room where Bettina perched on the windowsill, and a battery of beige machines were clustered around a bed. Alice sat holding a pillow to her face. An IV drip was taped to the back of her hand. The midwife touched Alice's arm and leaned close, a high-pitched whine covering whatever she said. The whining stopped. It had been Alice. She'd been humming.

She lifted her face, blotchy and tight with pain, from the pillow, and looked at him. "Why are you here?"

"Patricia asked me."

She twisted slowly to sit on the edge of the bed with her legs dangling. She was huge. From gaps in her gown, electrodes connected her to the machines. "But why are you here?"

He forced himself to meet her eyes. "I don't want to hurt you."

She snorted, rattling the electrodes.

"Patricia asked me to come. I'm here to help."

She waved her hand, shaking the IV tube. "My skin, it's on fire," and squeezed shut her eyes.

The midwife said, "Take another shower," and detached the electrodes, tossing them aside and guiding the IV stand forward. To Bettina, she said, "You hold her. I have to start the water."

Bettina slid off the windowsill, but Alice lifted her head to look at Rolly, seeming to take his measure. "Come here," she said.

She expected him to balk, her way of showing Patricia what a mistake she'd made bringing him in, but he walked toward her, his shoes squeaking on the tile floor. When he reached her side, he could feel her immense belly radiate heat from beneath her wrinkled gown, which now hung open. Since he'd last seen her naked, she had transformed into something primitive: bulbous breasts, belly, and thighs, strangely dark, mottled with veins, like a prehistoric Venus. On the other side of her body, he felt a space open up when the midwife withdrew, and Alice leaned against him, her drooping head barely reaching to the middle of his chest. He held her closer, accepting her weight, and felt her breathe, the rhythm slowing his thudding heart. Together, they walked forward, Alice clutching the IV stand. From within the shower's fog in the bathroom, the midwife waved come in, but he hesitated, not want-

240

ing to give up the balance he and Alice had just struck, but Alice pulled away and disappeared into the clouds of white.

He listened to the water splash and break, imagining a featureless man lowering himself over Alice nine months ago.

The midwife came out leaving the bathroom door ajar.

"The baby can't move in the position he's in. His head's down, that's good, but his spine is resting on her spine. That's bad. As you heard out there," she glanced toward the hall, "after this many hours, it's risky. If he doesn't turn soon of his own accord, the doctor will insist on a C-section."

"He? It's a boy?"

"Yes, and he's not too big, but he's in the wrong position."

"Why can't it, he, be turned with forceps?" His mother had told him of his own birth, the marks that took a year to disappear, her worry about brain damage.

"No forceps, no drugs, no surgery, all natural, that's Alice. She's insisting," Patricia snapped from across the room. "In my day, you were doped, you woke up, you had a baby in your arms. This is too hard."

The shower's drone filled the room as Bettina talked about Gia's birth and the midwife straightened the bed. An animal cry erupted from the bathroom and Alice's immense, dripping body swayed in the doorway.

"I think the baby turned."

The midwife pushed past Rolly and ushered Alice to the bed as a nurse appeared from somewhere, and another.

"Coming," the midwife muttered, drawing a cart into the circle that surrounded Alice, as someone slipped green sheets under Alice's hips. Rolly moved to where he could take Alice's hand. Something silver flashed in the midwife's hands, then disappeared between Alice's legs as she heaved and wailed. Sickened, he found Alice's hand and squeezed.

"He's here. He's coming. Keep pushing, that's it."

Alice jerked her hand from his. Through the tangle of nurses, he saw a blood-streaked bulge burst between her legs. Alice screamed. A yelp, a rush, followed by a gasp, movement shoving him aside, and the midwife held up a mangled red shape barely recognizable as a baby. More movement among the nurses, another howl, another rush.

Stepping back, he watched the midwife nestle the limp shape next to Alice's throat.

"We have to take you to another room now, dear," someone said.

"Why?" Alice cried. "What's wrong?" She twisted her head to look at Rolly as if he were supposed to answer, as they lifted her with the baby on her chest to a gurney, and then they—Alice, the baby, and the nurses—wheeled out of the room, and he was left with Bettina and Patricia, who was crying.

He rocked on his legs unsteady. A moment ago there'd been a malignancy inside Alice, then out came a *being*, an ugly red, unfinished, but stunningly alive *being*. It, *he*, was small enough to fit in Rolly's hand, yet *he* was vital, vital in a way that Rolly had never experienced, so vital that he'd realigned Rolly's body, his jaw, the tingling skin of his face, his hands and legs, all of him had tuned for a few thrilling moments to a new frequency. Now this miracle *being* had vanished, leaving Rolly hollowed out.

A nurse he hadn't seen before guided him, Patricia, and Bettina to a room with two empty beds. After a time, two orderlies steered in a gurney with Alice, but no baby. The orderlies shoved aside his gesture to help as they transferred her to the bed.

"A boy. He's beautiful." Alice smiled and fell asleep.

Bettina went home. He and Patricia stood watch.

"I'm glad you're here, Rolly," Patricia said.

"I'll stay until she wakes."

"I have to go home soon. Warren won't relax until I get home." She stood, her clothes wrinkled, a stain on her sleeve. "I wish Alice weren't on her own." It was the wrong thing to say. He could see that she knew it too. Embarrassed, she turned toward the bathroom and returned with fresh lipstick, which made her look worse.

When she was gone, he walked into the hall and looked toward the nurse's station, feeling as if he'd opened a wrong door and stumbled into someone else's life. Stretching his arms above his head, he tried to shake the toxic, surreal feeling. He wanted to see the baby.

A heavyset, black nurse rounded the corner, conferred with an orderly, then strode toward him.

"Would you like me to take you to the ISCU to see your son?"

"Son" stopped him.

"Becotte, right?" she asked.

"Yes," he said, glancing toward Alice's room, glad she couldn't have heard, then followed the nurse through a succession of corridors until they came to a door marked Infant Special Care Unit.

"The neonatologist has put him on oxygen."

"Why's that necessary?"

The doors swung open automatically.

"We need to scrub here."

The tiled antechamber held a stainless steel trough where shoulder-high faucets emitted cones of spray. Over the hiss of the water splashing his shirt, the nurse said, "His lungs aren't yet fully developed. The doctor will explain the details later, but for now, we thought you'd like to see him."

Rolly pushed up his sleeves and lathered to his elbow, scrubbing hard, so there was no chance he would carry any germs near the baby.

When the nurse said he could quit, he put on the gown she handed him. In the bright ward, banks of high-tech equipment were clustered around clear plastic bins, some of which were domed in plastic. Most were empty, but on his left two isolettes — that's what the nurse called the bins — held terrifyingly tiny red babies, too small for diapers, with plugs and needles taped to their heads and hands. Blue veins mapped the transparent, liverish skin that covered their skulls. Queasy, Rolly pressed his hands to his sides, afraid to touch anything.

The nurse pointed to the far end of the ward. Alice's baby lay inside a clear dome. He looked aggrieved, his tiny brows pinched, as if he were awake, but determined to shut out the painful world he'd been thrust into. An intravenous tube was taped to the back of his tight clenched fist, with his wrist tied down. Above the bandage that covered his umbilical connection, a quivering hollow in his small chest deflated, then filled.

"Is that normal?" Rolly asked, shaken to see how hard the baby had to struggle to breathe.

"Hyaline Membrane Disease. Each time he exhales, the sacs in the lungs collapse and stick together."

Afraid to ask anything else and his mouth dry, Rolly watched the hollow expand.

"You can touch him."

"I can't."

"Go ahead."

Rolly studied the pursed face with its bulging, closed alien eyes, then reached through one of the two holes in the dome's side to touch the closest leg, the size of his index finger. The leg felt rubbery. Rolly pulled away. A tremor jerked the tiny foot. Holding his breath and washed by a flood of tenderness, Rolly put his hand through the port again and

244

stroked the little leg. The baby's skin was hot. Another man should be touching this baby. Another man, not he, was this baby's father. Rolly had imagined this other man's imprint would be borne by this child, but he'd been wrong. This baby was not an offspring or a copy. Gaunt as a primitive trophy, and commanding, this being was entirely new. Though small and clenched, he'd pushed aside all of Rolly's expectations, and his fury, and had requisitioned for himself a new space, one unused and unsuspected by Rolly, until now.

At the other end of the ward, there was movement. A rumpled, middle-aged man in blue coveralls followed a nurse to one of the iso-lettes, the one with a pink ribbon. Rolly shifted to protect Alice's baby from view. Strangers should not be allowed a glimpse. How could a being part bird, part hairless mammal captivate him so? Kneeling be-side the domed shield. He stared. The baby trembled. Rolly reached through the hole again and ran his fingertips up the baby's skinny, flaccid arm. The trembling stopped. Holding his breath, he lowered his hand until the baby's shoulder fit into the hollow of his palm, like the knob of his favorite plane. The baby's pulse, heartbeat and breath, traveled through him.

When he returned to Alice's room, she was sitting up, hair combed. She'd been crying.

"Did you see him?"

"That's where I've been."

"Is he all right?"

On her bedside table was a chain with a Catholic medallion. He sat on the edge of her bed, careful not to touch her, and arranged the medallion's chain into the shape of a box.

She said, "The nurse said that his lungs aren't fully developed. No one seems worried about it."

"He looks fine. Beautiful, actually. They've got him in a special, domed crib-thing, to help with the breathing."

A muscle in her neck flinched.

The Venetian blinds rustled from a blast of air.

"I'm going home now," he said.

"Rolly?"

He stopped.

"Thank you."

∗∗∗

Wiped clean of thought, he drove home and fell asleep on his rental bed.

He woke, jolted by images of the baby, the small mouth struggling to breathe, the plum-colored eyelids, limbs twitching in distress. He sat up, heart knocking. It was still night. He called the hospital. A nurse in the ISCU said the baby had been put on a ventilator, but he was doing well.

Unsure what a ventilator was, but reassured by the nurse's calm tone, he showered, dressed, then prowled from room to room, turning on lights, until he found a box with his sketchpads, pried it open, discovered some Conté crayons, and began to sketch.

First he laid down a series of quick impressions of the baby, filling page after page, tearing through one sketchpad and another. Outside, birds began to squawk. When the sunrise began to color his window shades, he raised them and let the wash of pink light fall on the sketches he'd spread on the floor, his yet-to-be unpacked boxes, cheap coffee table, and rental couch. He turned off his lamp. His last drawing was of the curve where the baby's skull met his neck. Rolly picked it up, set it aside, and picked up another, of the baby's fingers, tipped with flower petals. He came to the one with the baby's head as blossom on a water lily pad. Dozens of drawings. He gathered them together, placing on

246

top the one in which he drew the baby complete, tangled in kelp and electrodes, his swollen face with eyes closed turned toward the viewer, toward Rolly. Behind the fragile eyelids a force called to him.

As soon as visiting hours allowed, he returned to the hospital. He wanted to go directly to the nursery, but understood that he had to call on Alice first. In the gift shop, he bought roses. She was sitting up dressed in a limp blue robe, face puffy. She'd been crying.

"Why'd you come yesterday?" she asked, noticing the flowers. He set them on the bedside table, pushing aside the Catholic medallion. Something had changed since last night. The connection had been broken.

"Like I said, Patricia called me. I felt some…I don't know…some residual…obligation. She made it sound necessary. I wanted to help you if I could. I don't know why."

She reached for a tissue and blew her nose. "It's not like you to throw yourself into the thicket of human entanglements, but thank you. I was glad you were here."

"I'm glad too." He wanted to say that he was back because something he had no name for had a hook in his chest and dragged him here. He wanted to say that everything else had dimmed. "After yesterday, I couldn't not come. I'd like to see your baby again."

A cart rattled past, the elevator chimed, a far away phone rang twice. He looked at Alice. She hadn't moved.

"The baby is my responsibility."

"I just want to see…"

"Just go."

"No, Alice."

"Go." She turned away.

"You don't understand."

"Go." She pounded her fist on the mattress.

He walked on stiff legs toward the elevators past the larger-than-life babies in the photograph who howled and jeered.

18

Sunlight sliced across Alice's hospital blanket. She clamped shut her eyes and traced the pain that enveloped her back to its source in her swamp-belly. She remembered a man's silhouette, not Rolly's, wavering over her. She struggled to see the bedside clock, then sagged against her pillow. The man was a doctor. The light from the hall had been directly behind him. She couldn't make out his features. He said his name. He'd examined her baby. He spoke of tests and rattled off nonsense syllables. She could now see his face. His deep-set eyes didn't blink as his mouth worked and his words flew at her. She tried to catch them. Something about low birth weight. Something about intracranial bleeding. She cried. He clicked his pen. Was this a message in code that she didn't understand?

She woke again. Rolly had been here, too, in the night, and again this morning, and now Patricia was sitting in a nearby chair, her lipstick fresh, a stylish white dress, not worried about blood or intra-cranial bleeding. Maybe everything had gotten fixed.

"You look better than you must feel," Patricia said, folding her magazine.

"Drugged," she mumbled, reaching for the water, "hard to talk."

"Don't talk." Patricia patted Alice's foot through the blanket.

"Rolly was here awhile ago. I sent him away."

Patricia shifted in the chair and exhaled slowly. She didn't approve.

"I can manage," Alice said.

"My dear, where is the baby's father?"

Wolf's face in the bus window, a ghost. Not the father, only the donor. The Virgin had shown her. Not immaculate, this conception, but what she'd wanted. And she'd botched it. The baby was damaged, because of her.

Patricia was talking. "I was scared…thought of Rolly….want what's right for you."

What's right? The doctor had said they couldn't know what had gone wrong. An infection. The difficult delivery. Errant genes. *I'm never sick*, she'd wanted to tell him. *I'm strong. I'm healthy. I was very careful*, but she was silenced as his echoing phrase "difficult delivery." She had insisted on natural, against the doctor's, the other doctor's, everyone's advice, so it was her fault.

The rushing in her head quieted so she could almost ignore it. She interrupted Patricia's yammering. "Dr. Petrillo stopped by. I'm supposed to go home tomorrow."

"That's good news."

Alice pulled the sheet up to her throat and clenched it there. "Another doctor came in last night. He said the baby's too small, even accounting for his being three weeks early." She swallowed. "There's a chance of intracranial bleeding. That's what he said." She could feel her head bobbing. She tried to stop it. She focused on the door to the hall beyond Patricia's shoulder. "This may mean cerebral palsy."

"Oh, dear. But they don't know for sure, do they? It's been less than a day, twenty hours. How can they know?"

"I don't know what cerebral palsy is." She dug her fist into her doughy belly, picturing poster-pretty kids with leg braces, and tried not to cry.

The air conditioner vent rattled.

"Are they sure?" Patricia asked.

"There are some tests. He asked for permission."

"So it's a possibility, not a diagnosis."

Alice nodded.

"Let's wait until the tests are in before we worry."

"Even then, they won't know. Not until after the first year. Can't tell" —
she fought the panic clawing at her throat — "the extent of the damage."

"Oh, darling." Patricia took her in her arms and stroked her head.
"Not for sure."

✳ ✳ ✳

She slept again. When she woke, Patricia was gone. She wondered
what kind of drugs they were giving her. She felt like she was under-
water. The blankets weighed too heavy. It took real effort to breathe. A
nurse came in to ask if she'd like to visit her baby.

"Not now. I feel weak." She ignored the nurse's concerned look by fixing on the TV where the anchormen grinned at each other, joshing, then
turned to give the audience a conspiratorial wink. The nurse adjusted Alice's pillows and left. Alice wished she lived in TV land. She would wear
a sharp suit, get a haircut, and swivel coyly back and forth in her chair,
before facing Wolf, who sat beside her. She would say, "I've had a baby.
He's four pounds, three ounces, eighteen inches long. That's considered
low birth weight and that's bad. And he has intracranial bleeding."

Wolf turned to her. TV land was gone, and they were in a gray, in-
definite space.

"Wolf?"

Could he not hear her?

"I've had a baby."

The expression in his eyes didn't change.

"He's your baby too."

Wolf's face quivered and his eyes worked loose from whatever anchored them as his mouth became a vortex that sucked his features away. His empty face stared at her.

"Wolf, come back."

Everything had become unhinged. Nothing was staying in place.

When she was little, about seven years old and before her father died, she slept out in their backyard one night. Fireflies looped around the dark shrubs, and not too far away, her parents watched television on the screened porch, their profiles outlined in flickering blue-gray. In her sleeping bag, she stared up into the sky. What would happen if gravity got switched off? She would float out of her sleeping bag, up into the overhead tree branches. Delighted by the rules being broken, she pictured her parents drifting up to the ceiling of the porch, bouncing lightly to the door, and calling her name. But she was safe. She would grab a branch and hold on. But what if she floated away from the tree and couldn't reach a branch? What then?

"Ms. Becotte?"

A fat, hillbilly nurse with a scraggly ponytail stood next to her bed.

"I've come to take you to see your son."

Son. A son. She wouldn't say "son" unless her baby was going to be all right. Alice sat up, noticing that she was no longer hooked up to an IV.

It hurt to walk.

"A few more steps, honey."

INFANT SPECIAL CARE UNIT stood out on the beige walls. Alice wanted to bolt, but the nurse guided her toward the double doors that whooshed open. Inside was a small antechamber lined floor to ceiling in stainless steel, cabinets on one side, a large sink with sprayers opposite, and at the other end more double doors, inset with windows, through which Alice could see what looked like a laboratory: white flexi-tubes hanging from the ceiling, monitors, machines, tiny gurneys, a few nurses in shower caps, rows of clear incubators, some that looked like little coffins.

She reeled back, knocking into the fat nurse. "Can't I look from here?"

"Wash your hands here, then we'll get you a gown."

"I don't want to go in." Her foul body leaking into a pad between her legs would contaminate the purity of this safe zone.

"It looks worse than it is." The nurse gave a little laugh. "You'll see once we go inside."

"Point to where he is."

The nurse's head was next to hers. "There, next to Connie, in the purple scrubs. She's checking his oxygen."

Alice fixed her eyes on Connie, then saw a white tube snaking down to something scrambled and red inside one of the coffins. She grabbed the doorframe.

"I need to sit."

That red thing wasn't her baby. They'd stolen her baby. Her baby was somewhere else, her perfect baby. She careened from the door toward the sink and began to wail, wanting to bring the whole place down.

＊＊＊

A rattling woke her. She was in her bed, and a hospital table was being moved in front of her. She waited until she was sure she was alone before opening her eyes. A meal. Pain uncurled from her center and swam everywhere. Her throat was raw. Her eyes were scratchy and swollen. Her breasts hurt. Pushing aside the tray and wincing, she reached for the card with phone numbers that Patricia had tucked under the vase with Rolly's flowers.

"Rolly, it's me."

"Yes."

"Will you talk to me?"

She heard movement, before he said, "OK."

"I want to know where the divorce stands."

"You want to talk about this now?"

"Just tell me."

"Everything's where it was. Your lawyer sent me papers. The court date is set for November. My lawyer filed a response. I get half our assets, including the house, I get what's in my studio, and you will buy my share of the house over the next ten years. And you relinquish all claims to child support. If you agree to that, it's done."

"It's done then. I wanted to make sure."

From the milk carton on her tray a cow beamed at her, a merry cow. Drink milk; be healthy. Nothing goes wrong if you drink milk. She tried to squash the container and squirted milk onto her blanket. She watched the liquid bead on the woven fibers, then seep in. "Did Patricia tell you?"

"She did."

"About cerebral palsy?"

"She called this afternoon. She said they wouldn't know for some time exactly what this is going to mean. She said it wasn't so much that he came early—"

"Do you think he's going to die?"

"They haven't said that, have they?"

Alice lifted her gaze to the sprinkler nozzle in the ceiling, wishing she could float away, and waited for him to add something consoling. If he did, she would hang up. He said nothing. She sipped air, ignoring the pain, and said, "Do you still want to see him?"

A sharp intake of breath. "God, yes."

His answer pushed her backward. Maybe she was wrong. Maybe he didn't understand she wasn't inviting him into her life. Maybe he didn't know this was just for now. Temporary. Until she was stronger. He *had* asked. He wasn't running away. She lowered the phone to her lap, beige, curved, the way her baby had looked in the five-month ultrasound, and sobbed. When she was depleted, she lifted the phone. "Are you still there?"

"Yes."

"You can come tomorrow, in the morning, around ten."

* * *

He barely slept that night and woke at dawn. After unpacking the last of his boxes, he vacuumed, cleaned the kitchen he hadn't used, and the bathroom, and when there was nothing else to do, he went out to breakfast, drank too much coffee, dawdling, then drove his rental car to the car wash. When he walked into Alice's hospital room, she was standing by her bed next to an open duffel. He'd never seen her such a mess, wan, hair disheveled, damps spots on her shirt, her breasts leaking. She stared at him. She couldn't figure out what should go in her bag. Packaged baby stuff lay piled on the bed and the bedside table. She hadn't thrown out his flowers. Whatever the reason for her call, he was determined not to do anything that might make her change her mind. He needed to see the baby again. He hoped this urgency would vanish as soon as he saw him. The baby should mean nothing to him, except as proof of Alice's betrayal, but Rolly yearned to see him again. He studied Alice, waiting to take cues from her. She was his access — only with her permission could he see the baby.

She pushed her hair from her forehead and looked directly at him, as if noticing him for the first time. She'd fortified herself with eye makeup, but carelessly. Mascara specks dotted the hollows under her eyes. She waved at the duffel bag.

"Patricia and Warren are coming at noon to take me home."

He started to say that was good, but she interrupted him. "The baby stays."

The way she dropped her eyes scared him. Had something gone wrong? Not breathing, he waited for her to tell him what had happened.

"Do you want to see him?" she said.

If there'd been a turn for the worse, she wouldn't have invited him. He nodded, guessing that almost anything he would say could set her off. She stepped around the duffel bag, and they walked in silence to the ISCU.

Unlike two nights ago, happy families and new moms holding babies crowded the hall. Alice walked with a slight limp, not seeming to notice anyone else. Down another corridor and around a corner, it was empty. At the ISCU door, a freckled nurse who looked about fifteen told them to wash. Beside him at the sink, Alice scrubbed with twitchy intensity. He remembered the morning after the miscarriage, when it was time to go home, how she'd jerked out of the hospital bed. Alice fought grief with physical action, but it took everything she had, then and now. His old sadness descended. He looked away, through the glass panel in the door. Gathered in the middle of the room was a Mexican family, a squat couple, the parents, and an even shorter old woman, the grandmother, her black dress visible under the green gown that matched the one the young nurse handed him. Beyond the Mexican family, where Alice's baby had been, the isolette with a blue bow was empty. His heart began to race.

Fighting panic, he pointed through the window toward the Mexican family. "Is that a new baby?"

"A preemie. Your boy's been moved over there."

The double doors swung open.

He and Alice followed the nurse through the ward. In addition to the Mexicans' baby, there were three others and several nurses. At the far end of the ward, in front a phalanx of machines Rolly hadn't seen before, big as refrigerators, with digital displays, Alice's baby lay on a small platform bed lit by a lavender spotlight. In the unnatural light, the baby's skin glowed hot red, as if a fire burned within. A white tube that led to one of the machines had been forced between his lips and taped in place. With his small mouth distended around the tube, he looked like a dying fish. Rolly tried to block Alice's view.

"It's not so bad as it looks," the nurse said. "Once it's in, it doesn't hurt."

"How the hell do you know?" Rolly demanded. "He can't cry with that thing jammed in his mouth."

The baby looked worse than he had a day and a half ago, like some mangled animal thrown to the side of the road. With each breath, his tiny chest seized and quivered. Nausea flushed through Rolly. Beside him, he could sense Alice shivering. He tried to fold her in his arms — he needed to hold onto something, to her — but she pushed him away, saying to the nurse, "He's going to die, isn't he?"

"He's doing fine, dear, just fine." She bobbed her head. She was one of those fucking cheery nurses. "The doctor was in a little while ago. He said everything is going well."

Alice spun away. "Going well? What does that mean? Why is this happening? I did everything right."

She clamped her arms to her sides and Rolly grabbed her to draw her to him, the saggy weight of her belly on his hip unfamiliar and disturbing, while the nurse repeated that Alice hadn't done anything wrong. Alice wasn't listening. The room tipped like a gyroscope, but he held on and stroked Alice's head until she stopped shaking and the shuddering in his own chest quieted. The nurse offered to call a doctor. Rolly shook his head.

Alice looked up at him, her blank-calm face streaked with mascara, her eyes glittering with hostility. She pulled away. "This isn't your problem."

"I know that."

"Why the hell did you come? Are you curious? Think this baby of mine," she held up her fist, "do you think he's some sort of *interesting* specimen, the kind of thing you might pick up in the woods, like your awful tree branches? Or some sort of tragic male shit, like what got you started on those stupid canoes?"

"Alice, please." He reached out. She lowered her fist, crossing both arms across her chest, defending herself. The milk streaks on her shirt made him nauseous, and the eerie light above the baby pressed on the edge of his vision, disorienting him. But he tried to concentrate on her face. He had to get through to her.

"I don't know why I care. That's the truth. All I know for certain is that I have to be here, if you'll let me. Yesterday, when you sent me away, I was furious. I was angrier than I've ever been. Can you believe that? All through this past year with you, I've never been more full of rage. Why now? It makes no sense. This — you said it — has nothing to do with me. But I know that I *need* to be here. This baby…I want to be with him."

She tilted her head, as if she might be listening to another conversation; he wondered if it was one they'd had long ago, where they'd said terrible things to one another.

"Let me stay," he said.

She didn't respond. He guessed she was tallying his shortcomings, his every failure. After a moment, the concentration required seemed to exhaust her, and her face went slack.

"OK then," she said, still not looking at him.

Grateful, fighting the sudden shudders of relief that threatened to erupt as laughter, he kept his eyes fixed on her. In the space between them, he sensed an infinitesimal movement and edged closer. When she didn't withdraw, he circled his arm over her shoulders. Barely touching, they stood together, the lavender light glancing off the top of her curls. He was afraid to move, afraid he would break this fragile accord.

A buzzing nearby became words. The obtuse, cheery nurse was speaking carefully, as if repeating herself. "What you need, dear, is to hold your baby."

Another nurse came up behind them and put her hand on Alice's wrist. "This little cherub of yours needs to be cuddled."

"No. No. No." Alice yanked away from Rolly, fluttering her hands. "I can't. No. Stop it."

The new nurse looked helplessly at Rolly.

Alice backed away, knocking a metal stand. "He'll die."

"He won't die, dear. He's a strong little fellow." The nurses surrounded her.

"He will die, if I touch him." Her face contorted with grief.

As Rolly reached for her, the nurses intervened. "Shh. It's OK... No one's going... Dear, squeeze my hand...shh..."

Behind him, something fell, not nearby, and there was the sound of feet. Rolly turned, expecting to see more nurses coming their way, but the noise came from the other family. Their nurse had dropped her clipboard. The Mexican family was leaving. Both parents smiled as they trailed their nurse to a desk near the door — nothing seriously wrong with their baby. The grandmother threaded her way between the empty isolettes toward where he and Alice stood. Her oily hair was knotted in the back, her skin pitted like an orange. Her dark eyes locked on Alice. He stepped in front of the baby's bed — he wasn't going to let this crone touch Alice's baby — but the old woman edged around an empty incubator and reached between the nurses to grab Alice's hand,

and holding tight, muttered something in Spanish. Then she let go. Shaking her head, she hurried away to where the parents waited.

"Alice, are you all right?" he asked.

She nodded, dazed, and the nurses flanking her relaxed. She held out a small white card with gilt words in Spanish.

"What is it?" he asked.

"A prayer." She turned it over to show the other side. A standing Madonna surrounded by colorful flames or feathers. "To the Virgin of Guadalupe."

The same as the medallion on her bedside stand and the postcard she'd kept for years. Alice had always maintained a web of superstitions against the world's cruelties, even though she claimed she didn't really believe in magic. He'd mocked her, but now he was grateful.

"I'm OK, Rolly." The corners of her lips lifted in an insincere smile, but she was no longer shaking. "Really. This is a sign."

One of the nurses moved to the baby's side, repositioning an IV tube, and said to Alice. "Are you ready to hold him now, dear?"

"No." Her smile was gone. She clutched the card to her throat above the gown. "Not now. Not yet." She turned to Rolly. "You, you take him."

"Me?"

"Yes. You hold him."

"Are you sure?"

"I want you to. He needs to be held, didn't you say that?" she asked the younger nurse, whose perkiness had taken a hit.

The younger nurse agreed as the other nurse walked away. Alice watched her, growing agitated, as if she were being abandoned. Would she fall apart?

"I'm going to sit down," she said, hobbling to a chair ten feet away. Before she sat, she moved the chair so she could face the baby.

"You, go ahead now, Rolly."

The nurse looked from her to Rolly, checking if he was willing.

He was, but he was terrified.

Alice called out, "He's my baby, not yours. Don't forget that."

"I won't."

The small, red, wrinkled baby, trailing strands that looped back to the machines and with a white hose taped into his mouth, floated out of the lavender light toward Rolly, who took him from the nurse, using both hands and arms to make sure the baby didn't slip or fly away. He felt weightless. Cradling him against his gowned chest, Rolly noticed a waxy glow along his shut eyelids, thin shining curves the color of candlelight. The perfection of these tiny gold crescents cast everything else — the baby's furious face with fish-mouth taped to pipe, his jerky chest, raw color, his warped legs, all of this — into irrelevance. Lightly, Rolly traced the almost invisible line of hair that bordered his red face up to the tiny widow's peak and down the arc of his temple. The baby's brows lifted and settled back. He liked Rolly's touch.

Rolly grinned.

Not far away, Alice sighed a half-laugh.

✳✳✳

From the beginning, the staff had insisted she name the baby.

"I can't," she'd told them each time.

"We need a name for the birth certificate."

How could she give him a name? A name implied a future. Christopher? Max? Toby or Zane? She would see little boys with stubby legs running on the playground and tears would come.

"Call him Baby Becotte."

✳✳✳

At home she slept in the living room, at the kitchen table, in the garden. The first few days, before she felt up to driving, she slept in Patricia's car, back and forth to the ISCU. Her breasts ached and leaked. She kept pads in her bra, but after ten days, two weeks, her milk dried up. She couldn't sleep enough. She slept late each morning and retired right after dinner, brought in most nights by Patricia and Warren; they ate together in front of the early evening news. She never dreamed. When she woke, she felt a pain, like a rubber band tugging her chest, a rubber band that connected her to her baby, which began to stretch as she drove from the hospital, and grew more taut with each mile, almost to the snapping point by the time she got home. But in the six hours she spent in the ISCU, that connection vanished. No pain. Only fear. Sitting by his bed, listening to the faint clicks of the machines and the hiss of the respirator taped to his cheek and nose, she watched his slight movements. All she could offer him was her attentiveness. Hope was out of reach. She couldn't imagine a future for him outside this ward. When a nurse would urge her to take a break, she wandered to the cafeteria or the gift shop and stared at the fleecy bunnies, the cocoa-colored teddy bears, and the musical crib mobiles made for plump babies who went home. She was sure her son would die. She was afraid to fall in love with him.

Rolly came most days. He would hold the baby, call him "big guy," and joke about his great grip. He chatted with the nurses and asked questions that didn't sound like accusations; but with her, he was careful. He didn't presume. He didn't claim an official role. Whenever they met, whether she was in the ward first or arrived to find him there, he looked at her in a way that made her understand that he was asking if he was still welcome. He was, which surprised her. They spoke, but only about the baby or what the staff said about the baby, nothing about where things stood with their divorce, nothing about his return to Haslett, the college, his time in Norway, never about the other babies who came and went, usually after only a few days. On some days, the nurses told her that Rolly had already come and gone. When that happened, she felt stranded. Not even Patricia's presence, nor Bettina's, not the nurses' kindnesses or their optimism could dislodge her sense of isolation.

✳✳✳

After another day in the ISCU and after dinner, a sandwich she'd picked up in the hospital cafeteria and brought home, she stared out her back door at her neglected garden and noticed that the sun was setting so much earlier than seemed right. Time had stalled for her, but the world moved, and the days were getting shorter. August 1. Tomorrow was her baby's due date, and she hadn't held him, not once, after that first day. Tomorrow he would be three weeks old. It was time. She didn't want to wait another day, especially not a day that would seem so significant.

In the ISCU the evening shift nurses were on duty, and the mother of the baby girl with the blood disorder sat by her daughter's isolette, in the same position as when Alice had left. At Alice's son's crib, Myrna, the kind Filipino, stood rocking him.

"He's about to doze off," Myrna said. "I'll just put him back."

"I'll take him. It's OK. Give him to me."

Myrna hid any surprise — Alice knew the nurses talked about her refusal to hold her baby — as Alice dragged a chair over, sat down, and held out her gowned arms. Saying nothing, Myrna draped the respirator hose and the trach tube over Alice's forearm, and then she was gone.

"Hello, Baby," Alice whispered, waiting for him to react to being held by someone unfamiliar. Air hissed through the tube that curved over his head, under his left cheek and below his nostrils. Was she holding him right? His eyes hadn't opened. Could he tell who she was?

He settled against the loose gown covering her lap, his small, diapered body nestled between her thigh and her arm, the back of his head in her palm, where it fit perfectly, like a peach. She avoided looking at the pulsing by the trachea tube in his neck. Wrapping her arms around him, she tried to stop trembling.

"You OK?" she whispered. His closed eyes didn't flinch. Was he aware of her? Was she the same to him as any of the nurses?

"Would you like me to sing you a song?"

He gave no sign that he heard. She shifted to nestle him closer and began to hum the tune to "Freight Train," the song her father had sung to her. It was hard to hum, the notes all sounded alike, but she kept at it — he wasn't asleep, that she could tell, even though he wasn't reacting — and soon the sounds she was making became vibrations that traveled down her throat and into her belly and into him. His transparent eyelashes fluttered. With pleasure, she was sure, and she laughed. "OK, we'll do that again."

Later, she would sing him the words, but for now, the music was enough.

＊＊＊

Rolly sat in a rocker with the baby balanced between his crossed legs, the respirator and trach tubes looped over his gowned thigh. She pulled up another chair and sat beside them. He looked as much at ease as if he were sitting in the beat-up chair in his studio. She envied him. Wherever she held her baby, she started shaking.

"What do you think of 'Gabriel'?" she asked. The baby's eyes were locked on Rolly.

264

"You named him?"

"They told me they're taking him off the respirator and putting him on a monitor, which is a big advance."

"Wow, fella, you're growing up. The question is: are you a Gabriel?" He snuggled his face next to the baby's, carefully moving the respirator tube, then looked up at Alice, giving an equivocal shrug. "Good, but foreign."

Foreign? She hid her dismay. Had he guessed about Wolf? But if he had, he wouldn't be here. She made a silly face. "Too un-Indiana?"

"Definitely. That's good, right? And it goes with Becotte, being French."

"I thought it was Spanish."

"Don't think so. If it becomes Gabby, can you live with that?"

The baby's arms flailed, and Rolly stroked his tiny limbs. He was focused on the baby. There was no hostile edge toward her. Foreign meant nothing.

She said, "Never. Not Gabby."

"Gabe?"

"Gabriel. Let's stick with that. And I'd like to hold him now."

"Sure." Rolly stood carefully, cradling the baby to his chest. "Come on, Gabriel, it's Momma's turn."

✳✳✳

The days passed in a blur. There were setbacks and advances, countless tests, a sudden fever that took Gabriel's temperature to 104.5 degrees, then a string of good days. He put on weight and finally began to track movement with his eyes. He smiled at her. The nurses assured her his smiles were genuine, not reflexive. They took out the tracheal tube when he could breathe on his own. He learned to suck from a bottle. He was thirty-two days old, and he weighed six pounds, five ounces when they said she could take him home. She was terrified.

She called Rolly that night — they'd spoken only once outside the hospital, the night of Gabriel's fever — to tell him the news. He alone had been certain this day would come. Gabriel's vulnerability had never shaken him. But she was overwhelmed by what lay ahead now, everything from scheduling nurses and therapists to buying the right kind of formula. Patricia would help in an emergency, and there was Bettina right next door, but only Rolly smiled when he looked at her Gabriel. She stared at the congratulatory cards plastered on her refrigerator and pressed the receiver to her ear. Hearing Rolly's voice flooded her with misgivings. In the hospital, he'd proven he could be trusted to keep his distance from her, but she worried about this next stage. They were still in the middle of divorce negotiations, with Reimus and Singer working on the details.

"Yes, it is great," she said, "but without the nurses, what if…well, you know."

"They wouldn't release him unless they're confident."

What could she say to the obvious, since she didn't believe it?

"So, OK, how can I help?"

Around her heart a vise loosened. "Could you drive me to and from the hospital?" she asked. "I've installed a car seat, but I'm nervous about this first time. You could come here, and we'll switch cars." She would have to invite him in, even though she didn't want him in the house. She would want him to carry Gabriel up the steps.

"I'll be there. Tell me when."

∗∗∗

With Gabriel at home, she went from sleeping most of the night to not sleeping at all. She moved a mattress into the nursery and slept next to his crib. If she brought him down to the mattress, his jerky

266

movements kept her awake. She dreamt that she crushed him. During the day, Fay, the practical nurse, took over, but whenever Alice fell asleep, the doorbell would ring, a friend, a therapist, a deliveryman — everything was delivered — or Gabriel's monitor would beep.

Rolly stopped by most days, even after his teaching began. After Labor Day, when Gabriel had been home for nearly a month, Rolly suggested that Alice get away for a few hours and leave him and Fay to watch over Gabriel. Why not? She raced upstairs and changed, then drove to the square, planning to drop in at the *Herald*. By the time she'd parked, a headache pulsed behind her forehead. The thought of talking to Fritzie, Barry, and her replacement, Weideroe, answering questions about Gabriel and when she might come back to work made her queasy. She walked to Holloway's and settled in the back booth, drank coffee, and decided she needed to get a cell phone, damn the cost, before she left Gabriel again. After an hour, the shortest interval that didn't make her seem like a foolishly distraught mom, she went home.

Gradually, she was able to leave Gabriel for a few hours. Her guilt headaches no longer flamed whenever she left the house. In early October, when Gabriel had been home two months and no longer needed a nurse, Fay offered her cousin Esther as a babysitter. Two weeks after Esther started, Alice returned to work part-time.

Alice was good at managing Gabriel's elaborate requirements: the daily muscle therapy, the frequent feeding, the medications, the doctor visits. While she remained on high alert every moment at home, couldn't relax when she held him, and slept fitfully with his crib nearby, her guilt and anxiety fueled unexpected new levels of competence. No breakdown in his sleep monitor undid her; no difficulty in scheduling the rotation of therapists vexed her; his choking episodes she handled with the skill of a nurse. She became good at being Gabriel's mother.

✳✳✳

She bought an overstuffed armchair for the nursery.

"This will be our reading chair," she said, settling him in her lap. "But for now, it's for singing." She reached for the warmed bottle she'd placed on the side table. She was beginning to relax. She no longer worried that he might die at any minute. "What would you like to hear? 'Twinkle, twinkle'?" He kicked his leg. "OK, we'll begin there."

Rolly was a steady visitor. With Gabriel at the center, she and Rolly struck an accord; Rolly lightened her load and, it seemed to her, Gabriel provided ballast for Rolly. They both wanted to maintain this accord, that was clear, because they never spoke about the divorce. Once Rolly had agreed to her buying him out of the house, the rest seemed inconsequential. Reimus would call with a question, and she'd tell him to work it out with Rolly's lawyer. Gabriel — what he needed now and what he would need in a month, a year, when it came time for school — occupied every cell of her brain. There was no room left to think about the divorce. Her job provided her only break.

Rolly taught morning classes only. He came over those two afternoons — he'd never been able to work well in his studio on teaching days — which helped with the cost of Esther, and, if Alice needed to go out on a story over the weekend or in the evening, she called Rolly. He rarely said no. She hated to ask Patricia who was too nervous with Gabriel.

✳✳✳

In late October, Alice had to cover the last session of the town council before the November election. From the living room window, she watched for Rolly, admiring the Halloween decorations the new owners of the Swenke house had put up, and was surprised when an unfamiliar silver-bullet car pulled up in front of her house. Rolly opened the passenger door and leaned back in to say something to the driver.

As he walked toward the house, the car made a U-turn, and she could see a woman at the wheel. Alice stayed staring out the window when he rang the bell.

He let himself in. "Hello?"

"I'm in here. Car in the shop?"

"Is everything OK?"

"Sure. I was just wondering why you got dropped off."

"Brake pads. I shouldn't have bought such a beater. It won't be ready until tomorrow."

She walked into the front hall — he had showered. After an afternoon of sex? — and ignored his effort to help with her coat. What right did she have to feel wronged after Wolf? And they were all but divorced. The court date was a month away.

"Gabriel's sleeping, and I'll be back around nine. I left some food on the stove, in case you haven't eaten."

At the council meeting, she sat in the back, taking notes, trying to tamp down her old feelings of being neglected, misunderstood, of being the drudge wife left behind while Rolly lived his real life elsewhere. She didn't want him, but his wanting someone else hurt. It shouldn't, but it did.

He was dozing in the living room when she got home, with a book across his chest and Gabriel's intercom on the coffee table. She'd often watched him sleep on the couch, just like this, and seen his closed face as a shield raised against her. Now, with his head twisted and his mouth slack, he looked capable of being harmed. She picked up the book on his chest and he woke.

"How did it go?" she asked, slipping his bookmark in place.

He struggled upright and told her about his evening with Gabriel, the bath, the bottle.

"He'll probably wake for his next feeding around midnight."

"Would you like some tea?"

"Sure, after I call for a ride."

"That new taxi company's number is posted next to the phone. Fay's husband drives for them."

In the kitchen she filled the kettle as he spoke into the phone. After he hung up, she asked if he still had time for tea.

"About a half hour. I called a friend." He sat at the table and straightened the newspaper he'd spread out earlier, when he ate the dinner she'd made. He didn't say whether he liked the chili.

"The friend who dropped you off?" What was she doing?

"That's right. Where's the sugar?"

She pointed to the counter, next to the coffeemaker. "I'm sorry I asked. It's none of my business."

He stopped to get a spoon and brought the sugar to the table.

"I was just curious," she said.

"Curious?" He stirred sugar into his tea. "I see. Well, in that case, her name is Clarissa McIlvoy. She's a new lecturer in history."

"Are you serious about her?" she asked, mortified. She was making a fool of herself.

Rolly sipped his tea, then put it down. "This is an odd inquisition, Alice. But since you're *curious*." She could tell he was enjoying this. "I would say that I'm serious in my terms, but not in yours."

"And those are?"

"For me, *serious* means sustained intimacy, and I believe, for you, *serious* means marriage." He reached across the table for her hand and he squeezed gently. "I'm not good at your kind of serious."

"What are you good at?"

His expression went flat. "You tell me."

270

"Why *are* you here?"

He looked up the ceiling, his lips twisting in a weary smile. "You have to ask? For Gabriel."

"He's not yours."

"No. You know I know that. But I *get* him." His thumb stroked her finger. "You can cut this off at any time. That's your right and you can sure hurt me that way, but why would you? Gabriel needs me."

"Do you love him?"

"You know I do."

He was right about her no longer needing to wound him. That ended in the ISCU.

"And I believe that you need me," he said, releasing her hand. "Tell me I'm wrong."

She expelled a breath, she didn't realize she'd been holding and glanced around the kitchen, at the sterilized bottles, the rack of prescriptions, the notepad with instructions, the penciled-in charts. She did need Rolly. She needed someone else to love Gabriel too.

He touched her hand lightly, and she looked at him. "I care about you, Alice, I do."

"But it's not the same as when we were married."

He shook his head.

"For me either," she said.

He looked away, at the baby intercom he'd brought in. The light still blinked green. For now, no emergencies upstairs.

EPILOGUE

Alice compiled a baby book. On the inside cover she put the bent-up postcard of the Virgin of Guadalupe and the prayer the Mexican grandmother had given her. Next came the early Polaroids the nurses had taken where Gabriel looked like various animals: fish, chicken, ferret, monkey. At first, she hated these pictures, but she'd saved them as reminders of the nurses' kindnesses. Letters and cards from friends went in, too, along with his blue plastic hospital bracelet, a clipping of the piece Fritzie had written for the *Herald*, and a copy of the birth announcements Bettina had sent out after Alice gave her permission, after Gabriel came home. She considered including the hospital leaflets on cerebral palsy, but instead put them in a file drawer labeled: *The Facts*.

The Facts is where she keeps the documents that govern her life: the folders devoted to Gabriel's medical matters, testing and evaluation, doctor's reports, insurance claims; her new will; her copy of the divorce decree. The divorce was finalized in December when Gabriel was six months old. In the legal documents she refused every angle Reimus had suggested that might formalize Rolly's devotion to Gabriel into an obligation, and, against expectation, the settlement of their property was easy. She kept the house and yard, with small monthly payments to Rolly each month for ten years, and he kept his studio. Pulling strings at city hall — a benefit from her good connections — she worked out a zoning variance to subdivide their property. *The Facts* are just that. The truth of her life lies elsewhere, in Gabriel's book.

The book is filled with photographs detailing his first year. After the nurses' Polaroids come pictures Rolly took: close-ups of Gabriel's hands, his turned-in feet, the back of his head with wisps of red hair, his wobbly smile. When Alice knew he would survive, they took him outside for his first drive since the hospital, and there's a snapshot of him wrapped in Fritzie's crocheted blanket, held in Alice's arms. They're in the woods. It's September and sunny. Then there's pictures of him nestled in a pile of pumpkins, several of him in Patricia's lap, and Warren's, on Thanksgiving, and close-ups of him in his Christmas pajamas, sleeping in the crib Rolly made. Alice took this picture and Rolly is standing behind the crib. There's a gap in the pictures, from when Gabriel was hospitalized in February. Next comes a page of pictures, him propped next to an Easter basket and swinging in a baby glider Rolly built in his new apartment. From the first hot day of May, there's a photo of Rolly holding him above Ariana's wading pool, dunking his feet, both girls stand back to watch, and Gabriel's eyes are wide with surprise. Rolly is Gabriel's favorite toy. He's more than that, but no one, not Alice, not Rolly, not Patricia, not any of their friends tries to name what he is.

He has decided to stay at Wesley and Alice is glad.

The lap-sized book closes with her favorite picture of all: Gabriel on his first birthday.

Gabriel is the tiny center of the crowd gathered behind the picnic table in the garden. He's in his infant seat, and he looks like a tiny smudge with a fan of cinnamon hair. Sunlight dances off the shrubs in the back and shimmers on the edges of everything. Around Gabriel, in front of the guests, the table is covered with brightly wrapped packages, so many gifts. Paul Faracci took the picture, and he must have been laughing because the table has a slant, like it's going to skid out of the picture. Everybody is laughing, as if they can tell that the table is about to slip away with the tilting birthday cake. Rolly made the cake. It's supposed to look like a train from Gabriel's favorite book.

That day the sun made everyone squint. On the left, Bettina has her hands on both girls. Gia is about to tear open one of Gabriel's gifts, and Ariana is stiff, embarrassed by her sister's antics. Next is Warren, slightly drunk and waving a glittering foil crown that someone brought for Gabriel, but that's way too big, and Patricia leans close to him, her smile brilliant beneath her glamorous sunglasses. Near the center of the group, Nan, from the hospital, smiles directly at the camera, then Fay, their first practical nurse, and Esther, the three back-up sitters, and Gabriel's physical therapist. A couple of nurses from the ISCU stand next to Barry who holds a mock edition of the *Herald* with the barely discernible headline: GABRIEL TURNS 1! Barry's newspaper throws a shadow on Fritzie, who beams from under her sun hat.

In the middle of the photograph, between the nurses and midwives, right behind Gabriel, Alice and Rolly stand side by side, the way they've been all year long. Alice has her profile to the camera. She's talking to Nan. Gossiping, Rolly says. Getting an idea for a story on home deliveries, Alice insists. But at that moment, Rolly bends over to straighten Gabriel's head. The cerebral palsy has affected Gabriel's control of his torso, and he has just learned to sit up, but his head flops to the side if someone doesn't help him. Rolly told Alice later that Gabriel called him "Raa," at that moment, his version of Pa, but Alice laughs and says that's just what Rolly wanted to hear.

Acknowledgements

My deepest thanks: to the Ragdale Foundation for giving me the time and space to find my way forward with this book; to Fred Shafer, a teacher without peer, who inspired and guided me; to the amazing writers in my closest circle, whose savvy advice, patience, and love of laughter carried me through; to Marc Estrin and Donna Bister, the generous souls of Fomite Press. This book is dedicated to Jeff, my husband and my love.

Book Group Discussion Questions:

1. Many couples have trouble conceiving. Lynn Sloan uses this particular couple's struggle as a lens through which to address questions of marriage and family. How is marriage presented in the novel? What does the book suggest about families?

2. Neither Alice or Rolly are religious, but Alice finds solace in her connection to the Virgin Mary. Why? How do the religious scenes work to advance the story?

3. Why is it important to the novel that it is set in 1999?

4. Do you think Rolly's choice of using ships in his art is symbolic?

5. Discuss the mothers in this novel.

6. Why does the novel have the title it does?

7. Sometimes Alice thinks of her life in terms of stories and headlines. Is she self-absorbed or is this a way of processing her pain or is this simply how she has been trained to think? Does it diminish her pain when presented as a headline, offering distance? Is this a commentary on how journalists respond to the people about whom they write?

8. Why do you think the author chose to set this novel in a rural environment?

9. Alice is scornful of her mother's decision to remarry. Her mother

wants Alice and Rolly to stay together. Why do they each have a stake in each other's marriages?

10. Part of the novel is about the commerce of art and the teaching of art. Does the competitive nature of his career affect Rolly's ability to produce good art?

11. Alice is critical of Rolly's work—his "baby," so to speak. Do you think Alice understands that Rolly, too, is trying to "birth" something?

12. By the end of the book, have your opinions about Alice and Rolly changed?

13. Do you think there is a healing in the end of the story? Is there forgiveness? What about hope?

14. The cover is striking. What scene do you think inspired it?

Fomite

A fomite is a medium capable of transmitting infectious organisms from one individual to another.

"The activity of art is based on the capacity of people to be infected by the feelings of others." Tolstoy, *What Is Art?*

Writing a review on Amazon, Good Reads, Shelfari, Library Thing or other social media sites for readers will help the progress of independent publishing. To submit a review, go to the book page on any of the sites and follow the links for reviews. Books from independent presses rely on reader to reader communications.

Visit http://www.fomitepress.com/FOMITE/Our_Books.html for more information or to order any of our books.

As It Is On Earth
Peter M Wheelwright

Dons of Time
Greg Guma

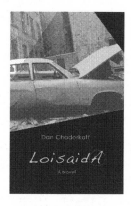

Loisaida
Dan Chodorkoff

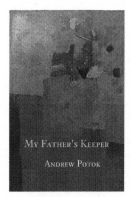

My Father's Keeper
Andrew Potok

My God, What Have We Done
Susan V Weiss

Rafi's World
Fred Russell

Fomite

The Co-Conspirator's Tale
Ron Jacobs

Short Order Frame Up
Ron Jacobs

All the Sinners Saints
Ron Jacobs

Travers' Inferno
L. E. Smith

The Consequence of Gesture
L. E. Smith

Raven or Crow
Joshua Amses

Sinfonia Bulgarica
Zdravka Evtimova

The Good Muslim
of Jackson Heights
Jaysinh Birjépatil

The Moment Before an Injury
Joshua Amses

Fomite

The Return of
Jason Green
Suzi Wizowaty

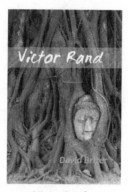

Victor Rand
David Brizeri

Zinsky the Obscure
Ilan Mochari

Body of Work
Andrei Guruianu

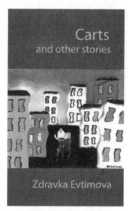

Carts and Other Stories
Zdravka Evtimova

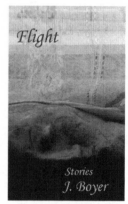

Flight
Jay Boyer

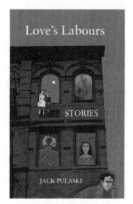

Love's Labours
Jack Pulaski

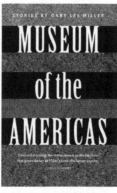

Museum of the Americas
Gary Lee Miller

Saturday Night at Magellan's
Charles Rafferty